EVERYWHERE AND NOWHERE

A SAM ABEL NOVEL

CLARKE MAYER

First Published by ROGUE STORIES LLC in 2022.

ISBN: 978-1-7355473-9-8

Cover Design by J Caleb Design

Editing by JD Book Services

*To my grandmother, Inge, whose help has been
immeasurable.*

1

———

Rain droplets pattered against the brim of Sam Abel's hat as he gazed into the second-floor window of the Spanish embassy. Two bodies danced jovially in dim light. The voices, muffled by the rain, informed him the two parties stumbling around the room had partaken of several beverages over the course of the night. Sam waited patiently for his cue: the lights would go off, and the window flanking the southeast corner of the building would open.

He casually lit a cigarette, though he knew the falling rain might snuff it out. That was alright, because he didn't believe he'd be waiting much longer. Sam, as always, kept his attention evenly split between the target ahead and his surroundings. He wouldn't have to worry about running afoul of the Nazis on this mission. His enemies this time around were far worse: bureaucrats.

Sam didn't understand all of the intricacies and loopholes of either international or domestic law, but he knew enough to speculate that this time, his commanding officer, Henry "Hank" Brandt, had probably crossed a line. Though the embassy was on U.S. soil, it was unlikely that breaking into it and stealing its secrets was fair game, even in wartime. He knew he'd broken a rule when last in Germany by sneaking around in the enemy's uniform, but Sam was accustomed to not asking too many questions of the man he had formerly only known as "the burned man."

A flurry of giggles and moans reverberated off of the concrete structure surrounding him, and Sam was sure that the woman and man had stumbled into the bedroom. A security guard paced around the front courtyard, but Sam wasn't worried about having to deal with him. He'd already been accommodated for his troubles by the man slurring his words on the floor above. The man, Salazar Moreno, currently served as the Consulate for Spain and, as its attaché, was keeper of many of its secrets. Spain did not have any spies embedded within the country—at least not spies of any competence. Of that Brandt was confident. Mr. Moreno, however, had been quite dirty as of late, and Brandt and his team of information gatherers suspected he had been funneling American secrets to his conspirators in the East, who in turn were providing them to their Nazi contacts. Though Spain had remained relatively neutral up to this point, Brandt and his colleagues were sure they'd been leveraging their position between Axis and Allied powers for personal gain—neutrality wasn't the right word at all.

Moreno was a handsome man, and well-liked by his Washingtonian contacts who knew no better. Preliminary scouting had revealed he was easily pliable and manipulated with wine and good food and certainly with any type of monetary coercion. The intel Sam's accomplices had gathered on him thus far suggested he was taking cash under the table from anyone who'd offer it and, as such, was a danger to American interests in the European theater. None of that had been proved—not yet—and that was partly the reason that Sam stood rain-drenched outside of the man's home away from home. Of all the things Moreno liked, his favorite by far was women.

A car approached, its headlight beams cutting through the steadily increasing rain and reflecting large illuminated pools of water on the street as it neared Sam. The spy tucked himself farther behind the brick wall he was using for cover, careful to cup the cigarette in his fingers and make sure its cherry was unnoticeable. Sirens wailed in the distance, and a dog barked somewhere to the south. Each of the sounds put Sam's senses on heightened alert. Just because he wouldn't be facing down platoons of enemy soldiers in the streets of Washington, D.C. didn't mean he was safe. In fact, the operation on native soil Brandt had recruited him for could be far more scrutinized than one on the war front. Sam had been able to operate with impunity in the Black Forest, but here in America, there were still rules.

When the car turned the corner, Sam stepped forward once more. The second floor was silent now, and after one last pull on his cigarette, the lights in the room went out one by one. He tossed the cigarette behind him—uncaring whether it had been properly extinguished since the rain was only growing more dense

—and focused his eyes on the corner window. The window slid open, and two curtains danced at its sides in the sudden gust of air.

He crossed the street, quickly surveyed the building behind him to make sure no one had seen his movement, then walked an abrupt diagonal line for the door located in the embassy's concrete wall. He quickly pulled black leather gloves over each of his hands, then headed straight for the door in the wall. He twisted the knob, which he knew would be unlocked, and stepped through. Now that he was hidden behind the wall guarding the structure, he had time to survey his route.

The architecture of the building had been designed in such a way that a drainpipe running along its corner was tucked neatly between stonework that jutted out at intervals of several feet. It was aesthetically pleasing, yet absolutely unsecured. He wrapped his hands around the pipe that led up to the gutters above and gripped it tightly with each of his hands. The pipe was wet—which he had not planned for—but the stone footing would still make the climb manageable. The guard ahead paced through the building's front courtyard, disappeared between several arches of trees, then out Sam's vision. Sam felt for the camera slung over his shoulder, tucked it behind his back and out of his way so he could navigate the climb, then placed both of his feet on the first two pieces of stone at knee-height.

The soles of his shoes would not aid him in any way. Not only were they wet, but they were completely untextured and flat so as not to leave any discernible prints. The tools spies often used weren't *always* the most efficient, but more importantly, they left little trace of their presence. Sam climbed rapidly, alternating his attention between the climb above and the building to his rear. He was confident no one was watching, but one could never be sure—after all, most people were unaware when he was watching *them.*

The climb wasn't particularly difficult, especially for a man in tip-top shape like Sam. His heart rate barely rose. When he arrived at the window, a soft, creamy-skinned hand reached out and offered assistance. He took it by the forearm, swiveled over toward the windowsill, then grabbed the concrete edge with his free hand. He tumbled as softly as possible into the room, wiped the rain from his face, and rose to his feet. In front of him, and softly glowing in the only available light coming from the lamp across the street, was a fair-skinned woman with long, fiery red hair and a satisfied smirk on her face.

"Well hello, Sam Abel. Fancy seeing you here," she whispered. Sam frowned at the use of his name. Still considered an international operative—who were often named according to three-digit-numbers—he'd have preferred she use his code number: 505. Then again, Sam wasn't *really* his name.

She handed him a roll of toilet paper, and Sam wiped his shoes vigorously before balling the used paper up and shoving it into the pocket of his pea coat. He removed his hat, placed it below the window, then turned the strap on which the camera hung from across his shoulder so it sat at the center of his stomach. Alley Cat, as she was known among Sam's cohorts, extended a finger toward the now-fast-asleep man she'd been with prior. He'd passed out face-first on the large king-size bed, fit for a royal, and was snoring. "My date fell asleep—couldn't hold his drink. You game?"

"Where is it?" Sam asked.

"You're no fun." Cat frowned, then strode purposefully on her heels toward a dark corner of the deep room.

Catherine McAlister, or "Cat" to those who were close enough to her to speak in shorthand, had been recruited by Brandt not long before the mission at hand. She'd been provided a fitting name within the animal kingdom like most of the other operatives on U.S. soil. The rosy-cheeked and freckled woman's spunk was matched only by her ability to infiltrate, but not in the way typical of her coworkers. She had taken on the role of "wealthy socialite" in service to the organization.

Her cover story was one of a misfortunate young girl who'd lost her parents—shipping magnates—shortly after arriving to America and was now one of the most desirable debutantes on the east coast. She'd inherited a fortune and had remained single into her late twenties, caught in a constant state of flux in her search for the perfect husband. No man had caught her eye yet, and if a party of the 'who's who' went down in New York or D.C., she was likely to be seen among the crowd. She played the part well, and Brandt's organization had given her quite a few resources and an initial injection of capital to sell the idea. Her tools included, but were not limited to, the finest dresses, jewelry, and cars.

Her true backstory was much more in doubt—she'd been scooped up by Brandt because of her charm—and her ability to crack safes. Sam didn't know much more than that. Brandt had vouched for her, and that was good enough for him. Though Cat was on the "team," Sam was still supposed to keep his eye on her.

She removed each of her heels as she moved toward a rose-wood armoire catty-cornered in the edge of the room. Her pine-green satin dress swished back and forth with each stride, and though she hadn't come from the royalty she would claim whilst among the powerful and influential, she could have fooled Sam. She grabbed the doors of the armoire, protected by the white and sparkling gloves that reached up to her elbows, and opened both doors. Inside, on a thick wood shelf, sat a large cobalt-colored safe with a single dial on its front door.

Sam followed quietly behind her. The man who'd been gleeful only moments before was now in a deep sleep and drooling onto the comforter into which his face had collapsed. A cartoonish snore reverberated through his lips as he fell deeper in slumber.

"How much did you give him?" Sam asked.

Cat frowned before responding with a harsh whisper, "He's a big guy! What they should have given me was a tranquilizer. The first dose didn't even make him yawn."

Sam shrugged, then redirected his attention to the safe. Cat grabbed the dial and twisted it once to the left. She pressed her ear to the door, then her eyes narrowed with intense concentration. She went on like that for several minutes, twisting and turning and pausing, then repeating the process. When she was satisfied she'd hit a mark, she glanced at the dial as if to make a mental note of the right number. Sam couldn't see any of the numbers she'd hit, and he didn't really care. What bothered the spy was that this was taking longer than he would have liked.

"I thought this was your specialty," Sam whispered.

Cat fixed him with a look of disgust, then said, "Quiet. It's bad enough I have to listen to his snoring."

"I didn't realize it would take this long."

"Just because I can do it doesn't mean I can do it with a snap of the fingers. Keep talking and we'll be longer." She turned the dial once more, now in the opposite direction, and noted the second number she'd arrived at. "If we didn't need to be so sly, I'd have just recommended a drill—much quicker, but that won't do, will it?"

Sam stepped over toward the window to make sure they hadn't been compromised. If he could have helped, he would've, but he didn't know a damn thing about safes. That was her job to figure out. He watched with fascination as she searched for the final number. Several more minutes went by, but he knew she'd done well when she pulled on the handle and the safe popped open.

"She's all yours," Cat said.

"How'd you do that?" Sam asked.

"Quite simple, really," Cat replied. "Most like this have imperfections. You look for those. Take into account the slop in the lock and there's not much else you need other than patience."

Sam wasted no time pulling the stacks of documents out from the safe, making sure to keep them in the *exact* order he found them, and Cat went to work closing the curtains on each of the windows behind them. Once they were out of view of any potentially prying eyes, Cat switched on a lamp on a nearby desk. Sam opened the first of several folders, stacked the documents neatly on the desk, then laid a series of papers in the center.

Cat popped the cork off of what was surely an expensive bottle of red wine, and Sam shook his head disapprovingly. "What?" Cat asked. "I'm supposed to be here anyway, right?" She tilted the bottle into her mouth and took a healthy swig like a blue-collar man coming off a hard shift. The behavior was unbecoming of a women of her status, but behind closed doors, Sam was figuring out Cat was anything but the character she'd become so good at playing. She shoved the bottle toward Sam, offered up the goods, and Sam took a taste as well. "Attaboy."

Cat went right back to the bottle, and Sam got to work checking the settings of his camera. He opened the aperture as much as he could to let in all of the little light present. He took a photo, questioned its sharpness, then adjusted the shutter settings to compensate for his shaky hands. He returned to his original position, mimicking his exact posture, and then once more adjusted the settings—this time the lens's focus—until he was confident he was going to take consistently usable photographs. Once he was satisfied, he began to photograph each of the documents one by one.

He couldn't pay much attention to the details. That would be the job of the worker bees back at The Yard. He was sure the information he'd come for was of value. The documents definitely concerned Spain's place in the war, and its status in the global theatre. He recognized the names of high-ranking German officials and military representatives of the Spanish army. Every time he photographed a document, he placed it face down in a pile beside the photographing area.

"Tungsten" was a word he caught briefly but frequently. It wasn't Sam's job to sort out why it was so relevant, but he took interest in those types of matters naturally because most information he came across in his travels often proved useful to his missions in some way or form. Some of the documents were written in Spanish, some in German, and some in English.

"What do they say?" Cat asked.

"Shush," Sam replied without removing his focus from the task at hand. Cat rolled her eyes and took another taste of the bottle. She'd almost depleted the entire thing before he'd even finished. Moreno let out a guttural growl from the bed, causing both spies to freeze, then murmured like a child and went right back to snoring. Sam finished photographing the first set of documents, then packed them up and laid the folder face down on the table. He opened another and went to work, repeating the same process. Though Cat had likely bought him plenty of time by incapacitating the Spaniard, there was no reason to linger in a sovereign nation's embassy while stealing their secrets any longer than one had to.

"So," Cat said, seemingly eager to make conversation, "how'd you get put on this one?"

"He points," Sam said. He snapped another photo. "I go."

"Huh," Cat replied with some confusion. "Seems like small potatoes for you."

"Why's that?" Sam asked, sure to keep his voice low.

"I've heard about you," Cat said. "About Germany, and that tank or whatever."

"Believe none of what you hear and half of what you

see," Sam said, his focus on the task at hand not wavering.

"Strange choice of words for our line of work," Cat replied. "It's just, taking pictures isn't so dangerous, you know? I figured a guy like you would be getting ready to head to Africa with the rest of the boys—or maybe the Pacific."

"Just because no one is pointing a gun at us doesn't mean what we're doing isn't dangerous," Sam replied. "In fact, it might be worse. Over there you'd catch a quick bullet. Here, they'll put you on trial."

Cat gulped, then took another long, hard drink from the wine bottle.

"But, I mean…" Cat said with hesitation. "What we're doing—it's all for the war, right? Don't the rules bend?"

"We might bend the rules," Sam said, then flipped another document onto the table, "but bend something long enough and it breaks."

Cat shrugged, then said, "What's a few secrets, am I right?"

"Stealing secrets is easy," Sam said as he worked diligently. "Keeping them is hard." Sam flipped the last of several documents over, collected them as neatly as he'd found them, and placed them back into the tan folder they'd come from. He slung the camera back over his shoulder and behind his coat to prevent it from getting wet on the journey home. Though his entourage had been given a bevy of new resources, and the money faucets seemed to be flowing into Brandt's operation, there was no use destroying good equipment.

As a matter of fact, Sam had grown quite fond of the camera. He'd found the process of looking over his developed photographs thrilling. Though stealing secrets was often a long game, photographs—after the bees in the dark room had their go at them—were quick, visible results. Sam never spent his time going through the nuanced information in the documents. The suits and ties at headquarters got paid to do that. He always made it a point of stopping by to check out the results of his work, though. If he could find free time, he'd consider capturing the next appearance of blooming cherry blossoms in the nation's capital.

Sam placed the documents back into the safe exactly as he'd found them while the Spanish representative fell deeper into sleep in the dark room. Cat closed it behind him and spun the dial with a quick whack of her palm. There was a brief moment of silence between Cat and Sam, then she placed both of her gloved hands on her hips, and said, "Say, I don't ever see you around at The Yard. What gives?"

"I'm more of a satellite operator," Sam replied. Sam maneuvered to the window he'd arrived through, grabbed his hat from the floor, then flicked it briefly out the window to rid it of any remaining water before he placed it back on his head. He eyed the sleeping man once more, then said, "You've got to stick around, eh?"

"Part of the job," Cat said. She motioned to the wealth of wine bottles sitting on a server at the far end of the room. "I've got plenty of friends to keep me company." Cat sat on the bed next to the slumbering man, then finished the last bit in the bottle in her hand.

Sam's eyes darted between the two of them for a moment, then he asked, "You don't—" He paused, unable to produce the words and instead pointing with his chin to Cat's "date." Cat looked at him briefly, then gazed back at Sam. "Do you?" he finished.

"We've all got to do things we don't always want to do to get the job done, right?" Cat asked. Sam nodded. "When he wakes, I'll convince him what a wonderful lover he was. He won't speak of it. I'm not *supposed* to be here."

Sam knew the feeling. Brandt had a way of plucking people with few options left to insert into his staff. Despite being in perpetually dangerous situations, for many recruits the promise of even minuscule amounts of freedom was enough to take the paycheck and do the job. Sam convinced himself—and he was sure Cat had, too—that when the war was over, it would all have been worth it.

Sam climbed out of the window, and as he did so, he caught one more glimpse of Cat staring at him. There was a forlorn expression in her eyes, as if the man she'd rather spend the night with had just told her she wasn't good enough, or not his type, and left her with a lesser caller. The empty bottle in her hand juxtaposed with the glamorous dress made the image even more depressing. Sam didn't have time to worry about that. He needed to get back into a safe place—he had precious documents on him contained in several rolls of film that needed to be protected at all costs. After climbing back down the drainpipe, which was even easier than climbing up it, Sam grabbed the handle of the door that led out of the courtyard and opened it. He took a good survey of the street ahead, twisted the lock on the door, then closed it quietly.

The rain had slowed. In the streetlight above, thin wisps of moisture danced in the glowing air. It was the type of rain he could see, but not feel. Summer had arrived and the weather in D.C. was getting warmer by the day, but that night's storm had cooled the area considerably. Sam would make the trek on foot to meet the recipient of the film. Getting the photos to the men ready and waiting to develop them was of the essence. The journey home wouldn't be quick without a car, but there was no use giving anyone a license plate to catch, and he'd use the alleys and cut-throughs of the closely packed buildings to his advantage to disorient followers; though he knew any would be unlikely. Cat would have to spend the night still "working," but Sam had a pint of beer at home with his name on it.

After his trek, when Sam stepped out of the shadows and into a predetermined pickup location, a black sedan slowed to a crawl in front of him. The window opened and revealed a dark figure in a fedora puffing on a cigarette. Sam dug into his pocket and grabbed the rolls of film.

"Nice night for paella," the man said. Sam handed the man the rolls of film through the window, then kept walking. The car never even stopped. It was hardly a brush pass, but the exchange was clandestine nonetheless.

He kept acutely aware of his surroundings for the trip home. The nature of his work work meant it was fraught with double agents and traitors, self-interested opportunists, liars, and people just looking to protect their own hides or make a quick buck. For all Sam knew, not even Cat could be trusted.

Brandt had kept most operations tight-lipped. Most of the people at The Yard didn't even know each other's names. It wasn't the type of job where people clocked in and discussed the latest college football games over Monday morning coffee. The fact that Cat had even known his name—and bits of his past—made Sam uneasy. That meant that people within the operation were already talking—and saying far too much. The Yard was rapidly expanding.

2

The Yard was located on the outskirts of the nation's capital. The building, camouflaged in a warehouse district composed of an offensive amount of brick, hardly seemed unusual in comparison to its neighbors. The Yard was named for the long, gated parking lot at its front. The days of scurrying around by boat and plane with the team the spymaster had assembled—which had seemingly grown exponentially overnight—had quickly ceased, at least for the lackeys. Brandt himself still disappeared for days at a time to God knows where. The operation—with its influx of new resources—had even been given a proper name: the SSD. Brandt thought it would strike confusion in America's enemies.

The acronym stood for the Strategic Service Department, but then again no one ever really gave that explanation out—it was purely for reference. It's primary concerns were reconnaissance, infiltration, disinformation, espionage, recovery, and sabotage. Now that the operation was going forward in an official capacity—though still operating off the radar with a secret budget—it had found itself needing a home suited to its activities. The number of cables coming daily were stacking faster than the men and women working inside the building could even decipher them. Sam had once seen a mountain of papers so high that they'd almost reached the ceiling of one floor and gave him the impression none of the employees had shown up for work.

What had started with only a microscopic operation had been turned into one that was growing larger by the day. Sam saw new faces every time he came to the location, and he was starting to wonder just how in the hell his superior could keep track of all of the comings and goings of employees. Some of the characters, like Cat or even himself, were hardly saints: liars, thieves, extorters, defectors, and even murderers—*good ones*. Brandt had been trying to work alongside the other branches of government as best he could, but he'd pleaded with his friend in the big chair—whose ear he had—that he needed complete autonomy so as not to jeopardize any of his missions. In other words, Brandt was running his own paramilitary group that had been okayed by the men on top for now. That hadn't always been the case.

Sam stepped through the opening in the chain link fence around the building's perimeter shortly after dawn. He had walked from home, not solely because he still didn't have a car—he didn't really have use for one—but also because he found the thirty-minute walk to be a good way of getting the day started. There was nothing noteworthy about the building. The windows on its second, third, and fourth floors were many, but dark. It had virtually no security outside. Any building that had armed guards and checkpoints was just screaming "secrets here," and D.C. was already full of places like that.

The lot surrounding the building was unkempt and comprised of pummeled stone and dirt that had probably seen plenty of action during the prior tenants' stay. The building had belonged to a food service of some sort. On hot days Sam could still smell the building's past, which could be nauseating to say the least. There were only a few cars surrounding the building—many of the drones would either take public transportation or hoof it on foot because the place needed to give the impression it saw little traffic.

The interior was a different story. Sam stepped through two brick columns which supported the building's front entrance, then entered through a glass double door that exited to a bare concrete hall. There was no artificial light, only the glint of sun coming through the glass door, and on the other end one man sat at a desk. He could see who was coming fifty yards away, and it was the only entrance anyone used to get in or out of the building. Despite the funnel of accountability, Brandt's eager recruitment still raised flags *outside* of The Yard.

The long walk down the hall was strange and quiet. Sam was only accompanied by the sounds of his shoes clacking against the stone floor while he plunged deeper into shadow. The man at the far end craned his neck to get a look at the approaching figure, and his hand reached down below his desk in response. He was closing the distance between his hand and a firearm. That was customary; the secrets and operations in the building were of high value. When Sam arrived at the desk, the man requested he put his finger on a small ink pad, which Sam did, then Sam pressed it onto a paper. The guard scribbled something on the paper, checked the prints against others contained in countless sheets in a large binder, then asked for Sam's "code."

"505," Sam said, and the man released his grip of the pistol from under the desk and waved him through. The guard knew Sam—he'd seen him countless times, but that was protocol, and everyone followed it. A freight elevator carried Sam up to the second floor, and when the doors opened, a flurry of action attacked his senses.

The sound of ruffling papers was an auditory assault. Phones rang, typewriters clacked, and voices spoke in intense conversation under a thick cloud of cigarette and pipe smoke. The smell of animal byproduct was pungent due to the warm morning, and so too was the whiff of ash. Even the floor was littered with discarded cigarette butts, most of which had been kicked to the corners of desks by the high volume of traffic. The lighting in the room was inadequate. Desk lamps in each person's space were what they were forced to work with, because little sun penetrated the windows and the ceilings were made of exposed beams.

Most of the people working looked tired. The men's ties were loosened, the women's dresses disheveled, and many had dark circles under their eyes and the glaze of days-old sweat. These people had probably been working for the better part of the night. War waited for no man —or woman. Brandt's initiative to make women a part of the team was unique and progressive. Though spy operations were traditionally comprised mostly of men, Brandt thought that they were just as useful —if not more so—than any man with a set of balls prepared to do that kind of work. Sam suspected Brandt's logic had more to do with the fact that the old man was a flirt and probably an adulterer. After all, Sam had seen him in action.

Sam lit up a cigarette. A few people took note of his presence, one woman even watching him with wide eyes as the spy stepped down the center walkway that split the room in half. The stories of his efforts in Germany to destroy the super tank known as *Erdschlag* had made the rounds amongst his compatriots, and though few people had asked him about the sabotage directly, Sam Abel was given respect when he stepped into a room. The employees in D.C. were paper pushers: intel gatherers, and decipherers—though good ones—and he was anything but.

When Sam reached the end of the room, he climbed up a flight of concrete stairs, then turned to ascend another. The third floor was unlike the first two. This was a series of maze-like hallways sectioned off to form private offices and cubicles, and it was where the most closely guarded secrets were kept. The SSD did not share information liberally amongst all branches—that was a recipe for disaster. The third floor was home to those who were involved in all manner of information sharing based solely on a need-to-know basis. Plans of attack, sabotage, and infiltration were prepared, monitored, and executed behind thick walls that were far more sound-proof than the halls of the floor below.

Sam climbed two more flights of stairs, then arrived at the building's fourth—and top—floor. Another desk barred entrance to the long hall ahead, which also contained a compartmentalized series of offices, kept private and away from prying eyes. A middle-aged brunette woman with a well-pressed white blouse and a charcoal wool skirt tended to the affairs of the desk.

"Iris," Sam said, and she smiled coyly.

"I heard you had a busy night," she replied. "He's been all sorts of excited this morning—he came in before the sun even woke up, or myself for that matter." She looked tired, Sam thought. Her hair was greying at the root, and even though her age was beginning to show in creases on her forehead, she still very much possessed the energy to keep up with the demands of the most important desk in the building. She wore no ring on her finger. Sam supposed she had been giving as much of her life over to The Yard as her superior, and there'd been rumors that she had been with Brandt before he'd even wound up in the capital, while he was still practicing international business law.

"That good, huh?" Sam asked. Iris's eyebrows rose into high arches that signaled surprise.

"He's in with someone," Iris said. "But he told me to send you over as soon as you arrived. 'Not a moment to lose.' His words, not mine."

Sam used the tray on Iris's desk to tamp out his cigarette. She was one of the few people in the building with whom he regularly had conversations, and the two were even on a first-name basis. But Sam suspected that wasn't even her real name, like his own. Brandt had once said to Sam, 'She's my second set of eyes. She sees *everything*.' Sam guessed that might have been how she inherited her name. She was responsible for previewing most of the information that crossed Brandt's desk and was also probably the custodian of the building when the boss was away—as he often was.

Sam had barely even seen Brandt since the Pforzheim debriefing. He'd been country-hopping by plane and boat like a madman, collecting assets and resources for missions across the globe. The documents that Sigrid Lang had provided were filled with details concerning Nazi troop movements and even information regarding those involved with the now-defunct project. Though Sam was still ripped up over the German defector's death, she'd done good. Valuable turncoats like Sigrid were hard to find. Brandt was learning that the hard way.

Sam continued down the long hall, the end of which banked left and led to a door that had been left ajar. Sam heard a gruff, accusatory voice coming from Brandt's office. He crept forward silently, eavesdropping as was his instinct. Sam could hear a voice he did not know speaking with a snake-like voice, then Brandt offering a rebuttal. As Sam got closer, the details were audible.

"And here you are running around D.C. without any accountability, all because you've got the big man's ear," the voice said.

"Our activities are conducted purely overseas," Brandt replied. It had been a while since Sam had heard his master's voice. It was tired, defensive even. "More importantly, our interests should be aligning. I would think the man *you* report to could respect that."

"He's about upholding the laws and regulations currently in place—"

"Phooey. I've got eyes and ears stretching across the globe, and they say otherwise."

"Are you spying on your own nation? That's treasonous—and an offense worthy of a court-martial."

"You couldn't if you tried," Brandt replied. "I'm not currently in the service. Of course, if you have a charge, I welcome you to bring it forward."

"Even better," the man replied. "It wouldn't be so difficult to convince a jury or judge of a private citizen's guilt; much less, in fact, than a man who has put his time in."

"Oh, I've put my time in," Brandt sneered. Sam heard the soft click of someone tapping metal, and though he didn't have eyes on the action, he was sure Brandt was reminding this combative man sitting across from him that he'd received the Medal of Honor, amongst others. Brandt kept it pinned to his suit jacket whenever he had the opportunity. It didn't hurt reminding people of just who they were speaking to, but Sam also believed it kept his ego nice and inflated. "Have you?" There was no response to the question. Silence fell, before Brandt said, "If your boss has got a problem with my outfit, you can tell him 1600 Pennsylvania is only a short trip that way. I'm sure he knows, though."

"See, that's the difference between him and you, though," the other man replied. "He doesn't need to ask daddy's permission to go out and play." Sam heard Brandt's guest rise abruptly from his seat before saying, "We'll be seeing you."

Brandt said, "Tell your boss to give my love to his wife—sweet lady."

Before Sam could even move from his hiding spot, the man turned the corner at a brisk pace. He wore a long, dark pea coat over a disheveled suit. He placed a fedora over his head before lifting his face to lock eyes with Sam. Sam froze up. He had been caught in the act of listening, and not by Axis forces, but by a D.C. suit.

The man's face was hardened and grumpy, as if he perpetually woke up on the wrong side of the bed. His nose and lips were contorted into an offensive snarl. He was bulky, but not toned, that Sam could tell from how his suit fit him. Whatever muscle the man had once had was softening as he crept into middle age, and his hair was a sleek black with a neat part at the side. When he saw Sam, he studied him briefly, then scanned him up and down twice over from his feet to his head—everything about the man's expression said that he had *recognized* Sam. Sam said not a word, but as the man passed, he smirked, then said softly, "*Auf Wiedersehen.*"

What did he mean by that? Sam's ethnicity could be misinterpreted easily. He'd pass for all sorts of European depending on the lighting in the room, how he combed his hair, or even how much sun he'd gotten lately. Did the man think he was German, or did he know something more? Sam again suspected far too many people had been talking.

Once the man had cleared the hall and found the stairwell, Sam turned into Brandt's office. He extended a thumb backwards, and the scar-faced man leaned back in his chair and folded his fingers over his stomach. "FBI—an empty suit, if you ask me," Brandt said simply.

"Don't they have better things to worry about?"

"It's a long story," Brandt replied. "Let's just say that though his boss and I both have the big chair's ear, we've got our own history. He's got it in for me and, in turn, *all of us*. Keeps sending his lackeys in because he's not man enough to come face me himself. If I didn't know any better, I'd think it was the mafia. Ever since we set up shop here, I've had his ilk crawling around and picking through our scraps. Now he's just pissed that he can't get the kind of work done that *we* do."

"Empty threats?" Sam asked.

"No," Brandt said. "Unfortunately, they have weight. Which is why you need to be extra careful, especially doing what you're doing." He gestured to the seat the FBI agent had just left. Sam took it, and suppressed his disgust at finding it was still warm where the man's butt had been resting moments earlier. Sam lit up a smoke, then pulled the ashtray on the desk closer to him.

Brandt packed a pipe, lit it, then took a deep pull of the smoke before saying, "Hell of a score last night, Sam."

"Is that so?" Sam replied.

"Damn right. The hive has been having a field day combing through that stuff since they developed the first photo."

"Were the exposures all right?"

"I wouldn't expect any less of you." He chuckled, then said, "Sam Abel: Master Photographer."

Sam wasted no time asking the question that had been taking up real estate in his mind. It was the first thing he'd wanted to ask Brandt since his return from Germany, and the one that had been keeping him up at night. "Anything?"

Brandt knew exactly what Sam was referring to, and he frowned in response, then said, "Not yet. If I found something, you know I'd tell you. Let's get something straight though, Abel—"

"I know," Sam cut him off. "Just because you find him doesn't mean I get to run back over guns blazing."

Sam had escaped from Lothar Eichler twice now. And the last time, he had taken the life of the woman Sam had gone to retrieve. But despite how eager he was to track the man down, his whereabouts still remained unknown.

Though Sam's efforts to destroy the super weapon and successfully bring classified and valuable documents home had been a grand success, Sam was bitter about the death of Sigrid Lang. It wasn't like him to get caught up in the emotions of the battlefield, but Sigrid had been a citizen gone rogue, and a brave one at that. She was also a knockout, and his memory of the night they'd spent together still lingered.

"You ask me every time we see each other," Brandt said. "We've got one of the finest operations going in the world right now. You think I wouldn't let you know if I found him?"

"I'm not so sure about that," Sam replied. "Who gets to hear about what around here is still up for debate."

"As it should be. Besides, we're changing the way we do things. Sending you in there, I admit, was probably unwise. It's very difficult to penetrate the fortress now, and we've got our eyes on trying to pull people down off the fence, the people already behind enemy lines, rather than our own men: resistance teams, dissidents, guerrilla fighters, that sort of thing. We've got be everywhere," Brandt said, then his eyes diverted toward the door where the FBI agent had recently stood. "And nowhere."

Sam didn't press the issue any further. He'd take Brandt's word for it. If Eichler could be found, he hoped the burned man would keep up his end of the bargain. He owed Sam one, anyway. Sam, one way or another, would figure out where Eichler was hiding, and when he did, he'd take a trip to the fatherland—in an official capacity or otherwise.

"How do you like our new girl?" Brandt asked.

"Seems up to the task," Sam replied.

"Good," Brandt said. "You'll be working closely with her while you're still home."

"She's a little chatty," Sam said.

"Part of the job."

The phone rang, and Brandt answered, "Yes?" His eyes fluttered rapidly as he processed the influx of information. He raised a finger to Sam. "Put him through." Sam checked his watch, and Brandt began pacing as far as the tether of the phone cord would take him. Sam rose from his seat, pointed downstairs, and Brandt cupped the phone then said, "Don't go too far. You're going out on the town tomorrow night."

3
—————

Cat woke to the feeling of wet, sloppy kisses running down her shoulder, then passing along her spine. It took her a moment to get her bearings. Waking up in unfamiliar places had been par for the course even before she'd joined Brandt's operation. Traveling along American roads and fleeing from law enforcement nightly was routine when she was much younger, and many of the following mornings were spent in shady motels and flophouses amongst criminals not unlike herself.

She turned over to find the hopeful, glistening eyes of Salazar Moreno staring back at her like a dog's. His hair was matted from a deep sleep, and his breath was foul. Cat, keeping up the act, produced a satisfied smile as if the man had made her night special. Little did Moreno know he'd been drugged and ransacked. She ran her fingers through the thick curls that fell around his ears, then snuggled closer to him.

"*Quieres más?*" Moreno asked.

Cat deflated, but didn't alert Moreno to her dissatisfaction. She said, "The least you could do is offer a girl some breakfast. What good are all these fancy rooms and servants if a girl can't get some eggs and orange juice?"

"It would be better, I think, that no one should see you," Moreno replied. Cat wasted no time tearing the covers from her body. It was bad enough she had to fake being a whore—the last thing she needed was to be treated as such. When she rose, the room spun. She'd slept poorly, partially because she'd had a hard time resting with all the heavy snoring spewing from Moreno's maw, but also because she'd take any opportunity to imbibe her fill of good, expensive booze.

She hated the morning part. Putting on the dress she'd arrived in and fixing her makeup to be acceptable enough that she was passable as a stand-up girl only reminded her of how much she loathed that part of the job. She didn't even have a damn toothbrush. Cracking safes was easy; keeping up the performance was loathsome. She was a respectable woman, anyhow. She hadn't slept with Moreno—not like *that*—but she would have. If she was going to have to do dirty work, she'd at least make sure the son-of-a-bitch was handsome. Moreno *was* quite dashing, as far as she was concerned, especially when he wasn't snoring.

Brandt wasn't a monster. If Cat was going to have to get her hands dirty, it was *her* say whether or not anything happened. Brandt actually respected her, and she owed him more than one for getting her out of a lifelong jam. The only problem was, she couldn't see the light at the end of the tunnel. What was the end—the end of the war? He'd never threatened her, but she suspected that if she fell out of line, he could send her right back to a Pennsylvania penitentiary of his choosing with a quick phone call. He seemed like a man with an infinite amount of important phone numbers at his disposal.

Cat reapplied some makeup in a mirror flanking the bed. She fixed her hair as well as she could, then straightened her dress and threw on a long fur coat that Brandt, of course, had paid for from what he called "The Lawn," then started slipping on a set of heels. Moreno rose from the bed, yawning obnoxiously like a bear preparing for a kill. He scratched at his hairy chest and went for the bathroom. When he wasn't looking, Cat took one more healthy swig from the wine bottle on the table beside the mirror. It would have to do for breakfast.

On the table near Moreno's side of the bed, a wallet sat open. Moreno had been busy brushing his teeth, his face now buried in the sink and his hearing obscured by the water rushing from the faucet. Cat ceased putting her heels on, then tiptoed over to the table. She riffled through Moreno's wallet, saw quite a wad of cash bursting through the seam, and grabbed a handful of bills. She'd been given plenty of money to galivant around D.C., but old habits die hard. She didn't take it because she needed it, but simply because she *could*. Besides, he was a scumbag, anyway. For all she knew, she'd been sent over because the man was either a Nazi sympathizer or Axis cohort. It was unlikely she'd have been sent for any other reason.

She finished the business with the heels, checked her appearance once more in the mirror, then grabbed her clutch and set off for the bedroom door. Moreno peeked his head from the bathroom before saying, "I can see you out."

"Not needed," Cat replied without even looking his way.

"Will I see you at the fundraiser?" he called out. His answer came in the form of a slamming door.

Her behavior hadn't been what Brandt would have preferred. She was never supposed to let her feelings get in the way, but her head was pounding something fierce. A bad hangover could handicap even the most adept spy.

Her first priority was to get a cup of coffee. She'd need to report to the office at one point or another to be debriefed. She'd been privy to information the night before while mingling with many of Moreno's associates: Spanish delegates, entrepreneurs, and even some celebrities from the film industry. She'd recognized one of the men at the party as one of those monsters from a horror picture. She didn't remember his name, but seemed to recall the costume involved fur or fangs or something like that.

She stepped down the stairs, then arrived in the marble-floored hall. The security guard who'd been aware of her arrival the night before had been pacing near the front entrance. He gave a disapproving nod. He'd understood the arrangement, and also not to speak about it, but he'd had no idea what she or Sam had really been up to. His face turned briefly, as if reminding her that the front entrance wasn't acceptable for girls like herself, and Cat turned on her heel and down another hall.

It was still early, and very few employees had arrived for work. It was better that way—the fewer people who saw her, the more incognito she remained. Leaving early was always important. She'd stick out like a sore thumb in an embassy during the bustling afternoon work hours.

Both Brandt and Cat were in agreement that she was trying to build a name for herself within the capital city. They'd settled on her faux identity only a few months earlier and agreed that, based on Cat's adorable charm and approachable demeanor, "wealthy orphaned socialite just looking for a good time" would work well. If she was perpetually single, the wandering eyes of men in power would soon find her. Brandt funneling money her way so that she could look the part helped. She'd had to take a class with a bitter old woman to beef up her skills in the manners and etiquette department, but she was a fast learner.

Cat's first priority had been to just "be seen" in the right places, and after being recognized at all of the right parties with the right people, soon she'd gotten to know the class of people that had been completely out of her atmosphere in her past life. Even Brandt was tickled at how well she'd integrated. Cat had always embraced her trashy side, but she'd taken a liking to dancing around with the elite. She was good at it, and any time she had a slip up, she was quick-witted enough to turn her misfortune or error into a joke that would color her the belle of the ball.

Dickering around with many of the powerful men she'd encountered wouldn't get her in much trouble, either. She was a good tease. The egos of suckers like Moreno were too fragile to doubt that they'd been too drunk to remember what happened, and more importantly, these types of men didn't kiss and tell. No one talked about their flings or extra-marital affairs, which gave Cat the ability to cozy up to quite a few of them in short time without any of the men exchanging information with each other. She'd even once been propositioned by the wife of one of her targets, but declined. She and Brandt had agreed that might raise a flag or two; otherwise she might have accepted the offer.

Cat kept her head low when she passed through the kitchen. Two cooks were busy prepping omelets, the smell of which made her mouth water. One of the cooks shook his head as if to shame her, but Cat paid him no mind and passed through toward the door that would finally let her out of the building. A small tray of glasses filled with orange juice sat ready and waiting on a stainless-steel table, and Cat grabbed one, slurped it down, then made sure to look the cook right in the eye before slamming it back on the table.

The courtyard Sam had crept through the night before was occupied only by the sounds of chirping. Cat called them "loser birds"—in other words, the birds that mocked men and women shamefully with song for the previous night's activities. Loser birds could only be heard in a small window in the early morning hour in which people with guilty consciences often travelled. If she didn't know better, she'd have thought they were tweeting right at her—maybe even laughing.

She opened the gate that led outside of the courtyard, a small iron door that was used to dispose of garbage and remained unlocked for quick exits—she'd known because she'd made use of it before. The street outside the building was still wet with a mixture of morning dew and leftover rain. A cool breeze swept around Cat, bringing with it the refreshing smell of petrichor. The weather had been getting warmer by the day, and the storm had brought with it a brief respite that would soon turn into unrelenting humidity. The sun had started to rise, but the tall buildings hugging the embassy on each side had not yet permitted it to shine where she stood.

She saw no one, though there was a black sedan idling at the far end of the street. She couldn't see through the windshield because of the way the glass reflected the grey morning sky above. Satisfied no one had spotted her exit, Cat set off down the sidewalk. A garbage truck tending to the waste sitting outside building façades roared toward her, and she clutched her coat in an effort to wrap it more tightly around her body.

Amongst the inventory of goodies provided by her organization was a car, but she hadn't used it the night before. She'd met Moreno at the event. He was a guest of distinction who'd shown his face to generate revenue for a fund Cat hadn't paid much attention to because Brandt was satisfied it was legitimate. She'd shown up as arm candy, and he had promised to introduce her to people. Moreno had done nothing of the sort, but rather mingled with smiling faces he was attempting to coax into emptying their wallets and purses.

Another forceful gust of wind pushed through the long street as the garbage truck passed by. A cool chill ran down Cat's spine, and though she didn't possess the uncanny instincts of the field operatives she worked with, she felt an overwhelming sensation that she was being watched. She turned to look over her shoulder, and the black sedan that had been immobile only moments before was now rolling slowly behind her. She still couldn't see who was behind the wheel.

She brushed it off, suspecting that it was the nature of the job getting to her, and continued down the street at a faster pace. Soon, the low hum of a motor drowned out the sounds of her heel spikes striking the cement. She turned once more over her shoulder and felt unease that the car didn't accelerate and pass her, but rather lingered behind as if following her. If the driver was attempting to monitor her incognito, he wasn't doing a good job. She'd been well aware of the car's presence since she'd first spotted it.

She stepped forward more quickly still. Not a soul was on the street ahead of her, and now that she could hear the garbage truck disappearing still further behind her, she was alone with just the stalking car. Ahead, another quiet street intersected with her course, but there wasn't any action going on down it either. She ran through her story briefly in her head. She and Brandt had prepared a sort of basic premise for her identity and whereabouts, enough so that if she ran into any real trouble with enemies or law enforcement, she'd be able to buy herself enough time that she could call in and get someone with real clout to get her out of a bind. She even had the manufactured credentials to prove her story:

I'm Catherine McAlister. Who's asking? If you've got a problem you can take it up with my attorneys. Unless you've got a charge, I'll be on my way.

The statement gave her no comfort as the car came closer. What good was a line of bullshit if she could be overpowered, or captured, or arrested? What if it was a reporter looking for a scoop? What if it was one of

Moreno's men trying to dispose of her as some kind of loose end to be cut? Did politicians have people killed? *Of course not.* But then again, maybe she was being naïve. This was war time, after all.

She took another look, this time doing her best to deduce just *who* was behind the wheel. She got her answer. There wasn't just one man—there were two. Both wore dark sunglasses, and they were looking right at her. There was no further doubt in her mind that they were on to her.

Not today. Cat McAlister is better than that. She eyed an alley to her left. Steam from a basement window funneled into the alley like a tornado, obscuring the long corridor and what lay ahead. It was better than continuing down the path she was on. She stepped off the sidewalk and walked diagonally across the street. While crossing the blacktop, she got one last look at the two men following, both of whom watched with unwavering gazes. She was confident once she'd cleared the whirling cloud of moisture she'd disappear. *That'll show 'em.*

For a brief moment, she saw nothing in front of her but a thick wall of tumbling clouds. She looked behind once more and saw the sedan disappear beyond the edge of the building. She smirked, then continued forward with a smug disposition. Before she could even celebrate her minor victory, she crashed face first into what felt like a solid wall and fell on her bottom.

The impact disoriented her, and she tilted her head up to see the bulwark that had blocked her path. Standing above her, a man in a black suit and tie stared. She couldn't see the eyes under the dark shadow of the fedora covering his head until he pulled on the cigarette between his fingers. The burning cherry lit the small circles of his eyes, casting him in a mysterious glow that only barely illuminated the details of his face as he puffed casually on the cigarette. The contents of her purse had spilled all over the asphalt, and she quickly gathered each of the items without saying another word.

"Cat got your tongue?" the man asked.

Cat rose after grabbing the last of the spilled items, a small compact mirror, and stepped forward toward the man in an effort to level the playing field. She showed no fear. He'd had the upper hand standing above her, but when she met his face, she discovered he wasn't so tall at all. Cat said, "What's that supposed to mean, buddy?"

"If you bump into someone, you usually offer an apology," the man replied.

"You bumped into *me*," Cat said, extending her index finger toward him.

The man inserted his free hand into the pocket of his slacks, and the displacement of his sport coat revealed a firearm holstered on his belt. Cat noticed it immediately. She dropped her finger, anxious to deescalate the situation. She was a woman alone in an alley arguing with an armed man she didn't know, in the wee hours of the morning, with nowhere to run. A cloud of steam shifted forward from her back and around the man in front of her. In that moment, she connected the dots and recognized that this man wasn't just some disgruntled passerby; he was in some way involved with the men trailing her in the sedan.

"Little early for a lady of the night, ain't it?" the man asked. He kept his hand idle near the weapon. Cat clenched both of her hands tightly, the one holding the clutch at risk of breaking the clasp and spilling the contents inside once more. "I suppose your work is done now, though, so you're probably on your way back *home*." The final word out of his mouth sounded with a skeptical sting.

He pulled on the cigarette once more, smoke trailing from his mouth in large tufts as he allowed her the next word. It was slow to come. Cat knew better than to start running her mouth. "Watch where you're going," she said.

"Same to you," the man replied. "See you around." He stepped aside to allow her to proceed forward down the alley, watching her with an uncomfortable glower as she moved forward. She stormed past him, unable to quell a feeling like an animal had its eyes fixed firmly on her back and might attack. After she'd gained some distance, she turned once more over her shoulder and caught a momentary glimpse of the dark silhouette of the man's torso disappearing into the cloud of steam.

4

———

Photos hung from clothespins in a red-hued darkroom. A technician handled the exposures with metal tongs as Sam admired his handiwork. He dipped the papers in a series of chemicals one after another, then he clipped each photo on its white edge and left it for air-drying. There were still several rolls of film to go. The room was a mess of piled photos. Despite rampant hiring, Brandt hadn't been able to meet the demand for bees to sift through all of the information the organization had been acquiring in a timely manner. Sam had seen several still-undeveloped rolls that were labeled with his own handwriting that he remembered acquiring several months earlier.

The spy had gotten pretty good at this part of the job, and it didn't require putting a knife to anyone's throat. He scrutinized his handiwork; he still needed to get the mechanics of the aperture down. He'd set his shutter between one hundred sixty and two hundredths of a second to compensate for the natural motion of his body, and his focus measurements were incredibly precise, but he still had some things to learn about changing light conditions and iris mechanics. A few adjustments in the development technique by the technician had compensated for Sam's imperfections, though, so the minor errors were just that. While most employees weren't even allowed in the darkroom, Sam had gained special clearances awarded to him by Brandt.

"Looking for anything in particular?" the technician asked.

"Where's the first roll?"

"The captain took it," the technician replied. If Brandt had already procured them, then something inside of the lengthy correspondence was of potentially high value.

"You might just have a career in this," a woman's voice said from behind Sam.

Sam turned to find Cat standing in the dark corner of the entrance way to the room with her arms folded. He said, "Didn't hear you come in."

"That's usually *your* specialty," Cat replied. "I suppose I've been hanging around you too much." Sam knew better than to think she'd actually acquired any skill. The dark room didn't have a door, but rather a long hall devoid of light so some of the employees could come and go freely through without risking early exposure of the film. "What's that?" Cat asked. She nodded to a photograph the technician had just clipped to the line others hung from.

"Are you supposed to be in here?" the technician asked. Sam vetoed his question with a wave, then turned to look at the photograph. There was a rocky substance, metallic, with sharp, jagged edges reaching in assorted directions. Where the light struck the mineral's surface, it reflected with a silvery sheen. It looked like some type of crude ore, one that hadn't been refined yet but which would likely go through such a process. Sam didn't even remember photographing it. He'd been turning the pages over and photographing all of the safe's contents at such a rapid pace that it blended in with the rest of the photos he'd snapped.

Sam cocked his head to analyze the picture further, then said, "Not sure."

"Oh, that's tungsten," the technician said.

"What's tungsten?" Cat asked.

"A metal," the technician replied. "I kept seeing the word appear in all the documents along with these images."

————

Both parties nursed cigarettes in Brandt's office. He'd become a hard man to find, constantly fielding calls and requests, traveling without a moment's notice, running back and forth between his office and hush-hush meetings at the White House, and gradually evolving into a tornado of energy and information. Sam, for the first time, had even read his boss's name in the paper. The article was scathing, scrutinizing and questioning Brandt's mysterious activities and his constant international travels. He'd been photographed with foreign dignitaries and allies of note. As a private citizen, the press had begun rampant and wild speculation regarding just what Brandt was up to.

Brandt tried desperately to keep his profile low. In light of his questionable activities, his hires were even more at risk of scrutiny. His rogues gallery of criminals, informants, lowlifes, expats, and moles was enough to fill a large museum, and the less people knew, the better. But regardless of the optics, anyone Brandt hired was good at their job, and if they did lack skill in a particular area, they made up for it with pure bravery. Never mind the fact that the men Brandt reported to had secretly syphoned taxpayer dollars directly into his pocket—a slush fund Brandt called "The Lawn"—and the amounts inflated month by month proportionate to the demand of his ever-growing spy network.

Not everyone on the payroll was a lowlife, though. Some were well-respected attorneys, accountants, business owners, and even artists. Brandt had hired engineers to dream up gadgets fit for science-fiction serials, artists to render maps of foreign and occupied territories, and even film writers and novelists to concoct propaganda leaflets Brandt was dropping over enemy territory. No idea was too loony for the network captain, though few that wound up on his desk actually came to fruition. Long gone were the days when Brandt could utilize only limited resources. Sam's efforts in Pforzheim had helped secure more funding—of that, the spy was sure.

Cat sat with one leg folded over the other, and the top one bounced nervously up and down as she smoked her cigarette. She was in a perpetual state of motion, which irritated Sam. His demeanor was calm and calculated, and the thought that he'd have to start working more closely with this woman made him feel more at risk than he ever had. Working alone was easy—working in conjunction with someone whose methodology differed so greatly from his own was dangerous.

She had no training that he knew of not the kind

that mattered. He was confident she couldn't hold a gun properly, let alone fire one. The last time he'd had an ally who didn't understand the playing field and the risks at hand, she'd wound up with a bullet through the neck and died bleeding and gasping for air on the dirt road to a Nazi stronghold. The fact that Sam was sitting in a room with Cat was confirmation that Brandt's tactics were changing, and men who had no fear of pulling the trigger on a gun weren't the only operatives of value in war.

Cat had ditched the glamorous outfit from the previous evening for a navy collared dress that stretched just above the bouncing knee. Though it was a more conservative garment, the tan stitching and buttons that had been sewn in told Sam that it was still high fashion. She wore tan heels to match the accents and had tied her hair into a neat bun at the top. If she was trying to be taken seriously to blend in with the men of status roaming the halls of the secret brick building, she was doing a good job. She still wore jewelry: earrings with small but charming diamonds, a series of bracelets on the right wrist, and several rings that decorated her fingers; except, as was fitting with her cover story, she did not wear any jewelry on her left ring finger.

Sam imagined she still had to look the part even if she was recognized outside of the parties she attended. Being caught out in the wild was always a risk for a spy. Judging by the type of work Cat was doing, she was probably more at risk than men like himself.

The door burst open with the force of a small explosion. Brandt eyed both of his employees, then said, "Good, you're both here," before touching a match to the pipe in his hand and puffing eagerly on the tobacco.

He flicked the match to extinguish the flame, then tossed it onto the desk like a slob. The sunlight filtering through the slats of the blinds was extinguished when he abruptly shut them. "You can never be too sure," Brandt said. "I just hired a lip-reader. Anything's possible." Then he sat into the chair and pushed himself toward the desk eagerly before splitting his attention between the two of them.

"Can you dance?" Brandt asked Sam. Before Sam could answer, Brandt turned to Cat, then said, "I know you can."

"Kind of hard with a gun on my hip," Sam answered.

"Have you got a suit?" Brandt asked. Sam frowned. "Didn't think so." Brandt tore the drawer open, grabbed a small envelope with cash bursting from its mouth, then retrieved several bills and handed them to Sam. "Go get something presentable—not too flashy, simple and classic. And black." Brandt addressed Cat, "For you, a gown of some sort will do."

"What's this all about?" Sam asked.

Brandt grabbed an envelope that rested on the desk, flipped open the cover, and slid the document toward Sam. Sam grabbed the paper. The spy quickly realized the document he was holding was a result of his handiwork. The document was in Spanish, but it had been translated into English in shorthand above each word.

"Moreno is going to a party tomorrow night in Georgetown," Brandt said. "There'll be some heavy-hitters there, but two in particular we're concerned with."

Sam scanned the document quickly, picking up the relevant words that had been underlined in order to accommodate a speed-reader; then he read aloud from it. "Event begins promptly at eight, though arrival for welcome words won't be necessary. The Carolinian will be in attendance. An introduction to Sparrow is of the utmost importance. Sparrow should have no trouble with travel credentials. Toro will make introduction and ensure meeting goes smoothly. Sparrow will make offer to Carolinian for materials. If Carolinian bites, Sparrow will travel south for survey. Toro will maintain communication and updates. Recommended that Sparrow present a whiskey as tribute—Carolinian is quite fond of that. Carolinian will be staying at The Regalia in Georgetown and is expecting car service both to and from event. Toro will be responsible for making the arrangements."

"Sounds like a children's folk tale," Cat blurted out. "What's a Carolinian?"

"That's a Carolinian," Brandt said, and slid a photo of a lanky man with a dark five o'clock shadow and a ten-gallon hat toward Sam and Cat. "We've been intercepting some correspondence between Moreno and him for some time."

"Who is he?" Sam asked.

"His name's Wade Ives," Brandt replied. "He's a landowner in Vance County, North Carolina, and he's got quite a chunk of property. He's got no activities that raise any flags. He grows tobacco, got a hefty bit of livestock, and a smattering of granaries from what we can gather. Fancies himself a miner ever since he started digging around his property. He's got a clean record. The question is, why is he coming up here to meet Moreno? And more importantly—"

"—who is Sparrow?" Sam said.

"That's right," Brandt replied.

"Sounds like a regular old business meeting to me," Cat said nonchalantly. "I mean, who's to say these gents are dirty?"

"Good men don't talk in code," Sam said.

"Unless they're us, of course," Brandt said. "You know, the good guys." Cat cleared her throat. Brandt corrected himself, "And gals." Brandt continued, "Innocent people conduct business meetings in broad daylight, not behind the closed doors of questionable representatives. Anyway, we've suspected Moreno was up to no good for some time. Spain has remained aggressively neutral during the war, and as such, we've allowed them to keep a tent in D.C. thus far. But I believe Moreno's been compromised, whether his people know it or not, and whoever this Sparrow is, well, he's probably a bad egg. If he's coming in from another country, it's likely Axis-loyal."

"Where do we come in?" Sam asked.

"Because it won't be a party if Cat McAlister isn't in attendance," Cat said proudly.

"And you've got a plus one to boot," Brandt replied. He addressed Cat, "I've secured you both tickets to the event—they weren't cheap. You'll be arriving, fashionably late, of course—with the distinguished real estate magnate Paul Rilyeh."

"Is that French?" Sam asked.

"It's European," Brandt replied. "Let's not get too bogged down with the specifics. You're not there to make friends, you're there to do what you do best. Cat will handle introductions, if any."

"Are we dating?" Cat asked.

"Why do you ask?" Brandt questioned

"Well, I need to know," Cat replied. "If we're dating, then I'll want to show him off. It will only work in my favor; most of the men at those things are threatened by a handsome young man, and they'll only see me as more desirable."

"Keep your attention on Ives," Brandt said. "It's unlikely they'll make any introductions in view of everyone in attendance. They'll probably have this 'Sparrow' in a lounge ready and waiting. I have a feeling 'Sparrow' doesn't want to be seen in public if it can be avoided. Ives is coming up solely to broker these goods, whatever they are. I'm sure he doesn't like us Yankees as much as the next southern man, so I don't expect he'll be up for mingling or anything like that."

"Looks like it's a date," Cat said to Sam, and she balled up a fist and punched him in the shoulder like a chummy old pal. Sam didn't react. He'd come a long way from penetrating the high security at *Flussrand*. Dealing with the wealthy and their phony smiles and overpriced jewelry was going to take more effort than disarming *Wermacht* soldiers.

"I'll have a car pick both of you up at Cat's place tomorrow at eight," Brandt said. "You'll have to arrive looking the part. Newton's got some gear for you to use during the op." Brandt turned to Sam. "No cameras this time—I just want your eyes and ears."

"I suppose it's up to me to figure out how to get in on that conversation?" Sam asked.

"I'd expect nothing less," Brandt said with a smile. "Don't do anything too rash, though. This is a classy affair." Brandt slid a paper invitation toward Sam and Cat. It had been written on a thick stock, heavier even than the paper on which Sam's photos were printed. The invitation was written in flashy calligraphy traced with a glittering gold finish. It read: *You are cordially invited to the tenth annual 'Dinner and Diamonds' event, a live auction and an evening of decadence hosted by The Montgomery Family. Guests are asked to arrive at 8:00 pm for cocktails and hors d'oeuvres, followed by dinner. Introductions begin at 9:00 pm, and the auction will begin at 9:15 pm promptly. Dessert will be served at 11:00 pm. RSVP not required.*

Brandt took a deep inhale from his pipe, and the tobacco crackled like a flurry of bullets from an automatic rifle. Sam noticed he was fidgety, more nervous than he usually presented himself. Brandt exhaled the smoke, pointed the stem of the pipe toward both of his employees, and said, "The party is at the Georgetown home of a Mr. and Mrs. Carlyle Montgomery. Both are very connected, especially in Washington circles, and though it's happening right under their noses, they're likely unaware. They're loyal party donors, and there'll certainly be press there to cover the event, so don't get into any trouble."

Sam understood now why Brandt was so uneasy. The papers had already had a field day with his activities, and any more noise produced from his camp was likely to set off even more alarm bells, especially among the Washington elite. Sam imagined that penetrating the meeting was worth the risk, and as far as he knew, no one was yet aware of just who Brandt's operatives were. He and Cat should blend in just fine—he hoped.

Brandt said, "Hell of a find you two managed. Had we not got in there in the nick of time, we might have missed this one. And now I need you two to perform this magic trick."

"The jewelry I have just won't do," Cat said. Brandt grimaced. "What? You expect a girl to show up to a classy affair like this and not be wearing the finest pieces?" She hadn't convinced him. "Costume, of course." Brandt dug into the envelope once more, retrieved several bills, then handed them to Cat while mumbling under his breath. Just how much Brandt had been spending was a mystery to Sam, but judging by the number of people working in the building, combined with the number of agents—both foreign and domestic—Sam suspected it had ballooned considerably.

"Take the night off," Brandt said. "I want you both fresh for tomorrow. We don't know just how late this thing's going to go or when these characters are going to get together, so expect a long night and plan on an immediate debriefing."

"See you at eight?" Cat said to Sam, batting her eyes.

"Not so fast," Brandt said. "Go see our friend with the spectacles in the basement before you leave."

5

Sam and Cat took the elevator to the basement level. The elevator was a rattling steel cage with a rusty finish and was only utilized by those seeking supplies from what had affectionately become known as "The Tool Shed." Sam didn't care so much for the naming conventions that had grown common at The Yard, but most employed in it and around the world had grown accustomed to the shorthand, primarily because most of them spoke in code when it counted. The machine was closely guarded by an armed guard and could only be operated by him. Inside the tight cube, there were no buttons—it would only go one place: down. The doors opened to a long, bare cement hall which was a far stretch from the brick style of the rest of the building.

Cat's nostrils flared. "Yuck," Cat said. "What is that?"

Sam inhaled deeply, then replied, "Gunpowder." The two parties continued down the hall, at the end of which was a single steel door with no handle. Sam knocked twice on the door, then a small plate slid open. Behind the tiny rectangular hole, a pair of glasses stared back at him, then the small plate slid shut to close the viewing window. A screeching noise emanated from behind the door, then the heavy metal barrier opened.

"As I live and breathe," Newton said with a large grin on his face. "How the hell are ya, mate?" He grabbed Sam's hand in his own and shook it vigorously with the same excitement he had the first time they'd met.

"Newton," Sam said, and a thin smile crept onto his face.

"I'd heard you were back in the states," Newton replied. "Didn't break my camera now, did you?" A boom sounded behind Newton with the concussive force of a small bomb, and a small cloud of smoke began to creep toward the doorway. A man in a lab coat appeared over Newton's shoulder, his goggles and face covered in black soot, and a small mechanism of twisted metal in hand. "Be careful with that, please," Newton called out. Then he turned to Sam and shook his head from side to side before saying, "Amateurs." Newton faced Cat, and his cheeks became as flushed and vibrant as the red of her hair. "Hello."

"Cat," she said, and she held her hand out for him to shake. He did so, but kept shaking it awkwardly as he gazed into her eyes. Cat looked to Sam, as if to ask, 'Is he always like this?'

"Newton," Sam said, then cleared his throat.

"Right," Newton replied, then stepped out of their way and gestured them in. He closed the door behind him, secured a heavy bolt the size of a two-by-four, then said, "This way." After turning the corner of a small vestibule area, he placed his hands on his hips proudly. "What do you think?"

Newton had been promoted to overseer of a large, warehouse-sized room for his operation. Long tables ran the length of the lab, and he'd also recruited a smattering of workers for his secretive operations. There were men and women in lab coats and coveralls, each deeply engaged in their tinkering. A glass wall on the left of the room provided a view of a laboratory with chemicals lining the walls, and the tables inside were covered in vials and beakers containing every color of the rainbow.

"Quite an upgrade," Sam said to Newton.

"Indeed," he said eagerly. "Beats a freighter. This setup's got more perks than the one back at school." Sam's best guess at the figure Brandt had been spending nearly doubled.

Behind another glass wall on the opposite side of the room, a man in military fatigues lifted a rifle toward a dummy opposite him. He took aim, released the safety, then fired on the body. Sam heard nothing of the rifle's report through the viewing window. The dummy, however, had felt every impact. Every round of ammunition tore through the dummy with extreme prejudice. It wasn't until Sam saw the shredded metal that he realized the dummy had been made of a durable substance which the ammunition had shattered.

"Where do I get one of those?" Sam asked. Just as he asked, the man firing the gun let out an inaudible shriek, and the gun fell from his hands. He skipped around the room like a madman, flailing his hands in the air and screaming expletives Sam didn't need Brandt's lip-reader to interpret.

"Not ready yet" Newton replied. "Can't seem to

keep the damn thing cool—armor-piercing rounds are quite wonderful, though the Germans have already figured that bit out, I'm afraid. That's why we're on their tail. Still more tweaks I suppose." A woman clad in similar fatigues ran toward the rifleman and cupped his hands with sacks of ice, and the man let out a sigh of relief from the soothing temperature change.

"Right then," Newton said, and he pointed toward the back of the room. "This way."

The group passed down an aisle of tables. Each of the tabletops was home to all manner of tools and gadgets, some of which were recognizable and others of a prototypical nature. Sam immediately spotted a rack of small glass vials: cyanide capsules, the same style as the one that had been provided as his fallback plan in Pforzheim. He was happy that was still one bit of technology he hadn't had to try out.

Through another glass wall, Sam could see a man tinkering with a potato. In front of the man, a large steel barrier designed like a shield covered most of his body. He toyed with the potato for a moment, and Sam watched with great curiosity, wondering just what the hell kind of a value a potato would have to an operation. The man tossed the potato at the far wall on the opposite end of the room, then ducked immediately behind the shielding. The potato hit the wall, then exploded in a massive fireball.

Newton noted Sam's interest, then chuckled before saying, "Not every idea is a keeper, but Brandt likes to hear them all. He leaves no stone unturned, that one. This one we're quite excited about." Newton stopped at the edge of a table on which a newspaper was unfolded. He grabbed the newspaper and displayed it for Sam.

"What's so special about it?" Cat asked. "Just looks like a newspaper."

"Indeed it does," Newton replied. A small brush rested in a beaker of liquid beside the newspaper. Newton grabbed the brush, let the excess liquid drip back into the beaker, then painted over the newspaper in long brush strokes. Slowly but surely, numbers began to bleed through the paper and become more intense with every passing second. Newton waved the paper back and forth to let it dry, then displayed it for Sam and Cat. "My own custom solution. Great for dropping into enemy territory without incident. Wonderful for ideas about sowing the seeds of disinformation under Axis noses, even better for transmitting code to allies."

"Couldn't they still break the cipher?" Sam asked.

"They're constantly breaking them," Newton replied. "Nature of the business, I suppose. Sometimes we're too late to the party once we've figured out the solution; sometimes they're just messing with us and they know we've already cracked the code. At that point, we're just being fed misinformation. If a code's broken, we've got to remain pretty tight-lipped about it. As soon as the enemy figures out a code's been broken, they change it immediately—then we're we're back to square one. Decoding a cipher is a bit like breaking into a bank vault, except if the code becomes defunct, the money in your vault is no good."

"Need better security for the vault," Cat said with a smirk. Sam watched as she scrutinized the numbers on the page, seemingly trying to deduce a pattern between the rows and columns.

"They're constantly rotating them," Newton said. Sometimes the Japanese even double-code—you'll need a code to crack the first solution, and that yields a further code that has yet *another* solution."

"Sound like a nightmare," Sam said.

"Not ours," Newton assured Sam. "That's up to the lads on the second floor. Anyway," Newton said, then continued forward toward a small desk on the far wall. He grabbed a small leather box from the table, opened it, and produced two tiny, skin-toned, pebble-like pieces of plastic with tiny rubber hooks extending out from them. He handed one each to Cat and Sam.

"Two-way-radios," Newton said. "Go head, try them out." Newton pointed to the area where the small hook met the mechanism, then said, "There's a small adhesive to peel off there so they stay snug." Sam and Cat took the devices and peeled the adhesive layers off of them. "Click once to activate." Sam and Cat pressed the small radios between their thumbs and forefingers, and both returned soft clicking sounds before they finessed them into their ears. Cat's piece matched the pasty coloring of her skin fairly well. It was barely visible. The olive color of Sam's skin did not match his as nicely. "We can recolor yours," Newton said to Sam.

When Newton spoke, Sam heard the conversation with a tinny, radio-like quality, but the mechanism worked well—it was Cat who was standing closest to the young tinkerer, and Sam was hearing Newton through *her* microphone.

"The throw leaves a bit to be desired," Newton said, "So you'll want to be careful just how far you travel. They're great for short distances, but they don't fare so well inside concrete walls or thick structures. Limited power means we can only do so much. A small microphone inside each will pick up your speech. We designed them for field work—troops speaking in limited ranges where gunfire and nuisance noises can make communication difficult. Some operatives have cited the loud nature of the war theatre being particularly problematic when trying to give commands in the field. With these, orders can be delivered directly to the ear."

"How long do they last?" Sam asked.

"We're lucky if we get an hour out of them," Newton replied. "The more you use them, the quicker the battery dies, so keep your conversations limited to the necessities."

Cat removed the piece from her ear, then asked, "How'd you get the batteries so small?"

"Can't give away all of our secrets now, can we?" Newton said with a charming smile. "Click twice to turn them off." Both Cat and Sam clicked the small mechanism twice each to silence them. "They're very fragile, so try to return them without damage. We spent a lot of money on these tiny packages. If you're too rough with them you'll damage the small mechanics inside."

"Do they transmit to our people?" Sam asked.

"We can't do *everything* for you," Newton replied. "That bit's up to you two. Sometimes you've got to just collect information the old-fashioned way." Sam went to light up a smoke. Newton snatched the cigarette out of his mouth with lightning-like speed, then stomped it with the heel of his foot. "Don't be daft!" Sam stared back wide-eyed. "We've got enough explosive chemicals and materials in here to level the capital. You want to win the war for the Axis from the inside?"

"Sorry," Sam said. "Hey, Newton, let me ask you a question. What do you know about tungsten?"

"Rare element," Newton replied. "And a valuable one at that. Very hard, high density. Has a very high melting point, as well. Useless if unrefined, but put it through the right process and you can do some nifty things with it. Most nations wrote it off as useless, but it's anything but. You usually find it in wiring, light bulbs, tools—very durable and sought after, *especially* by the Germans. Wolfram, they call it. That's why it's listed as 'W' on the periodic table."

"What would the Germans want with it?" Cat asked.

"What do the Germans ever want with anything?" Newton questioned. Cat shrugged.

Sam turned to her, then said, "Weapons."

"You're paying attention," Newton said. "The Krauts love the stuff. It's essential to the armor-piercing rounds they use in both their heavy weaponry and select tanks. The Brits found no good use for it—found it too unstable to work with. Well, pre-war they sold the stuff in bulk for fractions of pounds to the Germans, not real-izing that the stuff was rarer than gold and, in war, more *valuable*. They're hoarding it, and so are Spain and Portugal. We know the Spanish have been selling it by the boat-load to the Germans. In fact, our people have been buying it up at hefty prices just to keep it *out* of their hands."

———

Outside The Yard, Sam got to that smoke he hadn't been able to have in the basement. Cat asked him if he wanted a ride. Though he thought to decline—traveling alone was much wiser—the sun was already starting trouble, and beads of sweat began to run down the back of his neck. Huffing it back to the city on foot would see him drenched by the time he got to his destination. He agreed, then Cat went and retrieved her car as he puffed on the cigarette.

The car roared forward, spewing gravel and dirt out of its path. It was a sleek and clean vehicle that looked like it had never missed a day of polish, and though it attracted the certain type of attention Sam had no fondness for, it was exactly the type of attention Cat was tasked with drawing to herself.

"Toss the cigarette," Cat called out. Sam frowned. "Just because I'm not paying for it doesn't mean I don't want to take care of it. You'll burn a hole through the seat." Sam resented the statement. To suggest he might drop his cigarette implied that he was clumsy, and he thought of himself as anything but—*reckless*, sure, but not clumsy. He granted the request, then climbed in the car. "Where to?"

"Downtown," Sam said.

Cat accelerated the car with so much force it pinned the spy back into his seat. He couldn't imagine driving like that was necessary, but traffic in the area was hardly heavy and Sam considered it was her opportunity to "open the car up," as they said. They traveled down long, wide roads that were hugged on either side by warehouses not unlike The Yard. Deep in this industrial section of the city there were plenty of nondescript businesses, and The Yard blended in nicely against them.

"So, partners, huh?" Cat asked.

"What of it?"

Cat turned to face him. Her failure to focus on the road ahead made Sam uneasy. She drove—and acted—with an air of great confidence, and Sam possessed enough humility to know that though it was the exact type of personality The Yard attracted, too much of it killed men—and women. She said, "You know, you're a queer duck, Sam."

"Why's that?"

Cat mimicked him, speaking in a low, gravelly voice as if to mock him. "*What of it? Why's that? Give me a cigarette…*" Then, Sam laughed—he actually *laughed*. Cat said, "Oh so you *are* a human being?"

"Partners are baggage," Sam replied. "The nature of this game is solitary." Sam turned to her, and now neither of them paid attention to the road ahead. The speedometer only climbed, and the motor was begging for a break as the pistons struggled under the stress and heat. He said, as if attempting to defuse the situation, "It's just easier to look after myself is all."

"Well, you know I work better alone, too," Cat replied. "But I'm smart enough to know that sometimes two heads are better than one. You know things I don't, and I know things *you* don't."

"Is that so?" Sam replied.

"It sure is," Cat replied. "I don't need your help, and more than likely you don't need mine, but that's the way the boss man wants it, so seeing as you're stuck with me, I say we try to make the best of it. I've had disappointing partners, too, you know?" She fixed her eyes back on the road, then slowed the car down a bit and backed off the gas pedal. She sighed, then said, "If it wasn't for him, I would have never got caught. I was doing quite alright, thank you. I was on my way out. It was the one last job—it's always that *one last job*. I wasn't even the sloppy one."

"Should have got out when you had the chance," Sam replied. He was unsure exactly what she meant. He still didn't know where she'd come from or what her deal was. She spoke riddles. That she knew so much about opening safes only made her ethics more suspect. Sam didn't judge—*he* should talk.

"What's your excuse?" she asked. Sam didn't reply.

6

Cat dumped Sam at a Georgetown street corner surrounded by unfamiliar garment shops. She repeated the time at which they'd meet again and tore off after Sam agreed. The spy looked for suitable attire in a shop owned by an old Italian man. The man spoke little and moved around the room slowly, seemingly plagued by a slight hunch in his back. His hands and clothing were covered in smears of white powder. The culprit of all of the white residue—a small piece of chalk—was tucked in between his skull and his ear, and measuring tape was draped over his shoulders.

Sam told the man he wanted a dinner jacket with matching slacks. He mentioned he hadn't been measured in quite some time, so he didn't know what his size was. The aging man mumbled under his breath in Italian, none of which Sam understood, but took out a tape measure and acquired very specific dimensions with an engineer's precision.

The old man had white wings above each of his ears

where the hair color had started to fade greatly, as opposed to the top of his head, which was still a rich, dark brown. The shop was quiet, and Sam suspected that Italy's Axis alignment back home had perhaps caused his business a great deal of suffering. The man was likely off the boat himself, because every time he asked Sam a question, it was a broken mixture of English with Italian squeaking through.

After the man had taken the measurements and was satisfied, he asked Sam, "*Colore?*"

Sam responded with "Black," not just because that was the color that would suit him best, but also because it was what Brandt had specifically told him to get.

The man mumbled "*Nero,*" under his breath, limped with a soft step toward a rack in the back of the store, and waved his hand for Sam to follow along. The old man placed a second pair of glasses over the glasses he was already wearing, giving his eyes a large, bug-like appearance, then dug furiously through the assorted suits that lined the back wall of the shop on a double rack.

He dismissed all of the blue and tan suits. There was even a grotesque olive-color design that Sam was glad he'd have to go nowhere near. For once, he wouldn't be wearing any military fatigues—enemy or otherwise.

The man turned to Sam, squinting to get a look at his customer through the four-glass lenses, then asked, "*Lucente?*"

Sam shook his head, not understanding the question. The man pulled down two types of black suits, one with a glossy sheen, and one with a more subdued finish to the fabric. Sam pointed to the more subtle of the two. It had been a while since Sam had even had to put on a nicely tailored suit, and the only thing he knew he was looking for was something that fit in with the elite crowd but also wouldn't draw too much attention.

The elderly man stopped at a group of black suits with soft, matte finishes. He rubbed his thumb and index fingers against the materials of several, then pulled one off the rack and displayed it for Sam. Sam was no fashionista, but even he could appreciate the reserved, yet elegant cut of the one the old man had selected. It was classic, the kind of suit an eligible bachelor might wear on the town to show he was part of the crowd but not scream to be noticed.

The man took the suit off the rack and pressed it up against Sam's chest, then craned his neck to observe his handiwork in the mirror hanging behind him. The man said, "*Buona*," without even waiting for Sam's approval, then waved him forward once more. He instructed Sam with an extended index finger to stand on a small platform surrounded by a series of mirrors, then said, "You put it."

Sam quickly undressed and pulled the slacks over his legs, and the aging Italian man took a simple white shirt off a rack solely for fitting purposes. He handed it to Sam, who put it on, then the old man helped him with the jacket. The Italian tugged at the suit from all angles, first starting at the cuffs on the legs—which were too long—then the waist of the pants, then the sleeves of the jacket and the back flaps.

"Stand straight," the man said to Sam, then mimed how Sam should be standing. He puffed his chest up a bit, then dropped his arms to his sides, instructing Sam how he should present himself. Sam could tell the action took effort from the old man. He said, "You no stand straight, you look like me." The man resumed his arched posture, a warning to Sam that bad form might lead to scoliosis. Once Sam was in a position to his liking, the man pulled the small piece of chalk from behind his ear and started marking the suit up with faint lines where the garments would need to be adjusted.

"*Scarpe*," the man said to himself, then shuffled over to the corner of the room and returned with a pair of black, shiny dress shoes. He plopped both down in front of Sam's feet and waved his hand once more to instruct Sam to put them on. Sam did so. When the man saw how the pants fell in relation to the shoes, he wiped at the chalk briefly and made a new mark. He briefly pinched the back of the pants near Sam's rear where there was still some slack, scrutinized his choices with squinty eyes in each of the three mirrors, then marked the back near Sam's spine. He ran his hand along the inseam of the pants, decided that was acceptable, then checked the back flaps of the coat. He made one more quick swipe along Sam's back, then said, "Okay."

Sam put on the clothing he'd arrived in while the man gathered the garments, then hung them back on a wooden hanger. He said to Sam, "When you needa?"

"Right away," Sam said. Sam didn't think that would present a problem judging by the fact that he was the only patron in the store, but the old man grimaced briefly as if he couldn't be bothered. Perhaps it was not discrimination that had hurt the man's business but his own poor customer relations. Sam pulled the wad of bills he'd received from Brandt from his pocket, and the old man's eyes widened through the double set of glasses.

"Okay," the Italian man said and shuffled toward the back room. "You wait, okay?" Sam nodded, lit up a smoke, and paced around the store while the old man got busy.

When Sam arrived at the glass window which opened onto the street at the shop's front, he quickly noticed a man in a fedora and a black suit—far less tailored than the one he was currently buying—reading a newspaper. When his gaze and Sam's crossed, Sam thought the man was more likely looking right *at* him. The man quickly returned his attention to the newspaper opened in front of him, and Sam, always alert, *knew* something about the man was questionable. Sam turned his attention down to the corner of the street and saw another man in an almost identical suit—black jacket, black slacks, white shirt, black tie—puffing on a cigarette while looking in the spy's direction. When he realized Sam was looking at him, he, too, diverted his gaze down the opposite end of the street. The spy was being spied on.

Sam's focus returned back to newspaper man. He'd been watching Sam once more—and he wasn't doing a good job at hiding it. Sam sucked on the cigarette, let the smoke linger in his lungs, then flicked the ashes indiscriminately onto the floor below him. Though he hadn't asked the owner if it would be okay to light up, the shop already reeked of burned tobacco. On the far corner of the street, the other observer began watching Sam again. Any time Sam caught their attention, they both made like they had no interest in him, but Sam was sure that was anything but the case.

Who were these men? Likely spies themselves, Sam thought, but they looked American. Their suits were ill-fitting and frumpy, and the closest man's shoes could have used a good shine. He was balding at the temples, and his friend down the street needed a lesson in at least making it *look* like he was keeping busy. Sam stepped back from the glass window in an effort to ally himself with the shadows in the shop, but kept his focus split between the two men.

Sam surveyed the shop's entrances and exits. If the men were going to follow him, they were at least going to have to work for it. Behind the counter was a small open doorway through which the tailor had retreated to tend to the suit's adjustments. Sam tamped his cigarette out in an ashtray on the counter, then stepped through the doorway to search for the old-timer. In the rear of the shop, he was hard at work stitching at the seams of the suit.

"Do you have a back entrance?" Sam asked. The tailor looked at Sam like he had three heads. Sam turned over his shoulder and scoped out the street through the glass. The man sitting on the bench had vanished. Perhaps the aging Italian man sensed the urgency in Sam's demeanor. He pointed to an aluminum door at the end of a corridor. "I'll be back later," Sam said, and he wasted no time exiting the building.

He found himself in an alley lined by the back doors of other businesses. On either side of Sam, the alley led to unobstructed exits. The sun shined brightly in the sky, and Sam did not have the cover of shadows in which to move. He made for the exit which would lead north, the furthest from the men tailing him. When he arrived at the street running perpendicular, a bus was letting off patrons *en masse*. Sam disappeared in the crowd.

Sam returned to retrieve the suit some hours later when the sun had taken a break. Though it was a cloudless day, Sam chose to return during the evening rush hour when the streets were crowded. He wore the most unassuming clothing he could find: grey slacks and a grey jacket with a white shirt, black tie, and a fedora to match. He blended in nicely amongst the other men milling about the street on their way home to their families and loved ones. Sam encountered no one of interest.

———

He rested for the better part of the next day. The hours he'd been keeping stealing secrets for Brandt hadn't done his sleep schedule any favors. He'd been creeping about D.C. in the night, checking in with his captain in the wee hours of the morning, having a drink or two in the late afternoon, then collapsing in the early evening in preparation to be out and about late. He'd scratched the drinks this time around, fallen asleep at about six in the morning, then woken up again at four to eat.

He had two eggs, sunny side up, and a few pieces of toast. He washed that down with a glass of milk to coat his stomach. He was fully prepared to have some adult beverages at the party—not enough to jeopardize his mission, but enough to act like he belonged there. He skipped the coffee, if only to keep his nerves calm. If he was honest with himself, he was feeling nervous about the party. Sam didn't "mingle" well—not with that type of crowd, at least. He'd felt less nervous throwing on a *Wermacht* uniform and sneaking around Pforzheim. There, at least he knew what his enemy looked like.

When he put his suit on, his nerves relaxed a bit. He surveyed himself in a long, full-body mirror that had been hanging in his apartment when he got it. He looked *good.* The suit fit him well, and though he'd barely understood a word the Italian tailor had said, the man obviously knew what he was doing. The suit fit tightly in all the right places, but had room to breathe where necessary. At the very least, he was going to *look* the part.

He added one last accessory to the outfit: the watch Sigrid had given him in Germany. The classic piece fit well with the getup. Though it had one singular purpose —to tell time—the aesthetics of the piece were timeless. He applied a bit of black polish to the shoes to give them that finished sheen that made him look like he belonged. He didn't know much about real estate, but he figured he was smart enough to weasel his way around a conversation long enough and he could always step away if things got too detailed. He wasn't going there to sell property; he was going there to steal secrets.

Sam arrived at Cat's at eight sharp under the glow of a magnificent sunset sky. She had a glorious brownstone in Georgetown that kept up with appearances, and at this hour the sun bathed its face in an auburn glow. Sam didn't imagine she'd ever be required to bring a target home—that would be foolish—but if she was spotted in front of it, she'd need to continue to sell her identity. He mumbled a string of curse words under his breath. His setup was far less appealing than Cat's, and he wondered if perhaps putting his gun down and learning how Cat did what she did might not be a bad idea.

The building was three stories tall. There were only three buzzers on the panel in the front, and Sam tapped the one on the top that would signal his arrival to the third floor. The door clicked, and he stepped through and climbed the several flights of stairs to Cat's place.

The door was ajar, and Sam pressed it lightly, cautiously entering the apartment. Sam would never in a million years leave a door open like that, but Cat didn't have the same skill set he did.

"In here," he heard Cat call out. "I'll just be a moment." Sam snooped around as he waited for his date to appear. A serving tray in the dining room was host to several decanters, and Sam grabbed one, removed the top, took a sniff, and poured some scotch into a glass tumbler. He took a swig. Cat had the good booze—Brandt had probably seen to that. Was there any luxury she hadn't been awarded? The apartment was clean and well-maintained. Stained birch boards—probably very expensive—ran the length of the place, and it was fully furnished. Two large abstract paintings hung on the living room wall—Sam had no idea whose brush had graced them—but he assumed *those* were fakes. You couldn't cheap out on the good booze, but most people could be fooled by a phony painting.

A set of heels clicked against the floor, and Cat called out, "How do I look?"

Sam thought the right word was "stunning," but he didn't say it out loud. A long black evening gown ran the length of her body. The neck was cut deep, made that way to accommodate the large string of diamonds—also likely fake—that hung on her skin. On her wrists, she also wore diamond bracelets that matched the style of the necklace. The heels she wore made her taller than usual, and her hair had been done up in a tight bun that subdued the fiery red. A combination of blush, magnificently curled lashes, and subtle eye shadow completed the elegant look. She didn't look like a socialite, she looked like a *queen*.

Cat stared back at Sam with similar shock. Her lips separated, as if she wanted to say something but couldn't find the words. She looked Sam up and down, nodding her head in approval.

"Speechless, huh?" Cat asked. "I'll take that as a compliment." She spotted the glass in his hand. "You waste no time. Where's mine?" Sam retrieved another tumbler from the serving tray and poured her a drink. She grabbed it, held it out toward him, and said, "To secrets."

"To secrets," Sam replied, and both parties clinked glasses before slinging the drinks back.

A car horn tooted from street level, and Sam approached the window to see who it was. Below, a black sedan idled. The sun had fallen completely behind the tops of the buildings decorating the horizon line, and Sam got a good look at the nation's capital from Cat's eastern-viewing apartment. He'd never seen it in that way before—grand and alluring and full of possibilities.

"That's us," Sam said, nodding to the car below. Cat grabbed a purse and slung it over her shoulder. She motioned to a shawl draped over a chair, and Sam obliged, placing it over her shoulders. Taking the cue, he then opened the door for her. He was going to have to remember his manners for the night ahead.

The driver sat waiting, perched against the fender of the car. The car had a clean polish, reflecting the twilight sky above in magnificent hues of blue and turquoise. It had probably just seen a wax job, fitting for the guests who'd be using it for the night. The driver opened the door for both Cat and Sam, and both parties climbed in.

"Evening," the driver said. He shut the door behind

them, stepped around to the driver's side, and put the car into gear. "It's only a stone's throw away." The car accelerated, and Sam took a survey around the neighborhood in search of prying eyes. He's already been watched once in the last forty-eight hours, and as far as he was concerned, he would remain perpetually on alert from this point forward.

Sam suspected the driver was one of Brandt's men. For all he knew, he could be a spy much like himself who'd just been tasked with driving for the night. It would be unwise of Brandt to use anyone outside of the organization. Judging by the way the driver's eyes searched the street through the windshield, it was likely he'd been told to keep watch, too.

Both Sam and Cat lit cigarettes, each extending their arms out awkwardly in an effort to keep ashes off of their pristine clothing. Cat took the pair of small radio pieces out of her pocket and handed one to Sam. Newton had adjusted the color of Sam's. They placed the objects in their ears, sure to fit them correctly to ensure they wouldn't be visible. Sam and Cat tapped their ears in unison. A static hiss sounded in Sam's ear, causing him to cup his hand around his lobe momentarily, then with some slight adjustments, it settled. Sam heard Cat inhale from her cigarette, albeit with a tinny accent, and Sam asked, "Good?"

Cat gave him a thumbs up, then asked as well, "You?" Sam returned the thumbs up gesture.

The radio pieces were working. The team's successful —or poor—communication at the party would put Newton's new gadget to the test. Now Sam had to keep his nerves as sharp as his suit.

7

The car pulled up to the front of a large brownstone not so dissimilar from Cat's. The difference was the Montgomerys owned the entire building, which reached from one end of the block to the other. Oil lanterns bearing flames that rose up the stone architecture lit the building in a warm, gothic glow. A red carpet extended from the front door under a large awning with gold-leafed embroidery and met the curb where the car had parked. A short, balding man in a tuxedo stepped forward urgently to open the door on Cat's side.

"Madame," the man said, and he offered a hand to Cat. She took it with a dainty grip, and he escorted her out from the car as the driver opened Sam's door. All the formalities were a bit ridiculous for Sam, but it was part of the scene, and allowing the men to cater to them was just added camouflage. Sam met Cat at the edge of the carpet, interlocked his arm with hers, and set forward toward a pair of large wooden double doors. Two men standing by grabbed a handle each and opened the doors to allow them entrance. If Sam hadn't known better he'd have assumed that next there would be two men inside prepared to move their legs for them—maybe even hold their cigarettes while they smoked them.

Above, the muffled sounds of a party in swing echoed through the marble foyer. Several guests, also in glamorous attire, entered into the elevator. The elevator attendant held the door for Sam and Cat, guided them inward with a white-gloved hand, and they stepped in. As the elevator rose, the couple behind them spoke in hushed tones. Sam turned to Cat, who couldn't hide the smile on her face. She was enjoying all of it. Could he blame her?

The elevator stopped, the doors opened, and Sam and Cat stepped out from the lift and into a dimly lit hall. Overhead chandeliers, each of which was probably as expensive as the average automobile, cast intermittent pools of light down the hallway. The marble work in this hall was more magnificent than even that in the last, and they were flanked on either side by large candelabras whose flames flickered rhythmically in a romantic dance, seemingly in unison with the music coming from the ballroom ahead.

When they arrived at yet another pair of doors, a man bearing a tray of tall-stemmed champagne glasses offered one to both Sam and Cat. Sam waved his offer off, but Cat obliged and took a quick sip before the man and his partner opened the doors. Sam guessed the payroll for a party like this must be enough to pay a small factory's yearly salary. Six people had already been employed to assist in their arrival and they hadn't even gotten *in* to the party yet. "Here we go," Cat said. The two men ushered them through the doors and into the event.

The onslaught of noises, smells, and visuals was like an assault on the senses by an army of wealth. The band was in full swing. At the back of the room, and on a stage that looked more like it belonged in a theater than in a home, was a large group of tuxedo-clad men separated by section. There were groupings of string, percussion, brass, and woodwind instruments, and a solo pianist at the corner. Noisier than even the band was the sound of loud discussion and laughter.

The room was a sea of elegance. The men wore suits, all of which were finely tailored and expensive like Sam's own, and the women wore evening and ball gowns. Unlike the men's attire, the color of the women's dresses varied. There were hues of rose, evergreen, and sapphire. Sam swore he could hear the clinking of jewelry, but it was more likely the dinnerware. Even the glasses and silverware looked like they were as expensive as the jewelry the men and women had donned. Most of the women were older in comparison to Cat, and Sam understood why she had been so desirable amongst the type of men present—the lives of whom she'd been tasked with infiltrating.

The smell of cigarettes and pipes was ever-present, but it was the stench of fancy cigars which was most overwhelming. Above the band, a cloud of the collective smoke that had been dispersed from all of the party's guests hung like a gathering storm. Unlike the men, many of the women smoked their cigarettes through long-stemmed cigarette holders. Even the cigarette-holders screamed elegance, and many of them featured intricately detailed finishes like gold plating and painted designs. A tray of shrimp cocktail passed in front of Sam, and with it the whiff of shellfish.

A tray of oysters came from the other direction, and Sam took the liberty of grabbing one of those from the waiter and slurping it down. The oysters were tasty. Lemon shavings had been slipped inside the shell to keep the fish cool and provide a tangy bite. Cat swatted him with the back of her hand, retrieved one herself, then a napkin from the waiter as well as a small dish to put the shell on. She leaned toward Sam, then said, "Don't act like a heathen." Sam shrugged and placed the shell back on to the plate among the uneaten ones. The waiter wrinkled his noise, performed a curt bow to Cat, then whisked the tray away.

There were large round tables throughout the room ready to accommodate ten guests each. Nearby, a small table held place cards, and Cat pulled Sam by his inter-locked arm toward it. She scanned the table of cards, then stopped when she found the one that said *Ms. Catherine McAlister and Mr. Paul Rilyeh* in italic calligra-phy. She grabbed the card, opened the fold, then said, "Table ten."

Sam pulled Cat toward *him* this time and headed in the direction of the bar. Cat slurped her champagne down, then found a home for the empty glass on a tray in the hands of a waiter crossing their path as they moved across the room. Sam hated the feeling of being locked into this partnership, but this was the way of the crowd. Most of the women at the party were paired via some appendage to the men accompanying them, but Sam knew that if they were going to get the job done, they were going to have to break the link soon enough

They passed through a sea of people moving to and fro, many of whom had begun to dance and some who were in deep conversation. The sound of cackling made Sam uneasy. Everybody present seemed *too* happy to be at the party. Most of these fools—that was how Sam thought of them—were ready and willing to empty their wallets and purses on items of no real utilitarian value at all.

Cat nodded to several people on her way to the bar. Two women waved, and three men nodded, by Sam's count. At the bar, Sam said, "Scotch, neat for me, and… " He turned to Cat.

"Cabernet," Cat said.

"And a Cabernet for the lady." The bartender got to work on the drinks, and Sam surveyed the room for his target. He didn't see Moreno yet, or the Carolinian.

"Anything?" Cat asked softly.

"No," Sam replied. His eyes fell on her once more, and he was taken aback by just how magnificent she looked. Most of the women at the party wore layers of makeup to contour their faces into forced elegance, but Cat had a natural beauty that her makeup only amplified. He was currently standing next to the most sought-after-woman at the party. In Sam's typical environment that would be considered unwanted attention, but for Cat it seemed to be beneficial. While most of the women wore color saturated dresses that made them stand out from the crowd, Cat's subdued black did the opposite, and *still* she drew the most attention. The wandering eyes of the men lingering around the bar seemed to find their way toward Cat.

The bartender returned with a glass of scotch and a red wine for Cat. Sam took his tumbler and enjoyed a healthy taste, but Cat did not drink her beverage. Sam asked, "No good?" Cat shook her head. "Not up to par with Moreno's personal collection?"

"Red wine stains the teeth," Cat replied. "When you're at one of these things it's just for show. And the sugars in white wines give me a headache, so I can't drink those either."

Sam was amazed at how well the tiny mechanism in his ear was working. He could hear every word Cat had said with a crisp clarity, and yet the serenade of the band across the room was quite muffled. One of the band members stepped out toward the stage's edge and completed a saxophone solo, and the band leader swung his arms to signal the song's finish. The guests clapped in celebration.

The band leader grabbed the microphone and addressed the crowd: "Another fine number from Mel Pipes, ladies and gentlemen. I'm Stickey Buns and you're listening to the Sugar Gang." He was a greasy-looking Italian man. His slick hair was swept toward the back of his skull and looked like he'd used motor oil to set it in place. His voice was boisterous, yet charming. Sam got the impression he knew how to work a crowd, wealthy or otherwise. "We're not ready to slow things down just yet, folks. Here's another classic for you all to enjoy. If you're liking our music, clap your hands, and if your hands are full, just jingle your jewelry." The guests laughed, and Stickey turned back to his band and raised his hands. He swung the right one down with an excited swoop, and the band broke out into a jazzy number.

"I've got to do my rounds," Cat said. Sam nodded, rubbed his ear lobe between two fingers, and Cat winked. "How do I look?"

"Like a million bucks," Sam replied.

"Only a million?" Cat asked. Sam smiled, and Cat returned a smirk. "I didn't know you smiled, Sam Abel."

"Kitty Cat!" a frail old man yelped. He ran toward Cat with his arms outstretched, curling and extending his fingers as if to say "gimme."

"Mr. Donahue," Cat said, and she extended her hand for the man to kiss. He took her hand, pressed both lips firmly to the back of it, then raised it so that she might twirl to show off her look. She did, smiled cutely, then gave the man a curtsy. Sam found the display quite amusing.

"Looking stunning, my dear," Donahue said. He had thin wisps of white hair clinging for dear life to a nearly bald head, and large, rapidly blinking eyes. Unlike Sam, he wore a tuxedo. A gold pocket watch draped down from the inside of his coat pocket, over his cummerbund, and dipped on a long chain that reflected the light in the room. "Bidding on anything in particular tonight?"

"I haven't looked at the registry just yet," Cat explained. "But you can be sure—if it sparkles, it's got my name it." Sam was intrigued by the show Cat had put on. Her voice had changed, and her demeanor as well. Her delivery and posture suggested that she belonged here.

"I'd expect nothing less from a girl like yourself," Donahue replied. He turned to look at Sam, did a quick head-to-toe survey, then turned again to Cat. "Are you going to introduce me to your friend?"

Cat looked to Sam, then said to Donahue, "Why, of course. This is Mr. Paul Rilyeh."

Sam extended his hand to shake the old man's, and

Donahue gripped it tightly. For a frail senior, Sam was surprised at how firm the shake was. Donahue had shaken like he was attempting to crush the spy's fingers. Sam thought nothing of it—the old man was probably threatened by Sam's presence. Donahue asked, "Rilyeh —is that French?"

"Among other things," Sam replied.

"What do you do, Mr. Rilyeh?" Donahue asked. "Am I saying that right? *Ril-yay?*"

Cat took over for Sam and said, "He's in real estate."

Donahue brushed Cat's comment off and continued to address Sam. "Well, what kind of real estate?"

"Estates," Sam said firmly. He hadn't loaded a proper answer. Unlike Cat, he'd spent no time developing his persona. Why should he? It was a throwaway character that would have no value after the night's end.

Cat grabbed the reins of the conversation once more. "Mr. Rilyeh flew in yesterday from France. He's in search of properties to buy for some of his overseas clients looking to set up manufacturing operations in America—secondary homes, that sort of thing."

"Is that so?" Donahue asked. He looked Sam up and down once more. Sam knew he was unconvinced. "Well you'll have to tell me more about that some time, Mr. Rilyeh," Donahue said. "I surely could point you in the right direction if it's property you want."

"That'd be swell," Sam said, feigning appreciation.

"Shame what's going on over there," Donahue said. "What with that lunatic steamrolling through your country. Should have taken a stand, if you ask me. Now we've got to go over and clean up the mess." Sam was sure Donahue was looking to incite a reaction but, not *really* hailing from France, he didn't take the bait. Little did Donahue know the foreigner standing in front of him was involved in cleaning up the mess the jerk spoke of. "Well I'll let you to get to it." Donahue turned to Cat, his eyes wide with desire, then said, "Wonderful to see you again, Kitty Cat."

"You as well," Cat replied. Donahue set off and before long was doing the "gimme" gesture toward another couple nearby. He also broke into the same charm he'd offered to Cat.

"What's his deal?" Sam asked Cat.

"Investor," Cat replied. "Worth a fortune. He's harmless." Cat smoothed out her dress, then said to Sam, "Stay out of trouble." Cat took off, waving with a dainty hand to yet another aging man in a black top hat across the room. "Mr. Harris," Sam heard Cat say, only this time her voice couldn't be heard directly since she had moved away; he'd heard it through the earpiece.

Sam did his best to limit his attention to the conversation as he moved around the room. Cat was performing her character to its fullest extent. She'd turned on a charm he hadn't yet seen during his time with her. He clutched his scotch glass in his hand, letting his eyes wander amongst the crowd as he searched for either of his targets. Either Moreno or the Carolinian would do. He knew what Moreno looked like, and he'd assumed the Carolinian would still show up looking like a cowboy. He still wasn't sure who "Sparrow" was, or if he was an invited guest at the party. Sam could have walked right by him and he wouldn't have known him from the next guy.

As Sam drew closer to the band, the sound of percussion instruments beating grew louder. Cat's conversations grew more difficult to hear, and static soon obscured her words as she disappeared further from his view. He searched the balconies of the second floor. There were guests up there as well, and he still didn't see anyone of note. Most of the men in the room looked the same: varying shades of white skin and degrees of hair loss coupled with black suits and gold watches.

Sam's attention shifted to a tall, white-haired man nearby whose profile felt familiar. As the man spoke to several people in his sphere, his face turned, and Sam squinted to scrutinize the features more closely. It was at the same moment that he noticed Sam staring at him that the man recognized the spy—it was Abe Van Cortland. The two had met roughly six months prior on the eve of the Pearl Harbor attacks, and though their initial introduction had been dangerous to say the least, he'd been an ally of sorts.

Well look who came to the party, Sam thought. Without making a scene, Van Cortland nodded slightly to acknowledge Sam's presence. Sam returned the gesture, then went about his trip around the room. Though Sam normally could consider his cover blown, he need not worry about Van Cortland—Brandt and Van Cortland had their own arrangement.

An elderly woman in a beige satin gown walked past Sam, locked eyes with him, then looked him up and down briefly. Right as she passed him, she licked her lips, and Sam diverted his gaze to ensure she didn't get any ideas. Sam would grant Brandt many requests, but sleeping with one of those crows wouldn't be one of them.

"Mrs. Chartreux," Sam heard Cat say. "My name-sake." As Sam made his way away from the band, Cat's conversation grew clearer again. "What a pleasure it is to see you."

"Darling," Sam heard the woman reply with a long, drawn-out "A." Cat started discussing her jewelry with the woman, and Sam grabbed a piece of shrimp off of a passing waiter's tray. As he continued to tour the perimeter, he walked through a cloud of tobacco smoke that made even his well-adjusted lungs gasp for air. A man with a monocle puffed eagerly on a cigar the size of a stick of dynamite. Sam thought some of these people looked like parodies of wealth.

"Six o'clock," Cat said, and Sam looked toward her. She'd slipped the comment in with sly precision amidst her ongoing conversation. Sam locked eyes with her, even from the great distance across the room, and without missing a step in her act of entertaining her hangers-on, she nodded toward the door they'd entered through.

Sam focused on the double door entrance: Moreno had finally arrived to the party. "Good girl," Sam said, and Cat returned a charming smile and returned to her entourage of suitors. Sam maneuvered further toward Moreno, keeping out of sight and against the stone wall of the large room. Though his view was obscured by the crowd of people he passed through, he never once lost sight of Moreno. He didn't have to get close; he just needed to keep track of the man's whereabouts.

It wouldn't be difficult. Moreno's skin color stuck out like a sore thumb in the room of pasty white complexions. The only people with skin tones darker than Moreno's were playing instruments in the band.

Moreno tended to the guests who rushed him upon entry. It was clear he was popular with the crowd, despite not being "one of them." He might have the connections, the money, and even maybe some power, but he wasn't *really* one of them. The only real value Moreno had was his ability to liaise with people from his homeland to conduct business across the Atlantic. Sam suspected Moreno was easily replaceable, and none of his "friends" in the room would bat an eye if he was gone tomorrow. Sam could see right through him.

Sam got closer, but still kept a healthy distance. Moreno shook hands briefly with several more guests, then excused himself. Sam couldn't hear what he was saying, but the man looked like he had someplace to be, and after flashing some more phony smiles to the various party-goers, he made his way quickly across the room and toward a wooden door flanking the band.

"Great party," a voice behind Sam said. Sam turned, and standing behind him was the man he'd seen in Brandt's office. His expression was smug, and he'd ditched the frumpy suit for something a little more suitable. What was an FBI agent doing at a party like this?

"Sure is," Sam said. Sam was bewildered by the man's presence. He'd snuck up on him much in the same way the master spy would have approached one of his own targets: with the element of surprise. Sam searched for Moreno—he was gone. *Shit.*

"Looking for anything in particular tonight?" the FBI man asked. Sam didn't like the tone in which he spoke. He spoke with the smug sureness of a law-enforcement agent, always with a loaded question.

"I'm here with a date," Sam replied.

"I saw," the man said. "The redhead." The FBI agent reached his hand forward, then said, "Bruce Whelan."

Sam shook his hand, albeit reluctantly, then said, "Paul Rilyeh."

Whelan snorted. He knew Sam was a liar, but he played ball. "Great to meet you," he said, then paused before repeating Sam's cover name: "*Mr. Rilyeh.*"

As if an angel was speaking to him, Cat called on Sam's assistance through the earpiece, "Darling." Sam turned to find Cat miming a sip from her beverage. "Help." Some round woman with jewels in her ears so big they looked more suitable for a monarch was yapping in Cat's face.

"Excuse me," Sam said to Whelan, and made his way toward Cat, keeping his eyes peeled for Moreno. He'd been distracted by the fed, who was probably keeping as close an eye on him as he was *supposed* to be on Moreno.

The band finished another fast-moving number, and Stickey grabbed hold of the microphone once more. He addressed the crowd, who'd broken into applause. "Folks, we're going to slow things down a touch now for all those lovely ladies in the audience who might like a dance with that special man. If you've come here with someone you just can't live without, you go on ahead and grab them by the hand and lead them to the wood."

"Excuse me," Sam said when he arrived. "I'd like to borrow her for a moment."

"Please do," the woman talking Cat's ear off said, then her eyes fluttered a bit in response to seeing Sam. Cat offered her hand, and Sam took it gracefully and led her to the dance floor. The string section began with a soothing melody and Sam clutched Cat by the small of her back and pulled her in close, then the two began to sway rhythmically with the pace of the music.

"Thank you," Cat said. "That was Beverly Dodd, and the only thing worse than the sound of her voice is the smell of her breath."

"You saved me as well," Sam said as the two danced among other couples.

"Do tell," Cat replied.

"There's a fed here watching," Sam said. "I saw him at The Yard. He's got it out for Brandt and, by proxy, me. Name's Bruce Whelan."

"*Us*," Cat corrected. "I was trailed yesterday."

Sam looked her in the eyes with an expression of concern. "Does Brandt know that?"

"He does," Cat replied.

Sam suspected that might what be why the agent had been in the office in the first place. *Great*, Sam thought. *Compromised—and by our own people.* "Watch yourself," Sam said.

"Don't worry. I can hold my own. I think some of his friends saw me leave the embassy, but if they had anything on me, we wouldn't be having this conversation, would we?" Sam nodded. "Why the hell would the feds be working against us?" Cat asked.

Sam simply said, "Bureaucracy." He brought Cat in closer and searched over her shoulder for faces amongst the crowd. Cat did the same over his shoulder.

"You know, Mr. Rilyeh," Cat said, "I had no idea you were such a good dancer. If I didn't know any better I might think you were a romantic."

"You just watch the room," Sam replied.

Just as Sam made the request, Cat's attention landed on the entrance to the large ball room. She asked, "He couldn't be that cowboy right there, could he?" Sam turned her so he could get a good look. A man with a brown suit entered with a very "out of place" look on his face. He arrived with no date and was only accompanied by the cigarette hanging between his lips. He might not have been so noticeable had he not be wearing a ten-gallon hat that made him look more suited to lasso cows than attend a gala. The Carolinian had arrived.

8

The Carolinian stood awkwardly at the edge of the room. Sam watched his eyes dart nervously to and fro, beneath the shadowy brim of his hat. Now they were *both* looking for Moreno, and Sam guided Cat ungracefully in a circular motion to turn his attention toward the door through which Moreno had disappeared.

As if he had a sixth sense, Moreno walked through the doorway and straight for the Carolinian. Several people tried to get Moreno's attention, but he shooed them off abruptly. Sam tracked Moreno through the crowd like a hawk watching its prey. When Moreno met the man, he took both of the Carolinian's hands into his own and shook them eagerly. The Carolinian bit down on the cigarette between his teeth, pressed it between his lips once more, then took a huge puff of smoke before extinguishing the cigarette in an ashtray.

Moreno ushered his guest to the bar. He snapped two fingers at the bartender, then shouted something

Sam couldn't hear before whispering into the Carolinian's ear. The bartender poured a whiskey and handed the tumbler to the Carolinian. Moreno motioned toward the auction table, but the Carolinian waved him off. It seemed he had no interest in purchasing anything at the event. Everything about his face told Sam the southerner had come for one thing and one thing only: to conduct business.

Now the two men moved abruptly through the crowd and past the dance floor. Sam had been paying such close attention to the interaction that he hadn't even noticed Cat had come in closer to his body, and was even pressing her head against his shoulder. He was suddenly acutely aware of the smell of her perfume, a classy, timeless scent that suggested French elegance. Sam continued to lead her in a circular motion to keep track of the action. Both men had disappeared through the door.

"We're going to have to finish this dance later," Sam said. Cat's face grew forlorn.

"Something's better than nothing," Cat said, and kissed him lightly on the cheek. The sensation sent a chill shooting up his spine. "Stay in touch." Sam nodded, then took off through the crowd to follow his targets.

He pushed the wooden door open, behind which was a long corridor. As the door shut in his wake, the hubbub of the party died down considerably. He was left with the quiet isolation of the narrow hall.

"Can you still hear me?" Cat asked.

"Loud and clear," Sam whispered. He moved forward down the hall with a light step. The hall was dimly lit, and there were several sets of doors on either side of him. He pushed the first he found on the left open: it was an empty study littered with all manner of old books. He turned his attention to one on the right. There was nothing of interest there either, just a desk and some filing cabinets. A cover story would be in order in case he was cornered. He'd say he lost his way looking for the bathroom. Who wouldn't buy a story like that in a maze-like building like the Montgomerys'?

He wasn't even sure what the Montgomerys looked like. The hosts of the party hadn't made their presence known in an official way. Surely they'd show their faces before the auction began. Were they even aware of the meeting that was about to take place? Sam thought not, but Moreno surely knew his way around the building, and he'd been confident enough to host a gathering of select individuals to discuss something of a potentially incriminating nature.

The hall hooked right and led to a smaller, almost miniature foyer not unlike the magnificent one that Sam had seen when he'd arrived. At the end, a set of ornately carved double doors with golden handles beckoned Sam's attention. Every fiber of his being was telling him his targets had entered this room, and the smell of cigar and cigarette smoke creeping into his nostrils confirmed his suspicion.

Sam approached the door and pressed his ear against the thick wood, but he heard nothing. A tray nearby on which sat several wine glasses and scotch tumblers offered just the tool he needed. He grabbed the tumbler, for once using it for something other than slurping liquor, and turned it backwards so the base of the glass faced him. He pressed the mouth of the glass against the wall just beside the door, touched the base against his ear, and listened for evidence that the room in front of him was where he needed to be. The thick walls only returned muffled vibrations, but now he could hear the conversation of several men making introductions. Though the old trick would only work so well—he needed to get inside to hear the nuances of their conversation.

Sam grabbed the door handle—thankful it was unlocked—and pressed his eye against the small sliver of doorway he'd created. The conversation grew louder. He stepped through and found himself in a cavernous library fit for a king. The meeting was already in full swing. The men had gathered, standing around a wooden table with small lamps lighting its surface, and none of them seemed even slightly aware of Sam's entrance. He scurried to a nearby bookshelf for cover.

The high ceilings were supported with bookshelves that required a ladder to access, and at the center of the room a magnificent chandelier provided a warm, dim light that scattered across the books. There were so many books in the room, Sam couldn't even imagine there was that much in the world to write about. He suspected many of the titles were encyclopedias—updated and edited editions of the same books. Once he'd taken adequate cover, he removed one of the books from the shelf in front of him so he could watch the meeting. The book he'd removed to get a better view was, as he suspected, the "R" section of an encyclopedia series.

Moreno offered a cigar to the Carolinian. He declined it and lit up another of his own cigarettes, and then Moreno offered one to another gentleman in a tuxedo standing by. Two other men were also present, but their backs were to Sam and he couldn't see their faces. The chandelier above was casting dark shadows under the eyes of the men he could see, which only befitted the shady meeting at hand. The lighting made it difficult to see detail. Hearing them, on the other hand, was easy; the room echoed greatly.

It was so easy to hear, in fact, that Cat chimed in over the radio, "How's the party?"

"In full swing," Sam whispered.

"You let me know if you need anything," Cat replied. The last few words were accompanied by a staticky hiss.

"Keep an eye on that door," Sam said. "Let me know if any other guests are coming to the party."

"Only if you're going to finish that dance," Cat said. The radio was breaking up significantly now, but their conversation wasn't the one Sam had come for. Sam returned his attention to the meeting at hand. The Carolinian checked his watch impatiently, and Moreno kept fidgeting with his hands.

Soon the door at the far end of the room opened, and a man in a black suit stepped out from the shadows and toward the center of the room where his associates had gathered. The Carolinian asked Moreno, "This him?" Moreno nodded.

The newcomer, a tall man with luscious blond hair and a clean-shaven face, walked forward with an extended hand to greet the guests. He was fit, and his tailor had made sure his suit had been presented as well as Sam's had. When he got closer and the orange light of the chandelier kissed his face, Sam noticed a terrible scar that stretched the length of the left side from his hairline all the way down to his chin. The scar was old, and where it had healed it had left a long line of raised skin that suggested the cut was anything but clean.

Sam had noticed scars like that on some of the old-timers in Germany. Many men of power and wealth had them. They were the results of fencing injuries—*Mensur*, more precisely—most of which came from their time in universities. Even some of the men who'd made top brass in the Nazi party had been duelers, and many considered the scars badges of honor. A scar like that on a man could be a sign of extensive education, and considering the company presently in the room, Sam didn't think that was unlikely. Though many were only minor, the one this man bore was particularly gruesome. The spy was aware that the unclean healing process was the result of picking at the scab to make it more prominent. In his hand, he carried a large bottle of brown liquid—it was the scotch Moreno had advised him to bring. *Of course*, Sam thought. *Nazis.*

But to Sam's surprise, when the man spoke, he spoke in unaccented English. He said to Moreno, "Salazar, it is great to see you, my friend. I'd like to thank you again for arranging this meeting." He turned to the Carolinian. "Mr. Ives, I presume?" Sam had referred to the southerner by his code name so much he'd forgotten the man had a *real* name.

Wade Ives held his hand out and gave the man with the face-length scar a firm shake, then "Sparrow" finally introduced himself. "Maxwell Kearney," he said. "I owe you a great debt of gratitude for coming all this way, Mr. Ives. It's very hard for me to get to the east coast, just far too much to tend to back at the factory. I'm lucky if I get an hour away, let alone a night."

"S'alright," Ives said. "Let's you and me hope we're not wastin' our time."

Kearney presented Ives the bottle of scotch. "I'm told you're a fan. Regardless of whether or not we do business, take this gift as a thank you for attending the meeting." Ives took the scotch, placed it on the table beside him, then nodded in thanks. He leaned up against the table, then folded his arms and watched Kearney intently.

Moreno spoke up. "Maxwell, you remember Robert Brigham, and of course, Richard Thornton." He pointed to the two men whose backs were turned toward Sam. Each man shook hands with Kearney. "They'd be willing to help with packaging and transportation, respectively."

"If we can come to an agreement, I'm sure their help will be invaluable," Kearney said. "You must all be anxious to get back to your party, so let's get right to it. Mr. Ives, I'm told you've got what I'm looking for in abundance."

Ives clutched his cigarette between his teeth, dug into his pocket, and retrieved something balled in his fist. He placed it down on the small table beside the group of men. It was a piece of rock, and judging by the way it reflected the small lamp's light, Sam knew right away what it was: tungsten.

"Ah," Kearney said. "That's the ticket." Kearney grabbed the small piece of unrefined ore and scrutinized it under the light. "That's very fine indeed. How much do you think you've got?"

"No idea," Ives said. "We were out and about trying to blast and create some new paths in our mine, and next thing I knew the boys were hollerin' somethin' fierce—talkin' about how they've struck gold. Well, gold

I know it ain't. Got a Spaniard workin' on my property that says he knows a thing or two about it, and so I contacted my friend Salazar here to see what's what."

"No, it's not gold, Mr. Ives," Kearney said. "It's *better*." Kearney continued to analyze the tiny details of the ore, rotating it admiringly in his hand such that the light would touch it in different places. "Unrefined, and you've got a good-for-nothing rock. But after it's been processed to separate the good materials from the useless, you've got a very reliable compound."

"For what?" Ives asked.

"Appliances, of course," Kearney said.

Ives' curiosity was aroused. He asked, "Like what?"

"We use it for wiring and, when appropriate, durability," Ives said. "Right now, I'm going to see to it that it gets used for our new line of home-use fans, incandescent bulbs—that sort of thing. We've also utilized it for a new bake light. But I've got my sights set on bigger applications. You know these planes they've got, right? Well part of the reason they have trouble getting them to move much faster is because the stress of flight on aluminum is too great. Furthermore, when this stuff gets hot, it doesn't warp. A little help from our friends here in D.C.," Kearney nodded to both Brigham and Thornton, "and perhaps we can get some of those oh-so-sought-after military contracts. I'm of half a mind to start drawing up plans for a high-speed plane myself—not that I know a damn thing about flying." The men gathered all let out forced chuckles. Ives wasn't laughing.

The Carolinian looked Kearney up and down. Sam could sense he was trying to get a feel for the man; was he a bullshitter? Was he slimy? Ives inhaled deeply from the cigarette, flicked the ash in a nearby ashtray, then exhaled through his red-tinged nostrils. The man had clearly spent a lot of time in the sun. "So you're saying I can grab a pretty penny out on the market?" he said at last.

"I'm just a manufacturer," Kearney said. "Wouldn't know what to do with it otherwise. That said, if you've got a bidder that you're more comfortable with, then I salute your freedom of choice. As a businessman myself, especially in these trying times, I recognize that we're all just trying to stay afloat and get our piece. If you'd like to come to the factory, a visit could be arranged."

Ives adjusted his hat. He looked to Moreno, who nodded eagerly as if to give his approval. Ives waved his hand dismissively, then said to Kearney, "Not necessary. Far too much work at home to get out there myself. I'd like to extend the same invite to you, though."

"You can bet I'll be there, Mr. Ives," Kearney said. "If you'd in fact like to do business, then I'll oversee the acquisition of said tungsten and ensure it gets to where it needs to go. Of course, we'll have to bring in quite a bit of machinery, if that's alright with you. Harvesting such a rare metal requires a specific refinement process, as well as a team of men to ensure it's done properly. We wouldn't be in your way, that I can assure you."

"Not at all," Ives said. "The wife likes to cook. Your team would be welcome to come join in and get the lay of the land. We've got a guest house fit for a king. Mr. Moreno tells me you've already had a geologist test the mineral samples I sent?"

"I have," Kearney said.

"And it's viable?" Ives asked.

"It would appear so," Kearney replied.

"The question I'm more concerned with," Ives

began, "is just how much this is going to be worth to me."

"I'd have to see what you're working with first," Kearney replied.

"The vein my boys discovered must have stretched at least a few square miles," Ives said.

Kearney's eyes glowed like a child who's been offered unlimited candy. "I'd say it's safe to assume we're looking at anywhere between twenty and thirty dollars per kilo."

The cigarette nearly fell out of Ives' lips when he heard the offer. He stood up from the table he'd been leaning on, adjusted the waistband of his pants, then offered a firm hand to Kearney. Kearney shook it eagerly.

"When do we start?" Ives asked.

"Immediately," Kearney replied. "There's no time to waste. I can have my people there tomorrow and the rest of the equipment as soon as possible thereafter. Construction of a refinement facility will be a lengthy process, but that doesn't mean we can't get to work. Have you got a rail line near you, Mr. Ives?"

"Several miles from the farm's entrance," Ives replied.

"Good," Kearney said. He turned to Brigham. "Mr. Brigham, I expect you'll take care of those arrangements."

"Right away," Brigham replied.

"Mr. Thornton," Kearney said, addressing the man beside him, "we're going to need your trucks to make the trip from the site to the trains, and then offload them into our facility."

"How many trucks are we talking?" Thornton asked.

"As many as you have," Kearney replied. "I assure

you, it will be worth any temporary interruptions to your business it might cause."

"Where's it all headed?" Thornton asked.

"Very far," Kearney replied. He paused for a moment. Sam could spot a liar a mile away, and as Kearney struggled to find an answer, Sam could tell he hadn't prepared a lie for this question. "California, in fact. We've exhausted our resources on the West Coast, if you can believe it."

The radio crackled in Sam's ear. He heard Cat's voice faintly, but couldn't make out the words. He pressed the earpiece tighter to his ear. Cat said, "Sam," and the radio hissed once more. Sam thought he heard a tone of desperation in her voice.

"Cat?" Sam whispered. No answer came. He tried to contact her again, this time with a whisper as loud as he could produce without giving himself away, "Cat!" The radio only crackled further.

Sam refocused his attention toward the meeting. Something wasn't right. Brandt had known it, and now so did Sam. This Kearney wasn't at all who he said he was, and if Moreno was involved, there was no way in hell the man was manufacturing appliances for consumer use. The question was, did Ives know? Or how about Thornton and Brigham? Sam considered that each of these men could have been played by this Kearney fellow.

"Sam!" the spy heard his partner call out once more. The radio hissed, and then came a terrible screeching sound that made Sam want to rip the piece out of his ear. Now he was sure she'd gotten herself into some sort of trouble. *God damnit, Cat. Hold on.*

"I won't keep you any longer," Kearney said. "Let's

put this conversation on hold until we're at Mr. Ives' farm. There's no need to keep you from your party. Let's keep our arrangement limited to this room, gentlemen, shall we? My competitors would love nothing more than to outbid me." Kearney turned to Ives. "Mr. Ives, I'm confident you'll honor this agreement solely with a handshake?"

"Tell ya the truth," Ives replied, "I wouldn't know where to take the stuff otherwise."

"Good," Kearney replied. "We strike ground immediately." Handshakes traveled around the circle, then each of the men began to exit the room. Kearney left through the back entrance just as he'd come, and Sam scaled the bookshelf he'd used for cover to keep out of sight as the men left.

"Sam, I could really use some help here," Cat said. This time he heard her clearly. There was desperation in her voice. Had she been compromised? He hoped not. He was of half a mind to blow the joint right now if that was the case. There was no use putting both of their identities at risk. It was Sam's job to protect her, too, though. If she was one of the team, then her anonymity was just as important as his own—especially on home soil.

Moreno saw Thornton, Brigham, and Ives out the door Sam had come through. Sam exited swiftly, keeping behind the men while simultaneously lingering in the shadows. Through the walls, Sam heard the swell of a loud voice over the microphone and the echo of applause. The auction had begun.

9

"Sam!" Cat yelped. The cry drew the attention of several people near Cat, none of whom she knew. The sea of the crowd parted slightly for one brief moment, and through the moving bodies, the man she'd encountered in the alley the morning earlier stared back at her. He sipped his drink without breaking his gaze. This must be the Bruce Whelan Sam warned her about. Why was he *here*? Did it have something to do with her? Whatever his purpose, his interest was completely focused on Cat. Wherever she turned, she'd found him staring back at her with dead, accusatory eyes.

Stickey Buns grabbed the microphone and cradled it in two hands as the band's final notes trailed off. He spoke triumphantly, "And now, folks, the moment you've all been waiting for: your host, and the man who throws the best parties in this great nation, Carlyle Montgomery!" The percussion section broken into a rhythmic beat favoring the snares and symbols, and the crowd erupted in applause. Cat took the opportunity to snake through their bodies and ditch Whelan as best she could. The partygoers she navigated through started bobbing and moving to the sound of the drums, and Cat turned back to see Whelan fast approaching.

If his goal was to arrest her, she'd be dead in the water. Making a scene at an event like this would surely become a spectacle, and all the work she'd done would be for naught. Cat wouldn't be able to keep this hunt going much longer. She prayed Sam had learned what he came to discover and the two could get the hell out of there quickly.

Carlyle Montgomery climbed the steps of the stage and waved cheerfully to the cohort. Behind Montgomery, the stage lights showcasing the band dimmed, and a spotlight favored him. He was an old man, but maintained a healthy appearance complete with a head full of white hair and a charming smile of false teeth that could have stopped traffic. Unlike the subdued garment colors the rest of the men in the room wore, Montgomery wore a bright auburn jacket with a velvet texture. Behind him, his wife, Genie, ascended the stage-left stairs and waved to the crowd with a princess-like twist of the wrist.

Montgomery directed his hands toward his wife as if to display her for the crowd, and the people in attendance erupted in cheer once more. The silver gown covering her was, as expected, also fit for royalty and was bright enough to pull the attention away from her husband's teeth. The amount of light reflecting off the two hosts was offensive. Cat took the opportunity to put more distance still between her and Whelan—she'd lost him.

"Ladies and Gentlemen, Genie and I thank you all

for coming," Montgomery said. "We've had some fabulous offerings here tonight in the silent portion of the auction, and we thank those of you who've contributed for doing so. Without the donations and attendance of fine people like yourselves, we wouldn't be able to make events like this happen. This year's contributions will be benefitting our troops overseas, and a portion of the proceeds will go directly to machine shops stitching uniforms for the boys shipping off." The crowd cheered once more as if patting themselves on the back.

What a load, Cat thought. *Who's paying for all this shrimp and wine?* She found it all quite self-congratulatory and nauseating. For the first time since she'd started to play this game for Brandt, she felt shame for mingling with these people. The man tailing her through the crowd was another stark reminder of her past, and his presence only reminded her that she didn't belong—she'd never even have the money to bid on any of the fine jewelry herself.

"We're going to do things a little different tonight," Montgomery said. "We're going to start the auction with our most valuable and treasured piece. There's simply nothing like it in the world."

Cat was thankful when the overhead can lights followed the stage's cue and the large room became dark. The focus of the attendees remained on the stage, and Cat finally felt free to move about the room without sticking out. Her black dress was helpful in that regard, and she was thankful she hadn't chosen a more vibrant color. Now, keeping to the shadows, she actually felt the pressure placed on the other operators in Brandt's organization. Where once her job was to be seen, she now had to test her ability to hide.

"Ladies and gentlemen," Montgomery said, and a white-gloved man in a dark suit walked across the stage with a black box and presented it to the host, "Sierra's Pride." Montgomery opened the box—which held a necklace—displayed it for the crowd, and the people 'oohed' and 'aahed' with great admiration. The piece twinkled like an unobstructed view into a fantasized version of the night sky. If anyone's attention had still been focused on Montgomery or his wife, it had surely now shifted to the precious gems.

Even Cat took a moment to survey the necklace. It was the most stunning piece of jewelry she'd ever laid eyes on. Next to Montgomery, the white-gloved man pulled a large black sheet from an easel. On the easel was a picture of the piece of jewelry enlarged enough that all of the room could see it.

The necklace was a string of diamonds, the top ends where the clasps met starting off small with princess cuts of about a carat or so. Each diamond was fitted with a setting—either white gold, silver, or platinum, Cat couldn't tell—but what made the necklace so impressive was the fact that every several diamonds, the cuts grew larger and larger as they continued around the circumference of the necklace. The ones on the sides that would hang near the collar bones looked as if they might be two or even three carats, eventually reaching four carats near the bottom, and finishing with a single, magnificently large piece that would rest on the sternum. Cat thought it likely that the focal point of the necklace was easily a five-carat rock.

"What makes the item so special, my friends," Montgomery said, then handed the box back to the attendant and directed the crowd's attention to the photo, "is that each of these stones is near perfect. I only say 'near perfect' because it's impossible to judge a diamond as such. Every cut, as many of you know, is custom and unique in and of itself, and so one can rarely call any precious gem 'perfect.' One would be hard pressed to find a single inclusion in any of them. Though, I'm sure if there are any, Mr. Lefler will find them!" The crowd cackled. Montgomery pressed his hand above his brow to shield the light hitting his face. "Where is he?"

"Leave eet wiz me for zee night!" a Frenchman called out from the audience, and the crowd broke into even louder fits of laughter. Cat didn't know who Lefler was, nor did she get a look at the man cracking the joke, but she imagined it was he who'd spoken. She'd be sure to make *him* one of her targets if she had any influence on Brandt.

Montgomery started talking about the piece's designer, and Cat turned to look for Whelan. He'd found her again, and once they locked eyes, he made aggressive movements toward her. *God damnit, Sam. Where the hell are you?* If she didn't find him soon, Cat was going to make a break for the exit and take the car home with or without him. *Brandt will understand. I can't compromise my identity.*

As Cat continued to weave through the crowd, she heard the cries of several guests. Whelan had become a nuisance in his pursuit of her, and when she turned once more to check his progress, several guests had unleashed expletives in complaint of the man's actions. Whelan even shoved one gentleman out of the way forcefully, and Cat could see his face when the stage's light hit in just the right way—he was *enraged.*

Cat broke into swift steps and made her way toward the entrance. She'd made her decision: she was getting the hell out of the Montgomery household and getting into that car. The driver had been instructed to wait on standby on the corner of the street perpendicular to the home, so once she was out of the building, she wouldn't have to go far. Heels were not conducive to chases, so Cat made an executive decision to remove them. The room was dark enough that no one would notice. She pulled them off, clutched both between the fingers in her left hand, and then accelerated into a light jog.

She arrived at the edge of the dance floor, and was disappointed to find that a wall of people had formed. There was no way in hell she was going to shove through all of them. Doing so would cause far too large a ruckus.

"Should we start the bidding?" Montgomery called out. The room roared with approval, and an auctioneer —a squat, bald man with thick black horn-rimmed glasses—shuffled up to the stage and toward the podium beside the picture of the diamond necklace. The man struggled to ascend the staircase, gripping the rail tightly in an effort to prevent his shaky knees from buckling. He took small, baby-like steps across the stage, then placed several sheets of paper on to the podium and squinted through his glasses at the documents.

Cat turned to her side, seeking an exit. There, Whelan stood glaring—he was blocking it. The room's attention remained laser-focused on the preparing auctioneer, and in stark contrast to the rest of the party-goers, Whelan's was locked on Cat. She wasn't going to be able to go on like this much longer.

"Sam!" she called out once more in a breathy plea. The radio only returned a screeching static in her ear.

"God damnit." Whelan grabbed the shoulder of the man nearby and shoved him out of his way. Cat made tracks as the federal agent tore across the dance floor.

"Kitty Cat," the old man Donahue called out. He extended and curled his fingers yet again in his signature "gimme" motion.

"Not now," Cat said desperately, and brushed past the old man and behind a grouping of people flanking the edge of the dance floor.

The auctioneer cleared a grotesque amount of phlegm from his throat, then the sound of crinkling paper echoed through the room. The mumble of voices died down and there was a brief moment of silence, then the auctioneer said, "We've got a wonderful piece here, perfect for that lovely lady or someone special. It's a magnificent piece, one of a kind, none other like it in the world. Remember, folks, prices don't just reflect the value of the item but also the size of the contribution you will be making to a wonderful foundation you all know and love. We're going to start the bidding at the low, low price of fifty thousand dollars. Do I hear fifty thousand dollars?"

The auctioneer spoke with lightning-like speed. His speech pattern only added to the dizziness Cat was experiencing while evading the federal agent on her tail. Every word left his mouth rapidly, and though the old man looked like he'd be on his death-bed tomorrow, his vocal efficiency was still top-notch.

"Fifty thousand!" the man right next to Cat called out. The decibel level of his voice amplified through the microphone nearly gave her a heart attack.

"I hear fifty thousand in the back," the auctioneer called out. "Fifty thousand, a good number, an honest number. Can we do better than fifty thousand? Do I hear fifty-five thousand, fifty-five thousand dollars, folks?"

The speed at which the auctioneer spoke only increased. Cat thought now he was double-timing in an effort to get the crowd riled up.

"Sixty thousand!" a woman called out from the other side of the room. Cat recognized the shrill tone of the voice instantly. Cat looked to the source, and there was Beverly Dodd, the woman Sam had rescued her from earlier, smiling gleefully as people murmured at her lofty offer.

"Sixty thousand to the glamorous woman in the back," the auctioneer called out. "Will this magnificent lady bring this piece home tonight, or is there someone out there who can do better? Sixty thousand dollars and one cent is all it would take, folks—just one penny more. Do I see a higher number out there?" The auctioneer strained his neck to look at toward the crowd and search for the next bidder. "Do I hear sixty-five thousand, sixty-five thousand, folks?"

"One hundred thousand!" Montgomery called out. The crowd nearly fell over; audible gasps of surprise came from every direction. Cat knew the host of the party would never dare to bid on items at his own event —he was inflating the number to get the crowd going. She was thankful he had, because the distraction would continue to take the attention off of her as she searched for an exit through the pressing crowd. She looked over the shoulder of a tuxedo-clad man, and Whelan's eyes were darting frantically around the room in search of her.

Where the hell are you, Sam? Cat had spent so much

time developing her persona so she could get into these parties, and now all she wanted to do was get *out*. So many people had gathered for the auction that it seemed as if an exit didn't exist. The thought that the whole event was a fire hazard of epic proportions crossed Cat's mind. Should there be an emergency requiring the safe evacuation of the building, most of these old fogies would likely be trampled, or worse, burned alive.

"One hundred thousand dollars from Mr. Montgomery," the auctioneer yelled triumphantly. It was the first time Cat had even heard the old man slow his voice down. "Listen to that, folks. You're not going to let the host get away with a move like that are you? I know we can do better. Do I hear one hundred and fifty thousand dollars, one hundred and fifty thousand dollars for this fabulous item?"

"Two hundred thousand," another man at stage front called out, and the crowd shrieked in surprise. Now the ball was rolling, and the real value of the piece was coming out. The early minor increases in bidding only existed to let the people who never had a chance have a little fun—the real buyers had come out to play.

"Two hundred thousand dollars to this handsome gentleman right here," the auctioneer said, pointing to the man immediately below him. "This lucky man could walk away with this piece tonight if no one is willing to fight him for it. Do I hear two hundred and fifty thousand dollars? Just two hundred and fifty thousand dollars—a small price to pay for a glorious set of jewels like this."

"Three hundred," another woman called out.

"*Three* hundred thousand," the auctioneer replied. His question and response tactic was doing its job.

Amidst the chaos, Cat finally found a gap available for her to make a break from the dance floor. She wasted no time making her way for it, now breaking into a sprint. She was confident no one noticed, as the event had reached a boiling point. She squeezed between two men, both of whom she was sure she'd seen before among the circles she'd been traveling in, and took one more look over her shoulder—Whelan wasn't in view.

Cat looked to the door Sam had disappeared through when he'd begun his tail of the targets. The spy was nowhere to be found. Cat debated her options momentarily. Why had she been worrying? If anyone could take care of himself, it was probably Sam. *He'll understand.* He'd been well aware they were being watched, and he'd probably have done the same if he was in her position.

Cat gripped her heels tightly so she wouldn't lose them—they were a nice pair, after all—and turned to head for the exit. As soon as she worked up some speed, her face hit a fleshy wall so hard she thought she had broken her nose. She clutched her nose—staring back at her was Whelan. This was the second time he'd materialized in that fashion, and Cat was getting sick of it.

"Four hundred thousand!" a guest called out. The crowd had reached a fever pitch so loud it rivaled the band's music from earlier. The noise in the room was the perfect distraction for the interaction happening between the two parties flanking the dance floor, but Cat was screwed. Whelan had nothing to worry about; it was Cat who was hiding.

"Four hundred thousand, ladies and gentlemen!" the auctioneer yelled. "That's four hundred thousand dollars to the strapping gentleman with the hat. If anyone can beat four hundred thousand dollars, they'll be taking this incredible piece home with them tonight."

"Why such a hurry?" Whelan asked Cat. "The party just started."

"Five hundred thousand!" a voice called out from the center of the room. Cat thought she recognized the voice.

"Five hundred thousand dollars, folks!" the auctioneer said. "That's five hundred thousand dollars. Do I hear six hundred thousand?" The crowd's noise had now built to a roar. "Six hundred thousand dollars. Do I hear six hundred thousand dollars?"

Cat struggled to find words. Was she under arrest? Was he going to make a spectacle out of their interaction and reveal her true identity for all to see? How would Brandt react? A vision of steel bars flashed across Cat's mind's eye like a terrible fever dream. She wasn't going back to that cage in Pennsylvania. Cat balled her free fist up at her side. She was ready to strike if necessary. So what if she ran from the feds? Brandt could sort that part out, right?

"Five hundred thousand going once!" the auctioneer yelled. No one placed another bid. "Five hundred thousand going twice!"

Cat saw an index finger reach over Whelan's shoulder and tap it. Whelan turned to see who had requested his attention. Sam was standing behind him with a smirk on his face, and he cranked his arm back.

"Sold!" the auctioneer yelled cheerfully.

Just when the partygoers were at their loudest, Sam hit Whelan square in the face with a right hook. The impact sent the federal agent crashing to the floor, and

Cat sprang forward to make her escape with Sam. Whelan didn't even know what hit him.

"Five hundred thousand dollars for this incredible item going to the dashing man at the center of the floor!" The crowd cheered, and Cat looked toward the center of the dance floor as she hustled out with Sam. The attention of the people clapping and smiling had been focused solely on one man. Moreno had won the necklace.

Sam and Cat barreled through the double-door exit of the Georgetown home and knocked both doormen to the concrete in the process. The car they had arrived in was idling on the street corner as promised. As they leapt into the backseat of the car, Sam told the driver to punch it, and the car's tires spun with a deafening screech leaving burnt rubber and a trail of smoke lingering in the street.

10

Only a few streets away at another Georgetown home, Sam surveyed the dark avenue before allowing Cat to exit the vehicle. Now that Sam knew this Whelan character wasn't just on to him but to his accomplice as well, Sam felt a responsibility to make sure she got in safely. Once her door was locked and bolted, he'd sleep better, and he was sure Brandt would expect him to look out for her. In Brandt's eyes, Cat was as valuable as any other asset to the SSD—the information gathered the night prior had proved that.

Sam was satisfied that no one was waiting for Cat—and that no one had followed them—and he motioned for her to roll down the window when he'd arrived back at the car. Sam said, "Alright, let's go." Cat climbed out of the car, then Sam told the driver, "Hold on a moment."

Cat looked shell-shocked. Her eyes were wide black circles—the result of her body's response to a surge of adrenaline. The law, Sam thought, had brought something out of her, a *different* kind of fear. Sam could see her heels trembling in between her fingers. Sam asked her, "You alright?"

Cat nodded, though it was unconvincing. She said, "You just punched a federal agent."

"He was in my way," Sam replied. The comment got a giggle out of Cat, and that defused the tension. "Go straight up to your apartment. When you get up there, lock every window and door. If anyone knocks, don't open it—not even for any of our people."

"What if it's you?" Cat asked without shame.

Sam smirked. "Tomorrow morning, we'll go straight to Brandt."

Cat looked into his eyes with a hopeful expression. She said, "Stay with me."

Sam kissed her on the cheek and grabbed her shoulders. "That would be unwise," he warned her. "Better to stay split up. If anything happens to either of us, the other will still have a story to tell. If something happens to me, you tell Brandt that this 'Sparrow' is a man named Maxwell Kearney, and his plan is to get down to North Carolina to see about a wealth of tungsten that Ives has stumbled on. Moreno's in on it, too, and so are two others—Brigham and Thornton their names are. Kearney's a liar."

"What's really going on?" Cat asked.

"Kearney," Sam repeated. "North Carolina."

Cat nodded. "How do you know, she asked. "That he's liar?"

"Takes one to know one," Sam replied. Cat understood. She knew all too well the double lives both she and the other plethora of people employed in the operation had been leading. To be a member of Brandt's outfit was to become someone else entirely. Perhaps they'd be chasing people like that, too. "Flick your lights twice when you get in."

Cat walked up the front steps to the apartment and shut the door behind her. She turned back once more to look at Sam-who'd watched her as she disappeared into the dark foyer—then walked up the stairs of the main hall. Cat felt the uncomfortable sensation of being watched when she entered into her apartment. Though it was unlikely anyone had broken in, who knew what the feds were capable of? They were, after all, not so dissimilar from her or Sam—lurking in the shadows, watching their targets, collecting information.

She did a quick search through the apartment, opening every door inside and checking for any unwanted guests, then looked through the window to the street below where her handsome date stood waiting in the shadows in his suit. He was barely visible, and she might not have noticed him if she hadn't seen the glow of his cigarette cherry flare. She turned the lights on and off two times, then the spy made his way toward the car on the opposite side of the street.

There was no way Cat was going to get a good night's sleep. The thought of being cuffed again had tickled her nerves something fierce. On top of that, the fallen sun had not provided a respite from the heat, and the apartment was sweltering. She opened several windows in the hopes that a cool breeze would spring up, then poured herself a healthy helping of scotch—the good stuff—from the decanter and swallowed half of a glass before slumping into the couch.

A loud cracking sound went off nearby and almost made her leap out of her skin. Another followed, and that one rattled the foundation of the building with low a groan. She ran to the window, fearful that either someone had started firing guns or that the *Luftwaffe* had finally reached them across the Atlantic—or maybe it was the Japanese.

When she searched the skyline through the window, she saw no German or Japanese planes, but only a fading red glow against coming storm clouds. Another crack followed, then the black of the night sky lit up in a vibrant green. *Green?* Curiosity forced her up to the roof to see what the commotion was about.

The building's owner kept the access door to the roof unlocked, and Cat often went up there to admire the view of the capital. It was a far cry from the bare, cruel walls of the penitentiary in Pennsylvania she'd been pulled out of. She'd come a long way from prison rags and days-old slop. When she arrived at the edge of the roof, another explosion rippled across the skyline—this one a magnificent yellow—spreading outward until it dimmed along curling tendrils. *Of course*, Cat thought. *They're fireworks.*

It was Thursday, July 2nd, and one of the nearby towns—she believed the show was somewhere over Maryland, maybe Bethesda—must be celebrating early. Soon the intensity and speed of the display rapidly increased, and the black atmosphere was illuminated by a flurry of rainbow-like colors. Though the initial shock had only caused her further stress, the distraction was welcome if only to help her keep her mind off the realization that federal agents had nearly captured her earlier. She watched the entirety of the show—which ended with an explosive final act displaying nearly every color in the rainbow—and finished her drink in the process.

Back in her apartment, Cat finally felt some relief from the heat. Her nerves had calmed, no doubt from the booze rather than the passing of time. She felt tired, felt the comedown from the thrill of the party and a mountain range of adrenaline intervals. Perhaps there was some sleep in her future. She'd need to be up first thing in the morning and report to The Yard early, not only to debrief Brandt about the party, but also to warn him about her and Sam's new "friends."

The phone rang. The loud bell-like chime launched her out of a sleep she hadn't realized she'd fallen into. Cat checked the nearby clock on the wall: it was eleven o'clock at night. *Who the hell would be calling now?* The only likely answer was The Yard. Hell, they were the only ones who knew the damn number. What if *wasn't* The Yard, though?

She hesitated before answering, her fingers resting lightly on the receiver. It rang again. Cat lifted the phone, and before she could answer, an operator asked, "620?"

"This is," Cat replied.

"Transferring an incoming call to you," a calm, efficient-sounding voice said. Cat recognized her as the switchboard operator at The Yard. The method had been designed to intercept calls to lines given to special operatives. This benefit was two-fold: the calls could be transcribed for posterity and also protect the anonymity of those receiving them, Brandt had said. She'd given it to Moreno—among other targets she'd been assigned to. When someone dialed the line, that phone request would first stop at the switchboard, be flagged, and then be transferred to Cat's apartment when she confirmed receipt. Cat thought it was a well-designed system. And it was, of course, the brain child of Newton.

A series of clicks sounded through the earpiece, then Cat said, "Hello?"

"*Preciosa*," the warm voice on the other end of the line replied. It was Moreno. "You left early." She exhaled softly, not realizing she'd been holding her breath in suspense. Moreno she could deal with.

"Long day," Cat replied.

"I didn't get to see you," Moreno said. "I thought perhaps I was going to see you later tonight. Is that still a possibility?"

"I'm in for the night," Cat replied.

"But I'm not."

Cat faked a giggle, then said in a sultry tone, "Another night."

"How about several?" Moreno asked.

"Pardon?"

"I have some business out of the state," Moreno said. "Since we have a long holiday weekend, I'm thinking perhaps you'd like to come along with me."

"Do tell," Cat said with intrigue.

"Have you ever been to North Carolina?" Moreno asked. The phone almost fell out of her hand.

She hesitated, then said, "I haven't." It was a lie. She had been to North Carolina. She'd broken into a poorly guarded safe at a gas station while passing through the state, only to find it contained nothing other than a collection of worthless coins. It was the *last* time she'd been to North Carolina.

"Then I'd love for you to join me," Moreno said.

"I'd love to," Cat said without a second's pause. Surely Brandt would want her to go, right? She'd be in close on the action—that would likely mean being up close and personal with the Kearney fellow. She thought it was likely that *Sam* would be going, too.

———

Across town, and far away from the classic Georgetown architecture, Sam ensured the safety of his own apartment from the shadowy interior of the idling car before going inside. The feds had known how to find both of them—not once, but twice—and Sam suspected it was not because they knew where they lived, but rather because they had seen them coming and going from The Yard. Once he felt sure that no one had been watching, he waved the car off and tossed his cigarette into the street.

Sam was practiced at checking the interior of his own spaces for any signs of infiltration, and he was well aware of the signs of an amateur snoop. The first test, as always, was the small thread he secured to the door jamb for any signs of tampering or breakage. It was how he'd discovered Brandt in his apartment not long ago, *before* the burned man got the jump on him. The hair-like string, thankfully, remained intact.

The second test was a barely visible coating of dust just inside the entrance which would reveal footprints if it had been disturbed—there were none. The last, and final indication of tampering was a small thread across the seam of the fire escape window. It, too, had not be touched. He was safe—if only for the night—and did as was customary when he arrived anywhere and lit up a cigarette.

Like Cat, he assumed, he thought it unlikely he would be getting very much sleep that night. The highs of a good escape took time to wear off, and the blood pumping back and forth through his veins and arteries showed no signs of stopping. He stripped down to only his underwear in an attempt to cool down, poured himself a drink, and sat at the window while he nursed the cigarette. The smoke in the room at the party had been overwhelming, and if he was truthful he didn't even want a cigarette. Smoking it was purely habit. He'd recently considered quitting after inhaling so much burning debris. The raging fire of the defeated super tank during his last mission abroad should have been enough to convince a man, but he was a sucker for smokes.

A series of explosions echoed through the sky. Sam experienced no sensation of fear from the ruckus. He'd seen far worse in his travels. He walked slowly toward the window: a fireworks display was in full effect in the city outskirts. Sam always liked the ceremony. It had been one of his first initiations into being an American —even if it was unofficial—when he'd first arrived.

He thought of Cat and hoped that she was still safe. He half considered tossing the cigarette and making the trek back to take her up on her offer. If he'd been honest with her, he would have told her he *did* want to stay the night. Any man with a pulse wouldn't have dreamed of turning down a night with a woman like that, but Sam always had the mission in the back of his mind, and he didn't want to jeopardize Cat's safety—both for her sake and Brandt's. Starting up a fling with this girl now would mean trouble—he'd already failed in that department once this year.

Sam rested on the couch and watched the blank wall opposite him. He enjoyed looking at the empty wall. It was like a canvas for the mind, able to depict infinite images that almost appeared lifelike the more he focused on them. The effect was the most powerful that time of the night when he was half asleep, half awake, and half drunk, if that were such a thing. It was also the time of the night when his mind would usually wander toward Sigrid.

He still saw her face. Her *face*, with her eyes wide and full of fear and surprise and terror. The image was still frozen in his mind. Why *her*?

He'd spent the night with a woman, but when she'd lain there in the road to *Flussrand*, bleeding out through large holes the high-caliber rifle had ripped through her, she'd seemed like just an innocent girl. She was a girl that had gotten caught up in the games of dangerous men. She was a girl who'd come *back* for him.

She was a hero, and likely a far better one than he. Heroes weren't always the ones who came home with medals and stripes and pins declaring their victories, they were also the people rotting in trenches. They were the people who'd endured torture without giving up a single secret, the people who'd died before they'd ever even seen the enemy. They were the ones who went in guns blazing, not because they were asked to, but because they had to. They were the ones who came *back*.

She'd come back for him when he'd thought all was lost, and she'd paid the ultimate price because of it. No one knew her name, or would likely ever. Within her own people's history, if it would remember her, it would be as a branded *Verräterin*—traitor. The British, specifically those in London, where the dreaded super tank *Erdschlag* would have aimed its mighty barrel first, knew nothing of the woman who'd given her life to prevent it from firing its fearsome shells or rockets. Sam was hesitant about working with Cat not just because he wasn't sure he could trust her, but more importantly because he feared the same fate might befall her. That very fear of seeing Cat in harm's way had given him the guts to knuckle up and crack Whelan.

Sure, Sam had probably put a target on his back after that maneuver, but Brandt had that very same back protected. Just how much did the feds know, and moreover, would they be getting in the way? Sam suspected that discovering the true nature of this Kearney character and his nefarious business interests was not the only difficulty he was going to endure in the coming days.

11

———

Sam woke the next morning to a quiet capital. The fury of the evening's fireworks had been exchanged for soft bird songs and cheery, street-level chatter. The country would remain jovial—and oblivious—for at least the next several days while on holiday. Sam knew one of two possibilities was likely: he would be using the opportunity to continue to steal the secrets hidden in Washington D.C., or he'd be on his way to North Carolina to pay a visit to the farm of a notable Carolinian. He thought the latter likely.

Brandt wasted no time sending his operatives into action when the fate of the free world was at stake. He, unlike his other D.C. colleagues—both friends and enemies—would *not* be taking time off for the holiday weekend. He *never* did. Hell, he'd thrown Sam behind German lines only months earlier when it was perhaps the most dangerous place a spy could set foot. At least he'd be operating *alone* once more. In addition, he'd be on American soil, so a call for help wouldn't go unheard.

Sam, as he planned to reveal to Brandt in short time, believed that Kearney was anything but who he said he was. Brandt, of course, had already pegged "Sparrow" as nefarious, but Sam had confirmed it. The boss was the one who'd thought Moreno was bad news in the first place, and he'd been *right*. Brandt had eyes and ears for things like that, which was likely why he was the nation's current spy chief—publicly or otherwise.

The dueling scar stretched across Kearney's face was the first thing that had made Sam suspect foul play. It was possible that an appliance manufacturer from California could simply just have a bad scar. It was also possible that an honest businessman might want a valuable metal like tungsten for his engineering and production processes, but honest businessmen didn't speak in code with foreign embassies about closed door meetings.

The larger question Sam had was, just where was this tungsten really going, and who would be there to receive it? Of course, a warring nation could never have enough supplies, and the thought of stealing America's precious reserves from right under its nose would be enticing to the enemy. Sam still wasn't sure what Ives knew and what he didn't. Unlike Kearney, Sam did not sense anything dubious about Ives' character—he'd seemed like a farmer who'd stumbled upon some gems and was willing to sell them to another American for the right price. That was just good business.

Sam would know more soon enough. He arrived at The Yard, as was customary, while the sun was still low on the eastern horizon. The absence of light on the building's face at that time of day always gave it a mysterious, gothic appearance. One might suspect the damn place was haunted. It was fitting, because housed inside were secrets from nearly every nation across the globe and men who behaved like ghosts working inside of it. If America's enemies wanted to do any real damage, breaking in could cripple America's ability to wage war.

Sam did the routine with security, then arrived at the second floor after a quick trip on the lift. As expected, no one within the SSD HQ had the weekend off. The enemy wasn't celebrating a national holiday, and so Brandt wouldn't expect his people to either. The usual onslaught of shuffling papers and cigarette smoke welcomed Sam as he passed through the busy personnel.

He made his way up to Brandt's office, and before he'd arrived at the final staircase granting access to the fourth floor, Cat called out from behind him, "Sam!" He paused, took a pull from his cigarette, and waited for his partner.

She was flustered. Her cheeks were rosy where once they were pasty, and she looked as if she'd rushed to get ready. Her hair was still wet, and her clothing, unlike normal, was slightly disheveled. In her hand, she had a piece of paper that trembled between her fingers. "Did you get one of these?" Cat asked desperately.

Sam took the monochromatic picture from her, gave it a once-over, and was surprised to find that someone other than him was taking pictures, too; but theirs were of Cat—and they were damning. The picture featured Cat leaving the embassy the morning after their break-in to steal the goods from Moreno. Cat had a wary, guilt-ridden expression on her face. An unofficial operative—especially one who might be perceived as a lady of the night—leaving a location like that at the wrong hour might have some explaining to do.

"It was slipped under my door," Cat said. They *did*

know where Cat lived, whoever *they* were. Whelan, or one of his goons, had taken the photo. "I knew they'd seen me," Cat said in a panicked voice. "I mean, we *knew* they were watching, but what do you think they'll do with this? Who have they sent it to? Do you think Brandt knows? What if they've blown my cover?"

Sam clutched both of her shoulders. "Relax." He gave her a moment to catch her breath after her rapid-fire concerns. "If they want to do something with it, they'll do it—but they *haven't*."

"What do I tell Brandt?" Cat asked.

"You tell him exactly what happened," Sam said reassuringly. "You think he doesn't know this is a risk?"

"Right," Cat replied, unconvinced.

"That's why we have debriefings," Sam explained. "If we've got to do some shuffling, so be it. You didn't commit any crimes, at least not that *they* know of. If they did, we wouldn't be having this conversation, and there'd be steel bars separating us."

Cat blanched at the mention of bars. "But what about last night?" Cat asked. "That guy, Whelan, right? He *tried* to corner us."

"He tried to *scare* us," Sam replied.

"How do you know?" Cat asked.

"I'd do the same," Sam said with a reassuring smirk. He inhaled from the cigarette and offered it to Cat, who took a nice, long drag. She exhaled with a slow, ragged breath. "There you go," Sam said, and she handed the cigarette back to him. "Come on."

When they arrived at Iris's desk, Sam deduced that there had been more problems overnight. Iris quickly dabbed at her eyes with a tissue, composing herself nervously when the two spies approached her desk. Her cheeks were puffy, and her eyeliner had begun to run down the sides of her face.

"Iris," Sam said.

"Good morning," Iris said, her usual greeting shaky.

"Everything alright?" Sam asked.

"Yes," Iris replied. "Just some unfortunate family business is all. Nothing a day off couldn't cure—not that we get any of those."

It was a lie. Sam didn't need any high-tech gear or leaked information to figure that out. He wasn't one to console people or inquire about their problems, but something felt *off* about the coincidence. He was certain whatever was wrong with Iris had something to do with the FBI's activities through the night.

The lie also made him uncomfortable. Though the entire foundation of Brandt's operation was itself built on lies and secretive information, the woman who was one of the only barriers to the man in charge of those secrets was currently sobbing outside his office. Sam wanted to tell her to snap out of it. *Suck it up. You're the liaison to one of the nation's most powerful men.* He knew better than to say anything like that. Behind closed doors he'd been an emotional wreck himself, but he didn't bring it to *work*.

"He's waiting for you," Iris said.

"Thanks," Sam replied.

"I'm here, Iris," Cat said as she lingered in front of the secretary's desk, "you know, if you need to talk."

"I appreciate that, dear," Iris said. "You've got impor-tant business with the big man, I'm sure. He's all a flutter again this morning, and it reeks to high hell of pipe smoke in here. It *always* does when he's got a lot on his mind."

Sam and Cat arrived at Brandt's door, which was ajar, and Sam knocked. Brandt said, "Come in," but behind the door, Sam could hear the abrupt shuffling of thick papers. When Sam got his first visual of the spy chief, he was anxiously collecting the papers from his desk in an effort to hide them. A quick glimpse of the black and white print on the paper suggested Brandt had received some troubling photographs of his own. Sam didn't take Brandt's action of concealing things personally.

There were secrets floating about the office that even Sam didn't have the privilege of seeing. Not every operator got to know *everything*, even if Sam did often get special treatment—that was how the operation stayed efficient. Spies knew what they needed to know to get out in the field and get their jobs done. To know more than necessary was risky, whether the information be contained in the mind of a disgruntled defector or an agent undergoing torture.

"Sit," Brandt said after jamming the photos into his desk drawer. He folded his hands on the table, then just stared at Sam. Brandt's eyes studied the spy's, and then his lips and brows curled into creases of disappointment.

"Christ, Sam," Brandt said, then shook his head from side to side. "A federal agent?"

"Couldn't be helped," Sam said, then awkwardly cleared his throat.

"I told you not to make noise."

"With all due respect, sir," Sam said. He rarely addressed his superior as such, as the strange arrangement with certain SSD personnel suggested rank was irrelevant. "It wasn't exactly *noisy*."

"You two were supposed to stay under the radar,"

Brandt replied. "The only reason I even know is because I got a reporter who happened to see it and started asking Montgomery questions. And then you know what happened?" Now Brandt's eyes finally moved to meet Cat's.

"Montgomery called you?" Cat asked softly.

"No," Brandt said, and now he fixed his eyes on Sam's once more. He spoke with the conviction of a father disciplining his children. "He called Whelan—his *friend*—to see if he was alright. People talk, Sam—this *city* talks."

"Won't happen again," Sam replied. Brandt shook his head in disapproval.

"You see this?" Sam asked, changing the subject. He pointed to the photo held in Cat's hand, and she turned it over to Brandt.

"Bastards," Brandt mumbled in a low growl. Sam felt clever to have immediately reminded the boss about how much he *disliked* Whelan.

Brandt sucked at his pipe feverishly, as if the tool was broken and wasn't providing the comfort it normally did. The tobacco in the pipe flared with orange rage, and Sam noticed the remnants of a hill of ash in a small tray. The madman looked like he'd been at it all night. Two half-finished rye bottles now functioned as paper weights for the smattering of papers strewn across the desk. "If they had anything worth a damn they'd have already acted on it. This is fearmongering." Brandt removed the pipe from his mouth, and it darted between his two subordinates, then said, "But that doesn't mean they *can't* get anything—or won't. For God's sake, you committed a major crime just last night."

"I don't understand," Cat said, her head shaking nervously. "Why would the feds be working against us? Aren't we all on the same team?"

"There is no *team*," Brandt replied. "That's the problem. Sometimes I think we've got more enemies here at home than we do over there." He exhaled a thick cloud of smoke from the pipe. "No matter. We provide results, and soon enough they'll wise up to that. We haven't even gotten started. For now, you two need to keep your wits about you. If you run into any problems, you kill the task. It's not worth losing two operatives because there're birds in the trees. There's only so much trouble I can get you two out of, or *any* of my people for that matter. While you're home, you're simply to observe and report unless otherwise stated. Speaking of which," Brandt opened his palms to hand the floor over to his two spies, "tell me what you *did* accomplish last night."

Sam lit up a cigarette, then slid the ash tray over his way before he started to talk. "Well, you already know Moreno's into whatever it is they're doing, and as suspected, it's a tungsten mining operation."

"Go on," Brandt said.

"And it seems that Moreno pulled a few of his cronies into it as well—mostly for transportation. It's Maxwell Kearney who's got me intrigued—Sparrow."

"Kearney..." Brandt replied. He fell into a deep thought, his eyes wandering around the room as if to retrieve a memory he'd misplaced. Nothing came. "Don't know that one."

"I didn't suppose you would," Sam replied. "I think it's bullshit."

"I'd expect nothing less," Brandt said. "Moreno's pulling in some heavy money—off the books, of course.

He spends far more than any dignitary ought to be able to, even for an *infante de gracia*."

"*Infante de gracia?*" Cat asked.

"He's royalty," Brandt replied.

"Like a prince?"

"A little less," Brandt replied. "Third son. It's unlikely he'll ever rule over anything—he's too far down the line. He's still got the status associated, though."

Cat smirked, then said, "A prince, huh?"

"Remember whose side you're on," Brandt joked.

"That explains just how the hell he was able to win Sierra's Pride," Cat said.

"Who's Sierra?" Brandt asked.

"*It* is a piece of jewelry," Cat said. "He won the best piece at the auction—with a bid of five hundred thousand, no less."

"Going to take a hell of a payday to finance that one," Sam said. "Which would explain why he's the liaison for this transfer."

"That and the fact that the Spanish know a thing or two about tungsten," Brandt said. "Any idea what it's for?"

"This Kearney has been telling a fib about kitchen appliances or some such," Sam said.

"And Ives took the bait?" Brandt asked.

"Seems so," Sam replied. "They're on their way down to his mine as we speak. Kearney and a team of refiners, or miners, or whatever they are."

"It reeks," Brandt replied. "And if you ask me, I think the feds know that, too. That explains why they've been up your asses. They're watching this exchange themselves."

"So it's not just us?" Cat asked warily.

"Can't rule it out," Brandt replied. "The feds are concerned with matters on home soil, but I'd have to imagine you two aren't their priority, you're just a bonus. If they've caught Moreno's stench, then we're on the right track."

"Why not just let them sniff it out?" Sam asked.

"*I* want to be the one to bring this home," Brandt said. "We could use a good catch—over there, or here. There's another war going on right now, and it concerns who can do the job better. I've still got friends at the White House, but some people over there would like to see that change. We need a big fish."

"When do I leave?" Sam asked.

"Right away," Brandt replied. He turned to Cat. "Same goes for you, but your travel arrangements have already been accommodated, it seems."

A twisted expression of confusion crossed Sam's face. He asked Cat, "Travel arrangements?"

"You're not the only one worth a damn in this outfit," Cat replied to Sam.

"I was worried you weren't going to take that call. Now we've got someone on the inside, and we could use that," Brandt said to Cat.

Sam frowned. "What's her cover?"

"Mr. Moreno's invited her to join him as his date for a fabulous trip to North Carolina," Brandt said. Sam had no idea how this had all happened so quickly. Here he'd been thinking he'd go it alone, and now she was going to be right there in the middle of it.

Cat turned to Sam. "I've got friends in high places, too."

"Sam," Brandt began, "you'll be on a train to Vance County, North Carolina this afternoon. That gives me a little time get what I can on Kearney. I want you to infiltrate that farm and see exactly what this operation's about."

"What about Ives?" Sam asked.

"If he knows more than he's letting on, then we'll bring him in, too," Brandt said. "I want to connect Kearney to Moreno, or Moreno to Kearney. Whatever the connection is, they're both dirty. If Ives is aloof, maybe he'll prove to be an asset. We'll coax him into getting us information. Ignorance is no excuse as far as I'm concerned—especially at times like these. Spain is trying to remain neutral, but that's only going to last so long. Any country that wants to sit this one out is going to be sucked in eventually. They'll have their choice: side with the Allies and be on the right side of history or get trampled by the Führer. Spain has been sending off their tungsten reserves to the Nazis for some time now. Last time I checked, providing the enemy with resources isn't sitting the game out. Moreno's no good—call it intuition, but that's what we're running on these days."

Brandt took a great taste of the pipe. He exhaled, then a shroud of smoke clouded his face as he leaned back in his chair. Cat sighed deeply, as if the task at hand was far too daunting.

"What's wrong?" Brandt asked.

"These clothes just won't do," Cat said.

Brandt's eyes narrowed into thin slits of frustration. Sam could understand why the old man had such a great need to justify his operations: the money was flowing out as if from an open faucet. Sam and Cat were only two operatives, and Sam was confident Brandt now employed several hundred both at home and overseas. If Sam's code number was 505, then perhaps that meant there were at least that many operatives. Then again, the armed services were known to inflate their size with arbitrary company, division, and fleet number assignments.

Brandt opened his wallet, pulled out a handful of bills, then slapped them reluctantly on the desk in front of Cat. After Brandt had handed over the money, he said to Cat, "You just make sure you keep your eyes and ears open. Watch your cover and see how close you can get to this Kearney." Brandt turned to Sam. "And you— you're there to observe and take notes. Fire up that camera you've gotten so good with and bring me back a photo of Kearney. If anything, maybe a visual can help us figure it out. An identifying feature would certainly help."

"He's got a *schmiss*," Sam replied, and dragged his index finger down the left side of his face. "Hell of a job the other guy did, too."

Brandt raised an eyebrow. "I think that tells us quite a bit, don't you?"

"I do," Sam replied.

"One more question, Sam," Brandt said. "Did you at least knock him one good?"

Sam smirked. "I made it count."

The spy chief smiled. Brandt slid a folder toward Sam, the cover of which had had been stamped *Sensitive Information: For Entitled Parties Only*, then said, "Dispose of these after you've familiarized yourself with the lay of the land and your target's whereabouts." He turned to Cat. "You, Miss McAlister, are a guest of the enemy. Make sure they show you a good time. If you see a window of opportunity with which to dig, do so."

"Will do," Cat replied.

"For reference, we're calling this one 'Operation:

Shiny Toys.' Well," Brandt continued, "what are you two still doing here? There's nothing good going on in D.C. this weekend."

Sam and Cat rose from their chairs and made for the door. Brandt called out, "And Sam..." Sam turned to face his superior. "No fireworks this weekend. We'll have plenty of those as it is."

"I can't make any promises," Sam replied.

12

Cat had been picked up by four that evening for the overnight trip to Townsville, North Carolina. Moreno arrived—looking quite dashing—in a sleek black sedan fit for the transportation of a monarch. When he saw her, he said, "*Bonita,*" with a sensual purr. The man was charming, she admitted. She'd do well to remember he was currently under suspicion.

Cat was sure to wear her travel best, which consisted of a khaki pantsuit tailored to show off the finest of her curves, but conservative enough as to not draw too much attention. Her hair, red and vibrant in the bright summer sun, bounced around her shoulders with every step she took. She wore large, dark sunglasses—Moreno's idea, not her own—and finished the look off with a small red ascot tied into a neat knot around her neck.

Moreno—whose wife was at home in his native country—hurried the driver after Cat had placed her luggage in. Moreno said, "The quicker we get out of town, the better. No one knows me down there, but everyone knows me *here*." Cat felt the same way, especially considering the federal agents tailing her for the last couple days. She said nothing to Moreno about the watchful eyes of the black-suited G-men, though she considered broaching it to see if she could get Moreno to spill any information. What would Brandt have done? She was nearly as crafty as both him and Sam, but thought it best to leave that bit of information be. Both parties were living lies, which made Cat feel oddly at ease. Cat took a quick survey of the street to check for Whelan or any of his goons before the car pulled away from the Georgetown home—she saw no evidence of them.

She'd graduated to the big job. Here she was on the inside, now part of a *real* operation—or an op, as all the veterans around her called it—and she'd be expected to perform as admirably as any of the masters she'd learned from. No longer would she be tasked with simply ingratiating herself to the caricatures and cackling faces of D.C.—it was possible she was going to meet this Kearney face to face, dangerous as he might be. Cat tried to subdue the lingering feeling she was floating out to sea, despite being prepared, without a life raft.

The train station was buzzing with people. Cat was happy she'd accessorized to obscure her identity. She'd only been on the platform for ten minutes before recognizing several other travelers eager to escape D.C. for the vacation weekend. Many of the other patrons were as finely dressed as she and Moreno. They'd be traveling in a train car meant only for those worthy of its amenities.

The train that would usher them south was a stark red vibrant enough to rival only Cat's hair. Along the train and hugging the wheels, elaborate black and gold paint stenciled along its broad sides accentuated its elegance. Smoke barreled from the engine car when the vehicle blew its horn. The signal of a departure caused many of the people nearby to clamor for their belongings and board the train, and both Cat and Moreno took the opportunity to blend in with the crowd.

Soon after, they'd found their personal cabin. It was a sectioned-off compartment on one of the train cars complete with a couch that turned into a bed, several fine wines, hangers for clothing, and even a small private bathroom. Despite the danger, Cat often found this new life to be quite rewarding as far as aesthetics were concerned. The heat was still offensively uncomfortable, but most of the elite among them kept on their elegant dress. God forbid they be caught looking like the rest of the blue-collar passengers in the back cars.

Once the train started moving, Cat sensed Moreno had been put at ease. Neither took the opportunity to unpack any clothing—they would only be on the train for a short overnight trip, and they'd arrive at their destination as soon as the sun rose. Neither changed their garments for dinner when they ventured to the dining car. Moreno recognized several people in the dining car, but he only delivered waves of recognition. Cat didn't mind. The less she had to say to those people the better. She could talk their talk, but it didn't mean there wasn't inherent danger doing it.

Dinner was, Cat thought, magnificent. Their dinner consisted of a small salad drizzled with a light oil and vinaigrette, followed by a pea soup. Next came a main course of chateaubriand au jus served alongside green beans and carrots. It was the best piece of beef Cat had ever had. The edges were just the right amount of well done, seared to a dark brown, and yet the center was a luscious pink with the tiniest trace amounts of blood. As if the dinner presented wasn't special enough, the meal was finished with a small plate of chocolates and orange slices, "To cleanse the palette," Moreno had said. Cat was still learning.

Over the course of the meal, Cat inquired about just *where* exactly they were going and why. She'd plied the man with several drinks, and it was as good a time as any to press him. She couldn't forget what she'd been tasked with doing: obtaining any information she could to piggyback Sam's efforts.

Moreno explained that they'd be staying in the guest house of a business acquaintance, and that though he'd be working a bit during the day, at night there would be exquisite dinners and free-flowing drinks. He also promised to take Cat sight-seeing if possible. Cat didn't press the issue. Most girls probably would have questioned the nature of a trip like he described and wondered why they might not be going somewhere there were ocean waves or interesting culture, but Cat had to play it cool.

After the meal, which of course was also accompanied by several glasses of a bitter merlot—Cat was sure to order a second bottle—Moreno made brief rounds around the dining car to say hello to those of the evening's guests with whom he was familiar. He introduced Cat by her name, Cat McAlister, but was sure to make clear to all those who met her that she was his new administrative assistant and that she was accompanying him on a trip along the East Coast to inquire about property acquisitions for his Spanish friends back home.

"I can't be bothered with all that typing," Moreno told each of them. "And those dainty little fingers of hers strike the keys without error." Over the course of the introductions, Cat feigned a smile that made her cheeks ache.

Moreno indulged in a cigar back at their table, Cat in a cigarette, and they had another after-dinner drink Cat found entirely too sweet. The after-taste left behind the flavor of black licorice. Cat started to feel the motion of the train, which had picked up considerable speed along the American countryside, and decided one more drink might be dangerous. As it was, she was already feeling as if the room spun when she shut her eyes. Moreno said, "I have something to show you."

"What?" Cat asked. His eyes became wide and devious, not in a dangerous way, but rather one that was both charming and mischievous.

"It is back in our room," Moreno said, and he grabbed her hand to escort her from the table and bid farewell to several guests. On the way back, Cat bounced off the walls, barely able to walk a straight line. She wondered what Brandt would have to say about her heavy drinking, but she'd argue it was all part of the act and, if anything, made her feel she could perform the job better. Lying was easier when she was tipsy.

In their private quarters, Moreno locked the door behind him. He dug in his briefcase, then told Cat to close her eyes. Cat sat on the small couch, suspicious of just what Moreno was on about.

"Why?" Cat asked with a giggle.

"Because I have a surprise," Moreno replied.

"I don't trust you," Cat said playfully.

"I don't know that I trust you, *either*," Moreno replied. "So I think we can agree to trust each other, yes?" Cat obliged, closed her eyes, and listened to Moreno as he riffled through his belongings. Cat opened one eye, unable to resist, and Moreno said, "Close them, or you get nothing!" Cat did so, then lifted both of her hands and flattened them to cover her eyes completely. "Turn," Moreno said.

Cat shifted in her seat, turning her body slightly so her eyes faced the wall and her back faced Moreno. She felt his warm breath behind her neck, then felt the heavy sensation of cool metal fall against her neck and chest. Moreno clasped the jewelry behind her neck, then stepped back a few paces, and said, "Look."

Cat did, first allowing her eyes to fall down her neckline. The necklace returned blinding reflections, even in the dim light of the small cabin, and Cat knew immediately what it was: Sierra's Pride. She was left speechless. For several moments, she could only look at the piece, which she lifted with her fingers to get a better look.

Her bottom jaw hung open—she simply couldn't find the words. Cat rose abruptly, anxious to get a look at the stunning stones in the mirror along the broad side of the cabin. When the light above struck the piece, each of its stones twinkled like small galaxies. She let the piece fall once more and admired her appearance with it draped down her chest.

"*Magnifica,*" Moreno said. Up close, the diamonds were even more impressive than she'd imagined. Cat, witnessing the heavy jewels hanging from her neck, felt the familiar rush of *temptation*.

———

As the train carrying Cat rattled south along the tracks, another train making the trip concurrently trailed behind carrying Sam Abel. He had no fancy compartment to retreat in, no finely cooked steak, and mediocre wine options—Sam chose beer instead. He searched eagerly for a seat away from prying eyes. The train wasn't very full, and eventually Sam procured a seat with enough buffer around him that he could safely explore the top-secret documents he'd brought from headquarters.

Sam had inquired of Brandt whether there wasn't perhaps a plane on standby that could make the trip quickly and in turn buy him more of a head start. The burned man had made it clear that getting a resource like that would be a small battle in and of itself. Brandt had a plane in his employ, but it was reserved for the many trips he'd be making himself over the weekend and was unavailable to fly one lone spy on a mission, no matter how important it might prove to be. Of course, Sam's train fare was paid by the company, as was a small stipend for his meals, but his accommodations were a far cry from what he imagined Cat's were. He might have even been a little jealous, and he wondered if there weren't some questionable female operatives recruited by the enemy that he might have to court.

The file had been closed with a small piece of string wrapped around two hooks, which Sam unraveled as he puffed on a cigarette. The beer was a welcome change from the scotch whiskey he'd been downing and a better option for keeping his wits about him. For all he knew, Whelan, or any of his people for that matter, could be sitting in a nearby seat. He'd done a quick once-over of the train car he'd decided to occupy before taking his seat, and he was satisfied none of the characters seemed like anything to worry about.

The first piece of paper was a brief dossier on Ives. His full name was Wade Bartholomew Ives, and he'd been born in a small town called Buckholts, Texas, just outside of Austin. He'd relocated as a young man, first serving in the Great War, then inheriting his parents' farm. Both of his parents—Ives, Bartholomew Michael, and Ives, Maribell Jane, née Walker—had died in a tragic fire during his time serving in the nation's armed forces. Ives, returning from the war and inheriting quite a bit of coin, relocated to Vance County, North Carolina, in a small town called Muckside. He'd purchased the property quite cheap. He owned most of the property in the town, which was situated just south of the Roanoke River.

The wealth of minerals deposited by the river and numerous creeks and swamps, as well as quick access to water and fertile ground, prompted Ives to first begin a tobacco-growing operation. Soon after, he'd returned to his roots raising livestock, and it was only a couple years before he'd discovered some of the valuable ore deposits smack dab in his backyard. Since the valuable assets were on his property, he'd discovered he was living on a gold mine—even if there wasn't much gold to speak of.

Though Ives was one of the largest—and wealthiest—land owners in North Carolina, there weren't many other details about him to speak of. He'd apparently kept to himself, accumulating large amounts of money, and even donated quite a bit to community initiative projects in nearby counties. Most of the information that had been gathered on him was simply state or federal record. For all intents and purposes, he was just a good old American businessman looking to make another buck. He'd donated considerably to the war effort in the last several months—over three hundred thousand dollars, to be exact. No work by other agencies had been done to gather intel on him, so Sam would see to it that he'd learn as much as he could.

Sam turned the page and discovered the document containing their dossier on the next person of interest: Salazar Moreno. Moreno, on the other hand, had quite a bit of information gathered on him, specifically by the SSD. Brandt had trusted his senses about the Spanish dignitary, and so far, he'd been right. Moreno had sent quite a bit of questionable correspondence, much of it to and from Germany, in the last three years. Most of the information concerned shipping routes, specifically with regard to delivery into Germany. Still, the man had kept himself insulated by utilizing both informants and coded documents. He rarely had any direct contact with top Nazi officials, but via intermediaries, he was quite chatty. He'd maintained his position in D.C. because of Spain's hesitance to enter into the war, and by proxy, he had kept on good terms with the people in and around the capital.

On top of his shady dealings, he was worth a large sum of money—both at home and in Washington. Bank statements the busybodies on the second floor of The Yard had tapped into showed large transactions of cash, and Moreno even had one bank account within the country that was worth six hundred thousand dollars. *Enough to pay for Sierra's Pride*, Sam thought to himself. He'd acquired a beautiful Georgetown home, the picture of which showed an elegant brownstone Sam sensed likely rivaled Cat's.

One of the notes in the document also showed that Moreno had overseen a successful mining operation in the Spanish countryside, and they'd been selling tungsten to private German companies at healthy rates. Sam, and certainly Brandt as well, knew that those businesses were likely shell companies that functioned as go-betweens for those resources to be delivered to the German military. Of course, nothing had been proven, but Brandt's team was good at putting two and two together, and since most of the German workforce had dedicated its attentions to the war effort, it was highly suspect that suddenly there was a demand for the processed tungsten to manufacture anything *other* than weapons.

There was a bit in the document about Thornton and Brigham, neither of whom Sam had gotten a good look at the night before, but mostly they were both just entrepreneurs involved with transportation and didn't raise any red flags Brandt had felt noteworthy. What was more concerning was that Brandt had phoned Sam before leaving town, to tell him that a preliminary search by operatives around the country had yielded absolutely no evidence about Maxwell Kearney. In fact, though there was proof an American named Maxwell Kearney existed, he ran a small diner in Maine and was completely accounted for.

The folder did, however, contain a detailed topographical map of Ives' property, which took up the bulk of Vance County. There was a large spike in elevation on the western side, specifically where a range of mountains had collected and flanked the river. A large swampy area of creeks and small rivers split the county in half from the northern side almost to its center. In total size, Ives' property measured about three miles wide by seven miles long. There weren't many roads leading around the property, most of which Sam imagined were dirt and unpaved access—it was, after all, predominantly a farm. Sam did suspect the map was outdated. There was no way Ives' mining operation would be carting precious minerals away in bulk sizes if some pathways didn't exist to do so.

The next page, which did seem more up to date judging by the recent pencil shavings scattered about, was a document that looked like it had been sketched by a skilled artist. Sam knew that Brandt had employed many within the building, whether to design propaganda for use in the field or to sketch accurate maps for agents' use. Mapmaking was a huge part of the operation. "The small details," Brandt said, "will win the war."

Brandt put a lot of stock into information collecting —not every valuable operative was like Sam. Brandt had been passing many of those detailed maps on to Army and Navy higher-ups to show just how valuable his team was, but his intel was rarely put to the test. The allies had barely scratched the surface of the European theatre, and though Sam knew reconnaissance-based strategies were inevitable, Brandt had remained tight-lipped about many of the details.

The setting sun beating down on Sam through the window was becoming uncomfortable. He shuddered to think how he might deal with the harsh heat of the south. He reasoned it was better than the punishing cold of Pforzheim, and had prepared for such. Unlike his usual attire, he'd tossed his suit jacket for more comfortable clothing, specifically a thin white collared shirt and a pair of grey slacks which were the most comfortable he owned.

He did a once-over of the property map, taking particular interest in landmarks that the artists had made it a priority to include. The farm, or at least the portion where the livestock congregated, was near the river. Near that, there were dormitories made from converted barns for the farmhands and workers to sleep. Sam considered that detail important, since it was possible that Kearney's men would be resting there after they'd done their work. The main house was just north of the dormitories, and just south of that was the guest house Ives had spoken of. It was likely that Kearney would be invited to stay there to be close to Ives and his family—Moreno, too.

The property was large and, due to its wide open and prairie-like landscape, did not provide the normal cover Sam looked for when infiltrating. The manicured farm plots were separated by rows of foliage Sam guessed were probably a mixture of tobacco and vegetables. The northwest corner of the property line, specifically in the areas where the elevation rose steeply, was home to the mines, which, unlike the rest of the property, had not been well-mapped. The snaking veins and arteries in the mountains were likely carved into the area, and therefore were not visible to whoever had done their quick research.

As usual, Brandt hadn't given Sam a plan of attack. "That's what the money's for," Brandt always said. Sneaking around didn't concern Sam as much as knowing Cat would be on the inside. His risk of danger if discovered was twofold: he, as usual, could be captured, tortured, or killed—that was par for the course. Cat, on the other hand, he was worried wasn't equipped with the tools necessary to handle a high-stakes meeting like this. He'd felt the same way about Sigrid back in Pforzheim.

Sam saw something in Cat he did not see in Sigrid, though. Whereas Sigrid had a moral compass aligned with ensuring the safety of her people—among others—Cat did not. Cat's hard drinking made Sam suspect as much, and her unknown past only confirmed it. Sam thought perhaps Cat might have a little more fight in her if she got herself into trouble, and her capability to lie and steal might be her best source of protection. The spy's biggest fear was one he hadn't encountered before: that Cat would bring home better intel than *he* would.

13

───────

When the train departed the derelict station the next morning, Sam found he was the only soul present on the platform. As the locomotive traveled into the North Carolina countryside, the local noise grew clear. "Heat bugs," as Sam called them, signaled the arrival of what was sure to be a warm day. They might have been cicadas, or locusts—Sam wasn't sure. Birds chirped from the trees, courting each other from obscured perches within the dense leaf coverage. The train had finally disappeared from sight, leaving behind only a sharp screeching along the rails.

A breeze that was anything but cool whipped across the wooden platform: another promise of the incoming heat. Sam lit up a smoke, stepped under the nearest tree which offered shade, and took inventory of the landscape. A broken-down wood shack whose windows had been shattered sat at the edge of the platform. There was no attendant present, and Sam wondered just how anyone boarded the train from the location—or if they did at all. He welcomed the sounds of nature. The insects carrying on in heavy conversation were a far cry from the hustle and bustle of Washington.

Sam heard the approach of a motor from the distance. A battered pickup with rusted wheel wells tore down the dirt road passing his position, leaving a long trail of dust in its wake. Unlike his new home in D.C., there were no cars to hail or mass transportation to speak of where he'd been deposited. Sam was going to talk to Brandt when he got back—he always convinced himself he would before a mission—about better transportation options. He'd had to hoof it to The Whispering Oak in New York state, and he'd traveled across the Black Forest on just two reliable feet. Brandt had made it clear that a car waiting for him at the station might bring too much attention, and that even if Sam had been provided one, it wasn't like the conveyance could drop him off on Ives' front porch. Sam checked the watch Sigrid had given him—it was 8:00 am. Without any other option, Sam took a deep drag from his cigarette and set off across the field perpendicular to the dirt road.

He was sweating profusely within ten minutes. With no cover to speak of, and the July sun beating down on him, the spy decided to forego another cigarette. The body wasn't so dissimilar from a radiator, and smoking under those conditions only added unwanted warmth to an already taxed machine. Though he found the warmth repulsive, Sam did admire the lush greens he saw from every angle. The sky was a deep blue, and unfortunately cloudless, but it was the first time he'd really encountered Americana, and he did his best to enjoy the little time he'd have exploring it. He had a canteen packed in the rucksack slung over his shoulders. The water wouldn't last long, but it was probable he'd see that river with his own eyes to grab a refill.

The rucksack, as usual, didn't carry nearly enough of the items Sam felt he needed. He'd brought his camera, an Xposé model 100—a very high-end piece of equipment the average photographer wouldn't have the luxury of using—five rolls of thirty-five millimeter film, the canteen, one change of clothing, several bars of rations, the small ear radio—which was the sister piece to Cat's own—and a .38 revolver. Though Brandt had made it clear he should be making no noise while working—and Sam preferred a knife—the spy wouldn't dare be caught without a firearm in the war climate.

Leaving the piece at home for his missions within D.C. was acceptable, but roaming the American countryside and digging into "dirt" was a different story altogether. Sam checked the pistol, made sure it was loaded, then deposited it behind his waistband to conceal it alongside a small combat knife tucked in a small leather sheath. The danger involved in trespassing through private property before he'd even arrived at the Ives' farm was real. Who knew what unsavory character's land he might be traipsing through?

Newton had also given him a kill-pill. Unlike the last model, which was a small glass vial designed to be broken with the teeth, this one had been designed to just be swallowed. He'd sewn it into the collar of his shirt this time. Sewing it into the cuff wouldn't have been a terrible idea, but if his hands were bound, he'd never be able to access it. Without free hands, he'd be able to bite at the collar and tear it out with his teeth if he had to. He'd never actually had to do it, but in a matter of life or death, he was sure he *could*. After all, what was some temporary pain in the teeth and jaw if you'd be dead momentarily anyway?

Once Sam felt the sting in his calves from the rising elevation—which came after several miles of walking—he was sure he'd gotten closer to Ives' property. He'd cross the ridge just before he was officially on it, which would give him a good vantage point from which to scope out the terrain before he actually descended down into it. He might even be able to get a look at one of the aforementioned mine entrances—maybe even snoop around a bit and cool down before he got down to the *real* work.

Even after arriving within range of the property line, Sam still had quite a bit of walking to do before he made it anywhere real action would be taking place. Once there, he'd have to move even slower to avoid detection. Just getting the lay of the land would take some time if he was to make sure he wasn't noticed.

The first order of business would be to deduce just how accurate the map he'd been given was. Though a map was helpful, no amount of thoughtful planning could help once he was in the field. Humans were prone to error—spies included—and all that mattered was what Sam saw with his own eyes.

Sam arrived at the peak of the ridgeline. Below, he could see the valley where Ives' property sat, a sprawling and lush landscape with farm plots, barn structures, and what he assumed were the Ives' home, the guest house, and the dormitories. Beyond that, a large pond reflected the sapphire blue sky, and a bright twinkle shimmered from each of the water's ripples. The map was relatively accurate. The dimensions might have been off, sure, but that was to be expected, and there were some structures that were unaccounted for. Sam thought they probably belonged to the tobacco operation. He sat for a moment to give his legs a break and get a sense of the land. Quite a bit of sweat had accumulated on his face, and he splashed the last bit of water in the canteen on it to cool off.

Judging by how high the sun had climbed into the sky, Sam guessed it was about noon and that he'd been walking for nearly four hours. A quick check of his watch confirmed the time. A good spy always had a sense of time, regardless of whether or not they had a way to confirm it, and the sun never lied if you knew what time of year it was and where you were on the globe. Cat would probably be arriving soon if she hadn't already. He guessed she would be staying in the guest house with Moreno and Kearney.

Sam surveyed his surroundings. The ridge he'd ascended was robust and rocky, though it was still littered with fertile plant life. He could understand why the region was so rife with value. Elevated ranges like that often bore precious or valuable minerals—such was the case with the Sierra Nevada. Ives had just so happened to be sitting on a rewarding one.

Sam took cover under a large swath of trees and lit up a smoke now that he'd found shade. He *saw* the caravan arriving in the distance before he even heard it and positioned himself behind a rocky lip. Though it was unlikely that anyone would notice him at such a great distance from the farm, he couldn't rule out the possibility that Ives had security of his own. The first automobile, a large truck whose chrome finish reflected the glistening sun, led the pack. Behind it, several more trucks followed. *Here come the troops.*

Following the first grouping, there was a small break in the action, and the growl of the type of diesel truck designed solely for moving large materials rippled across the wide farmland. This truck, too, had been followed by a series of others just like it. So many industrial-grade automobiles traveled down the dirt road that Sam began to lose count. The cloud of dust whipping up around the frenzy of vehicles wasn't helping. More and more trucks continued to materialize from the small dust storm. Though the land was fertile, if Ives' farming business suffered problems, the army of people arriving to whisk away his unique goods was prepared to create a revenue stream comparable to a small country's.

The trucks turned left toward the main house, then traveled along the road past the guest house and continued deeper into the property. *The trucks kept coming.* After the dump trucks had passed through, flat beds followed behind carrying large industrial tools Sam could only imagine were for drilling. The spy had no idea what any of them did, but he guessed boring holes into the hills might require such machinery. The line of vehicles traveled through the property as if mounting a military campaign.

Kearney had wasted no time preparing for this transaction, which meant he'd been ready to strike before Ives had even given the go-ahead. Brigham and Thornton, the ones who'd be responsible for carting away the goods, had probably been ready to send out a fleet at the drop of a hat. Hell, they'd probably been waiting on standby judging by how fast they'd arrived on the scene. Had Sam taken any longer to get to Ives' farm, they might have beat him to the punch.

Sam removed his camera from his bag. In addition

to providing photographic evidence, the camera functioned as a makeshift form of binoculars via the 70mm-300mm telephoto lens he'd brought with him. He was excited to try the new lens out. He'd had no use for it before while breaking into D.C. haunts—only the small, 50mm prime he'd often used to photograph documents. He replaced the primary lens, enhancing the optical distance with the telephoto—which was far heavier—and rested the edge of the lens against the rocky formation he'd used for cover. He grabbed the barrel and twisted the focus ring until the image was sharp.

He adjusted his exposure—f22 would be the sweet spot for an outdoor photo in broad daylight—then snapped a photo of a passing truck. Through the viewfinder, Sam caught sight of an emblem that had been painted on the door of the truck: the words Thornton & Sons, and under the lettering the text had been underlined by an artist's rendering of two crisscrossing thorny branches. He snapped another photo of the logo for posterity.

Sam took photos of everything he could. He tried to obtain a photo for each truck present, *all* of which bore Thornton insignias. The whirling dust made getting perfect photos difficult. He hoped that when the trucks came to a halt, the dust would follow suit and settle. Now that he had a closer view of the tools on board the flat beds, he also saw boxes with DANGER written in bold red lettering, and below that, the words BLASTING MATERIALS.

Satisfied, Sam redirected his lens toward the main house. Ives waited on the porch with a cigarette tucked between his teeth as he watched the cavalry arrive. The cowboy hat, once again, made him instantly recognizable. Sam snapped a photo of the Carolinian, then trained his lens on the dormitories—there was no one present. After redirecting his camera, his focus landed on the farmhands working on the tobacco fields. He snapped a photo of them, too. Most of them looked like poor or working-class folks covered in sweat-drenched overalls. The job looked grueling, and though being a spy was perhaps the most dangerous job one could do, he harbored no jealous feelings for the poor, sweaty bastards.

Sam followed the trail of trucks to its tail-end. The last truck had arrived. Sam counted—between the hauling trucks, flat beds, and small vehicles—a total of at least thirty trucks of varying shapes and sizes. A flicker of light under a canopy of trees was the next visual that captured his attention.

Two black sedans made the encore, both following the dust path carved out by the caravan of trucks. Sam zoomed the lens in further, and though it was difficult to catch a good exposure from the glaring passenger window, some patience finally revealed Moreno in the back seat of the front car. Sam homed in on the other car following the Spanish dignitary's, which carried Kearney. Sam redirected the camera back to Moreno's car once more: Cat sat in the back seat at his side. She wore a tan, large-brimmed hat fit for a lady out on a hot summer's day. Dark sunglasses obscured her eyes. Sam secured photos of both Moreno and Kearney before redirecting his camera to the meeting point and watching the action play out.

The trucks all stopped near the main house. All of the vehicles remained idle, and the driver in the front truck hopped out of his seat and wiped the sweat from his brow before making his way toward Kearney's car. Sam aimed his camera at the driver. He was a tall man, muscular and blond and far too polished for your average working-class miner. He looked more like a soldier than a truck driver. Ives approached Kearney's car and greeted the group of men with handshakes all around—Moreno included—but Cat remained seated. They were discussing something, though Sam was barely close enough to see them let alone hear what they were saying. He tried to read their lips through the camera's viewfinder, but he had no success. He'd regretted not learning that tactic from the lip-reader Brandt had recently employed, and he'd make it a priority to do so when he returned from the mission. Any tool added to the spy's repertoire could prove valuable in the field.

The truck driver towered over the group of men, making them all look like children in his company. The greetings ended, and Ives pointed directly toward Sam. The action made Sam's heart skip a beat, and he pulled the camera from view and retreated behind the rock covering. His jumpy reaction had gotten the better of him, and he felt foolish for a moment. *No one* knew he was there. He grabbed his camera, refocused on the gathering once more, and watched as Ives directed the men—all of whom were now looking in Sam's general direction—toward the mountain.

He's giving them directions. Ives wagged his finger toward the range, demonstrating the zigs and zags of what was surely either the route or the pathways of the mine, and Moreno, Kearney, and the driver observed his gestures closely. Sam snapped one more photo, this one sharply displaying the faces of all of the conspirators in one single shot. Each of the three men nodded, then

Moreno and Kearney followed Ives back to the main house. The driver, on the other hand, made his way back into the seat of his truck, closed the door, and put the truck into gear. His truck started moving down the road flanking the main house, then turned right down another dirt road. Each of the trucks followed, then Sam removed his eye from the viewfinder and surveyed the gathering's route. The road, and the trucks on it, were both heading right for him.

14

Cat rolled the window down in the car as Moreno spoke with Ives at the base of the home's front porch. The heat was agonizing. How she was expected to maintain a healthy glow under the conditions was beyond her. Brandt, with all of his master spy techniques and training, had no tactics or tools to make the sweltering heat any more bearable. Couldn't Newton have manufactured some clever type of coolant? At the least, she'd throw Newton the idea of makeup that didn't run when she returned back to The Yard.

Moreno had not allowed Cat to wear Sierra's Pride any longer than the time she'd modeled it in their private compartment. Wearing it in public would have drawn far too much attention. Cat didn't need any more convincing. Wearing the jeweled necklace made her feel for a moment the royal glamour Moreno had probably been accustomed to for the better part of his life.

Yet, as the night on the train had gone on and she was kept awake by Moreno's snoring, she contemplated how difficult it might be to pilfer the piece from him and vanish into the night. Never mind the strings Brandt had pulled to get her out of prison or the target that would appear on her back if she disappeared with the precious item—the thought of pocketing the piece and fleeing for the hills was incredibly tempting. She had not a clue where the train was on its journey. The moon shined brightly through the glass window, but beneath it lay only a mysterious, dark countryside littered with rolling hills and plentiful trees. Even if she got off at the next stop—and the train made plenty of them through the night—a young girl walking around alone with six hundred thousand dollars' worth of jewelry on her was a scenario just begging for trouble.

Suppose she was robbed, or stopped by the authorities, then what? What would happen when Brandt got wind of her absence? Moreno himself probably had the ability to deploy resources to seek her out much the same way the spymaster did. Would Sam be the one tasked with looking for her? The thought of it only made the act *more* enticing. Though her name might be Cat, if Sam was involved, she'd certainly be playing the part of the mouse.

After an hour of tossing and turning, both physically in bed and with the plans in her mind, she finally decided that blowing her opportunity at doing some good for once was foolish. Not only had she been given a second chance, but she was actually making a difference in the world. She knew it was risky to work for Brandt, but with it came thrills that made her feel more alive than any of the jobs she'd done on her own. She'd see the operation through, at least long enough to ensure that Brandt got what he needed and Sam made it out alive. But if Cat was honest with herself, her thoughts were mesmerized by the reflections of those jewels and just how valuable they might be on the open market.

Once the gentlemen had finished their greetings, Moreno waved Cat over. The thick cloud of dust formed by the brigade of trucks they'd followed to the property had partly subsided, but Cat waved some of the debris from her face in the way an elegant girl unfamiliar with the grit of the country would. Most of the time she was adding little details like that to her persona because they helped sell her lies—she was plenty familiar with the grime of tooling around in the dirt and sleeping under the stars. As she approached, all three men stared in unison. She couldn't help the fact that her good looks, coupled with her uncanny style, drew the attention of men from all angles.

"Miss Cat McAlister," Moreno said as he introduced her to the other two gentlemen. "Mr. Wade Ives."

Ives took Cat's hand, shook it gently with a soft grip that only held the ends of the fingers, then said, "Howdy."

"And Mr. Maxwell Kearney," Moreno said. Kearney grabbed Cat's hand much in the same way, but he bowed slightly, arching his back gently and tipping his head.

"A pleasure," Kearney said. Cat's attention instantly homed in on the scar covering the better part of the left side of Maxwell Kearney's face. Staring wouldn't be noticeable—the sunglasses covering her eyes would hide her interest. She'd seen Ives already at the party, but only Sam had seen Kearney. She'd heard the spy mention the *schmiss*, whatever that was, and she considered that whatever duel this Kearney had been involved in, he'd lost. The scar was old. The sensitive tissue of the face had left behind a pinkish line where the skin had never quite healed properly. Cat suspected that the abundance of muscles in the face had made a perfect healing process difficult.

"For me as well," Cat replied. Kearney's head tilted slightly, as if he'd taken great curiosity in her presence.

"You didn't tell us you'd be bringing a guest, Salazar," Kearney said to Moreno. His eyes never broke contact with the dark circles of Cat's glasses when he made the comment. The man's gaze *already* made her uncomfortable. There was something wicked about his presence, and she was instantly convinced that whatever her partner had sensed as devious in the man was accurate.

"Ms. McAlister is discreet," Moreno replied. "I can attest to that." Moreno guided a hand behind Cat's lower back and pulled her in tightly.

"I'm sure she is," Kearney replied. The creep was still staring directly at her. "We wouldn't want any of our competitors making Mr. Ives a better offer, would we?"

"Certainly not," Moreno replied.

"I'm just a girl looking for a good time in the country," Cat assured the mysterious Kearney. "You boys go about doing whatever it is you need to do. I'll join you all when it's time to get social. Perhaps Mr. Ives can show me some of his farm?"

"I'd be happy to do so," Ives replied. "The missus'll be happy to have another lady around. Lord knows we don't get too many."

"Ms. McAlister has quite an operation of her own," Moreno said. "She's a specialist in *transporte*, to be exact." Moreno let his native tongue slip in as he often did.

"Is that so?" Kearney said to Cat. "I do look forward to hearing more about you, Ms. McAlister. Later you might be so kind as to regale us with tales of your enterprises."

"I look forward to it," Cat said. "Where did you say you were from, Mr. Kearney?" Cat immediately took the opportunity to throw the ball back into Kearney's court. Damn if she was going to let a guy like him push her around. She'd handled much tougher boys in her youth.

"California," Kearney replied. "At least, that's where our manufacturing headquarters are. I'm originally from Massachusetts."

"Wonderful state," Cat replied. "Massachusetts, that is. California I could take or leave. Whereabouts in Massachusetts?" Cat pressed further.

Kearney paused, then said, "Boston," unconvincingly. He moved on quickly, breaking eye contact with Cat, then addressed Ives, "Should we all make our way to the guest house so Mr. Ives can show us where we'll be laying our heads?"

"Right this way," Ives said, gesturing toward the guest house. The main house was a mansion, a plantation style home of two floors with multiple columns supporting a roof that extended outward and provided a perimeter of shade. An archway of finely manicured trees led down a carved slate path to the home's front entrance, and a smattering of tall windows decorated its face. The home's coloration was all white, only deviating in the dark navy shutters and a set of red double doors. A small gravel path broke away from the main house, which was producing a smell sweet and savory that Cat couldn't put her finger on, but suspected was some type of baking fruit. Neither she nor Moreno had

had any breakfast on the train, and she was already hankering for both a decent meal and maybe a finger of booze.

As they passed the main home, the guest house came into view. It, too, was impressive, rivaling most normal folks' homes in size, and had a custom-carved slate path similar to the one leading to the main house and ending in two beautiful Romanesque columns with ornate carvings. Cat could tell that Ives wasn't your average farmer. Whatever type of business he'd gotten into, he'd been doing it right. The guest house had two floors as well and was surrounded by large trees reaching high above the roof which Cat hoped would provide a break from the scorching heat.

The property was incredibly tranquil. Far away from the hustle and bustle of D.C., Ives had carved out a quiet—yet productive—small town of his own. To the left Cat spotted large plots where the tobacco plants resided. Some were wilting.

"Been a bit since it rained down here," Ives said as the group continued toward the guest house. "We're just hoping' it's nothin' like '31. Unlikely anything like that would happen on this coast—part of the reason I set up shop here—but you never know what God can get up to. He's mysterious like that."

"Don't I know it," Cat blurted out. The thought came abruptly, and without warning. The filter she'd typically applied to her thoughts had cracked if only momentarily. She considered that the country twang of Ives' speech pattern had awakened a persona inside her she'd repressed, and walking the territory reminiscent of her childhood had broken her character.

"Are you a Christian woman?" Ives asked Cat.

"Most days," Cat replied.

Ives reacted with a chuckle, then said softly, "Ain't that the truth? The wife runs a tight ship—prayer every evening, no drinks on weekdays, and worship with the congregation on Sunday mornings. You'd all be wise to watch your tongues around her." Ives slowed a bit to direct his conversation to include both Kearney and Moreno, then said, "Fresh milk every morning—eggs as well. Most of our breakfasts come from right here at home, as is customary when you're a farm man like myself." He turned to Moreno. "Huevos, am I right Salazar?"

"*Si,*" Moreno replied. "*Estoy deseando que llegue.*"

"Good man," Ives replied. "You'll find you're in good company here. I employ quite a few of your people on the property. Cheap labor, but more importantly, good workers."

"I think you're confused," Moreno said. "I noticed several of them when we arrived—you've got some people of Mexican decent."

"Same difference," Ives said as he sauntered along. Cat could tell Moreno took offense at the comment, but as a passive man, he pressed the issue no further. "Now that every able-bodied man is ramping up to head across seas, good help can be hard to find. If they're not getting rifles slung over their shoulders, or enlisting down at the recruiting office, they're taking those precious factory jobs."

"Someone has to feed the factory workers," Cat replied. "Right?"

"I think those boys over there are going to be hurting for a cigarette more'n anything," Ives replied.

"Did you serve, Mr. Ives?" Kearney asked.

"France," Ives answered. "My campaign was brief, but explosive. Landres-et-Saint-Georges," Ives said in a barely acceptable French pronunciation.

"A decisive battle," Kearney said in admiration.

Ives sighed as if reminiscing, then said, "One of many. I was of half a mind to enlist again myself, maybe take a command post away from the line of fire if they'd give it to me. But this is a young man's game now. These kids are out for blood ever since the Japs did a number on us, and I can't blame 'em. Give 'em hell, I say—that little fella with the loud mouth, too." Ives rapped on his legs with balled fists. "Besides, these kickers ain't what they used to be, and I think the wife'd give me hell if I even stepped foot off the farm. There's far too much work here, as you can see." Ives nodded toward the guest house. "Here we are."

A black woman opened the front door, patted her dress to make it presentable, then nodded to everyone individually. Ives said, "This is Adelaide."

"How do you do?" Adelaide asked. Cat shook her hand eagerly, which seemed to surprise the woman, but the rest of the men delivered curt nods.

"Cat," Cat replied.

"I'm pleased to meet you, Mrs. Cat," Adelaide said with a jovial smile.

"Just Cat," Cat replied. She waved her hand to show a ringless finger.

"My apologies," Adelaide said with the flush of embarrassment coloring her cheeks.

"Not necessary," Cat replied.

Ives pointed to each of his guests. He said, "Adelaide, this is Mr. Salazar Moreno, and Mr. Maxwell Kearney. See to it that they've got everything they need and nothin' they don't." Ives nodded to the main house. "You all have any trouble and you know where to find me, but I suppose we'll be seeing a lot of each other between today and tomorrow—at least until Mr. Kearney gets working."

"We'll waste no time, as you can see," Kearney said. His eyes focused on the brigade of trucks climbing into the hills. Where once they'd created quite a commotion, they were now relatively silent in the distance. "I'd like to have my men blasting and carting away as soon as possible."

Cat began to fan herself. Moisture had gathered in the small of her back, and she was eager to change her outfit. "If you all don't mind," Cat said, "I'd like to get into something more comfortable. This heat is doing a number on me."

"Mr. Ives," Kearney said, "if we could, I'd like to go see the entry shaft to help my men formulate a plan of attack."

"Can do," Ives said.

"Salazar?" Kearney said to his friend.

"Let's see what all the fuss is about," Moreno replied.

"Well, then," Cat replied. "If you boys will excuse me, I'm going to get acquainted with the accommodations."

"Adelaide," Ives said to the woman, "gather all of our guests' belongings and see to it that they get where they're going, then go see that Mrs. Ives gets started on some lunch."

"Yes, Mr. Ives," Adelaide said, and she hurried to grab Moreno and Kearney's bags.

She made for Cat's as well, but Cat said, "No need. I've got two arms." Moreno kissed Cat on the cheek before she left, and Kearney continued to glower at her as she heaved her bag under her arm. She considered that perhaps dealing with her own belongings rather than allowing Adelaide to do it was unladylike in the man's eyes, and furthermore, that this Kearney could see right through her. Cat averted her gaze from Kearney, then made for the front door of the home.

The interior foyer was far cooler than the conditions outside. Just being out of the harsh sun's rays was a small relief. Many of the windows in the home had been left open to allow for a draft, which was pleasant and cooling.

Adelaide said, "Right this way," then directed Cat up the large staircase that led up to the second-floor balcony in a semi-circle. Cat chewed her lip at the sounds of the groaning wooden floors present in the home. They screamed of the home's age and its history. But despite their charm, they'd be anything but helpful if she needed to sneak out to rendezvous with Sam. She could foresee herself creeping about in the night while Moreno was asleep.

She hoped that Ives and Kearney weren't so old fash-ioned that they'd prefer to spend their nights without the company of women and discussing the business at hand. She'd have to make an attempt at proving to Kearney just how good her own business acumen was within her own entrepreneurial pursuits so that she could have her own seat at the table if that was the case. All this deep thinking about the job at hand made her acutely aware that she had another important, imme-diate job to see through—one for which she'd need to ditch Adelaide.

"This is your room right here," Adelaide said, and

offered Cat a bright smile.

"That one's Salazar's," Cat said, pointing to a brown leather suitcase. Adelaide placed it next to the bed. She then moved for the window, slid it open, and started to fuss with the drapes. "Don't worry about all that." Adelaide stopped immediately. "I'm going to tend to our belongings and find a more accommodating outfit. If you'll give me some privacy."

"Yes, ma'am," Adelaide replied, and she quickly retrieved Kearney's suitcase and shut the door behind her. Cat hated being so short with the woman, and she'd had no intention of offending her, but there were pressing matters at hand—and a window in which to tend to them. Cat listened for Adelaide's trailing footsteps, and when she was satisfied the woman had made it to the other side of the house, Cat got right to work.

Brandt had taught her to inspect a room for any type of equipment that might be eavesdropping. "In this day and age," Brandt had said, "everyone's listening —*everywhere*." She surveyed the room briefly, unsure just where to start. The first order of business was ensuring that the room hadn't been bugged or planted with listening devices of any sort.

Cat started in the corner of the room, first lifting an empty vase and checking under its base, then looking inside of it. She moved to the drapes, folding them and inspecting them acutely, then checked the dresser, opening each of its empty drawers and running her hand along the tops and bottoms of the hollow wood bins. After sliding the furniture out from the wall and guiding her fingertips along its rear, she scrutinized the bedside table, including the lamp that had been resting on it, then the closet door and the sitting desk opposite that.

On her hands and knees, she inspected the underside of the bed, then rose and pulled all of the linens off of the bed and checked the pillowcases, in turn making a mess. That part, she considered, might have been a little overboard, but Brandt preached the value of thorough searches. Luckily, other than the available furniture and linens, the room was quite bare. An oil painting of what seemed like the main house in its original condition, probably many years old, hung on the wall above the bed. Cat removed it from its picture hook, checked its back—as well as the wall it had once occupied—and confirmed there was no threat there either.

Satisfied she'd done the best she could, she then took interest in the window on the west side of the bedroom. The open window provided a very clear view of the mountain where the trucks had gathered. Was Sam there? Hopefully he'd known that they were headed his way if so. She felt a brief moment of worry for his safety, but quickly quelled the feeling. Sam could take care of himself.

Cat had far more to worry about regarding her own infiltration techniques than Sam did. Keeping up the act around Moreno and his cronies was easy, but this Kearney seemed to have a better sense of smell. Cat removed the large hat that had been shielding her eyes from the sun, then rested it on the windowsill. If Sam came looking, he'd know where to find her.

15

———

The mining caravan led Sam straight to the source: a horizontal cavity bored into the angled ridge face. A base camp of sorts had already been set up where the trucks gathered, large enough to accommodate a small town of people. Where there had likely once been fertile lawns, there was only a well-trod dirt lot. The team wasted no time—several men had already been dragging aluminum and plywood across the dry base of soil for what Sam could only deduce were soon-to-be-erected structures.

Sam had a good vantage point from where he was standing, which was roughly one hundred yards away from the site. The ridge in question that lay to the north was still quite high in comparison to where he stood, and he was already looking down on the action below. The position wouldn't yield good information; he'd need to do better. Most of the men gathered around the site wore tan or navy coveralls, and each was also equipped with a hard hat.

He fired up his camera once more—which was proving even more valuable for its telescopic features than for its ability to take a nice photograph—and aimed it at the site. In addition to the standard garb, many of the workers had also been given goggles or glasses that hung from their necks, and the faces of quite a few were obscured by masks. A uniform would prove valuable for the spy's purposes—camouflage was *always* on Sam Abel's mind. The trucks had been set up in a maze-like arrangement, parked wherever their drivers had seen fit and without rhyme or reason. Sam immediately recognized the opportunity to use the vehicles as a means to navigate the site while remaining invisible. He'd have to use the opportunity now, rather than later, because soon the foreman of the site would likely organize them more particularly, and the infiltrator would be walking around in plain sight.

The good news was that Sam wasn't expecting to meet as much resistance as he traditionally might have. There were no soldiers or massive weapons or war-torn countries to traipse through. There'd be no need to arm up or clip grenades to his belt. He needed to get in, get as much evidence on the mine's interior as he could—and perhaps on some of its occupants—then see what he could capture on Kearney. But Cat might have a better chance at success than he did.

Sam trained his lens on an approaching truck as the cloud of dust the caravan had kicked up began to settle. He was able to see through the windshield with great clarity. He snapped several photos: Ives, who was driving, was transporting Moreno and Kearney to the site. When they exited the vehicle, the driver—whom Sam assumed was the aforementioned foreman of this operation—greeted Kearney specifically, then directed his attention to Ives and began asking a series of questions that Ives answered.

Ives pointed toward the mineshaft, then directed his finger up and down the mountain in sweeping motions. Sam thought that meant that the mine shaft was likely vertical, that the shafts which had already been dug climbed up the ridge, and that the materials would be delivered back down via gravity. The four men all agreed to something in unison, then proceeded forward. Spying without all the senses was not an easy gig. Sam wished he could hear what everyone was so eagerly discussing, rather than only acquiring visuals. Brandt would value that, too.

Sam followed the men through his lens toward a makeshift canvas tent that had been rapidly set up at the center of the outdoor site. Shielding from the sun seemed to be a priority for the crew. Sam himself was already feeling the telltale sting of overexposure, and the temperature had not even reached its peak for the day, so his next priority was getting into the mine. Not only would he be better poised to acquire evidence, he'd get a break from the solar assault. He'd survived enough spy campaigns to make even the most thrill-seeking soldier weep, but he was facing another nemesis in the weather. It still beat the cold temperatures of *Flussrand* and Pforzheim.

The tent provided yet another obstacle: at best Sam could only see the feet of the men gathered under its shelter. They'd probably be going in themselves shortly, and Sam would need to be trailing along right behind them. Sam tossed the camera in his sack, slung it behind his shoulder, and made for the base of the ridge. Navigating the steep slope was not particularly difficult. He kept low to the ground, and utilized trees for cover where necessary. He didn't foresee any eyes would be on him, because all attention had been focused on the southern-facing side of the mine. Once he got to the site, it would be a different story.

A truck parked along the edge of the site gave him a perfect barrier on his approach to the camp. He checked the passenger side door for anything that might be of use. He'd need a change of clothes if he was going to get inside without drawing any unwanted attention, preferably one of those sets of coveralls and a hard hat. If he could get the goggles and the mask, he'd really been in business. There was no way he could be sure whether any of the men working the mine already knew each other. If there was already a sense of camaraderie among the team, they might pick Sam out as an outsider. He prayed they'd been cherrypicked from around the country and that no one would recognize him from the next guy.

Most of the men present had gathered around the tent, while the others got to work carting supplies from the trucks. Sam was relieved to catch a break from the sunlight while navigating the shadowy sides of the trucks. Shadows were where Sam thrived. He dropped to his hands and knees, surveyed the undercarriages of the trucks nearby, and looked for feet. There were none present, which meant he was free to move around the outskirts of the site until he found some better clothing to accommodate his entry.

He turned around the front end of the first truck, then made his way around another. He checked its cabin as well: no dice. The fear that the workers had brought their own uniforms set in, and if that was the case, there would be nothing for him to use. He continued down an aisle formed by two of the larger truck's containers, stepping softly but quickly, as he split his attention between his surroundings and the undercarriages. He passed another flatbed, which was loaded with long steel beams which stretched almost the entirety of its length. Next to the truck, a flatbed carrying bundles of wood piled as high as two men provided still more cover.

Sam dropped low once more, this time to his belly, and retrieved his camera again. The meeting in the tent was still going strong, and he recognized the opportunity to do some more searching. As he directed the lens around the site, he discovered a series of boots in a straight line standing in front of a shipping container. One set of boots stepped forward, followed by another, then another, and all traveled back toward the tent. If boots were the types of visuals Brandt was looking for, Sam would be in business. They weren't; however, the process piqued Sam's interest, and he tossed his camera in his bag once more, rose to his feet, and made for the edge of the truck bearing the wood stacks.

He craned his head around the corner. *That's the ticket*, Sam thought. In front of one of the containers, a line of men had been formed, and they were stepping inside the container one by one. All of them were in plain clothes, but when one entered, he soon left with a pair of coveralls, a hard hat, and a pair of goggles. *Thank God.*

Sam slung his bag over his shoulder, grabbed a handful of soil from the ground below, and dirtied up his clothes to blend in a bit better. Most of these men looked like they'd seen a hard day's work and few pints of beer in their lifetime, and they had the tan, weathered skin to prove it. They possessed the hardened, blue-collar aesthetic of men who had perpetual dirt under their fingernails, and Sam looked too manicured in comparison.

Sam searched further around the corner to ensure that no one would spot his arrival. He got his first good look at the tent area, which many of the men had now attended, and each of their faces was focused on a table where Ives and Kearney held court. Ives was pointing to a map, and Kearney scrutinized it closely as he did so. Ives had mentioned that they'd already started to dig out the mine back at the party, but Kearney was probably going to amp the operation up quite heavily—and in short order.

Sam saw a moment of opportunity and walked as casually as possible to the back of the line. No one paid him any attention until he arrived at the tail end, then the man in front of him turned to face the spy and said, "Hiya." Sam nodded, averting his eyes away from the worker in an effort to discourage conversation, then the worker turned his attention back to the quickly dissi-pating line ahead. Sam was the last person in line. Although it made him feel like a sitting duck, at least he'd slipped in relatively unnoticed and without setting off any alarms. The sooner he changed clothes, the better. Bringing his bag was a safe choice—many of the men at the site had their own sacks and lunch pails, and bringing some personal belongings into the mine was probably not out of the ordinary.

Sam turned his attention to the tent again. Now Kearney was hunched over the table with a pencil in hand and delivering orders to several men standing by.

The driver, whose unmistakable height was still the only thing more noticeable than Ives' cowboy hat, was right at Kearney's side. Sam would do best to avoid that man. He was likely in charge of the operation in Kearney's absence and would certainly be milling about the mine to ensure a successful dig.

Sam looked forward. An awkward, sizable gap had formed where the men in line had once been. He'd been so focused on retrieving more details that he hadn't been paying attention to the minor task at hand. He shuffled forward, several steps closer to obtaining a uniform, then got a look inside the container. The uniforms hung from racks cascading away from him from smaller to larger sizes. There were also hard hats hanging on the wall opposite the clothing, and a small table with a slew of goggles.

The man in front of Sam retrieved a navy coverall, gave Sam a nod once more, then Sam stepped forward into the container. Once again, the brief respite from the sun was welcome. He looked to the navy coveralls, then the tan ones, and paused with reservation. What was the difference? Sam grabbed the tan suit, quickly placed it over his body, then strapped the hard hat to his head.

The uniform felt bulky and wouldn't have been the spy's choice if he had a say, but Sam's occupation required him to be a chameleon—instantly changing his skin to blend in where he was needed. Among other things, he'd once become a waiter, a construction worker, a court clerk, and a deep-sea-fishing excursion's deckhand. Though he often felt uncomfortable in the costumes of his target's environments, he'd always been able to perform his duties. The mining attire was no different than the finely tailored suit he'd worn only the night before—it was uncharacteristic, but necessary. Should he find himself in a situation involving hand-to-hand-combat, he might say otherwise. At a minimum, he'd have to lose the hard hat.

Sam shuffled his way toward the meeting at hand and kept his eyes low to avoid any contact with his "coworkers," but he kept his ears open for any information of interest. The gathered crowd made seeing the focus of the discussion—a map of the portions of the mine Ives had already begun work on—difficult. Among the other grunts, the spy was small in comparison. They were men with muscle to show for their hard work. He actually felt self-conscious about his stature standing among the group. Though his physique was trim and taut, next to the crew he looked like a rag doll. Despite his feeling of inadequacy, Sam knew that in a fight he could easily disarm or kill any of them with proper close-quarters skill. What Sam lacked in bulk and muscle he made up for in speed and technique. The bear-like man he'd killed in Pforzheim had easily been double his weight and looked capable of lifting a small car, but Sam had handled him nonetheless.

Sam inched his way forward, circling the crowd and searching for a Goldilocks-like pocket between shoulders in which he, too, might be able to witness the plan of attack. He wouldn't need to take any photos yet—to do so here would just be asking for trouble. Though he hadn't found the sweet spot, he could hear Kearney speaking very clearly amidst the attentive men standing by.

"Here's our main vertical shaft," Kearney said, and Sam caught a glimpse of him dragging his finger up the large paper spread out on the wooden table. "Our first order of business is boring out this section here, at roughly six hundred feet of elevation. Then we're going to cut across horizontally, roughly around sixty square feet. That'll be where we construct the next vertical shaft that will lead to our tributaries. If you're wearing a blue jumper, you're part of the structural team. Secure infrastructure, lay track, and coordinate the delivery of the ore. If you're in tan, you're going to be working with the boring team. Rudy here," Kearney said, and he pointed to the Olympian-esque driver Sam had been watching, "will be in charge of blasting. If you've got any questions about blasting procedure, he's going to be the one to ask."

Sam finally found a small sliver between the shoulders of two burly men with a field of view adequate to watch Kearney dead-on. Beside Kearney, this Rudy character stood stoic and expressionless, his cold, robotic eyes never breaking his forward-facing gaze. Kearney pointed to Rudy once more. "Listen to his orders if you'd like to keep all of your arms and legs and see your families again." The comment prompted laughter among the men. "I run a safe operation, and a tight ship. My last job saw one injury and no deaths, so I'd like to beat my last numbers if that's alright with you gentlemen." Kearney shifted his attention among the men in tan suits, then said, "I'll also want our infrastructure set up here at the base. I know this situation is a bit ramshackle in comparison to the jobs some of you may have worked, but supply is in high demand and so we're going to start our work before all of the separating and refining materials arrive."

Kearney pointed to the vertical shaft on the map

once more with the tip of his pencil. "After we've secured the second shaft, we're going to start working our way through multiple levels both north and south. After the blue group has successfully cleared a passage, tan group will be developing ore passes. Once that's been done, you guys in blue will go back in and secure the stopes if necessary. We'll be tunneling and hauling as we go." Kearney directed his attention to the mine entrance, then said, "We've already got some room to work here at the entrance thanks to Mr. Ives." Kearney turned to him. "How far in did you say your men have gone so far, Mr. Ives?"

"Roughly eight hundred feet," Ives mumbled through cigarette clenching teeth.

"Alright," Kearney said. "So we'll want to lay this track first so that we can start getting man-trains inside." Kearney turned and searched among the group of trucks. "Ah, there are our first ten cars," he said, then pointed to a flatbed that had hauled the small covered steel cars designed for carrying men into the mine via rail. "Blue team, we've got enough steel on these beds to erect a skyscraper, so you're going to want to go in and augment the work Mr. Ives' men haven't done to standard." Kearney turned once more to Ives. "I mean no offense, Wade."

"None taken," Ives replied.

Kearney started again, "After you've secured that track and the entrance, you're going to continue north, roughly one more mile before we create another shaft and some more passes and ramps."

"We got a schematic?" one of the workers called out.

"We're working on that," Kearney replied. "Mr. Ives here has been kind enough to get us some topographical maps from the local office, and the rest we're going to be developing as we go. John?" Kearney called out as he searched the faces in the crowd, "Is John here?"

"Right here," said one of the men beside Sam.

"Right," Kearney replied. "Everyone get to know John here, who'll be in charging of mapping the mine. Any geographical questions you've got should be directed toward him. Another important item on our agenda is to start running electrical. For now, we're going to be stringing temporary lighting throughout on an overhead system. You can all look for Fred if you've got electrical questions. Fred, can you raise your hand?"

"Howdy," a sweaty, bearded man said from within the group.

"Hello, Fred," Kearney said. "Fred will be in charge of air flow, as previously discussed."

Sam was impressed. Whether or not Kearney was who he said he was, he obviously knew a thing or two about mining operations. There was no way he was going to finesse his way around the group of men gathered, who'd surely be able to see right through him if he proved he could not speak the lingo. Sam didn't know a damn thing about mining, but he felt he'd already gained a crash course that might help him while inside.

"This is Mr. Moreno," Kearney said, grabbing his friend by the shoulder. "And don't do anything stupid, boys—he's a D.C. man and he'll get us shut down in no time if that's the way he wants it." The group chuckled once more. "He's already facilitated the ore testing, and if the information we've gathered so far is accurate, we've got quite a haul ahead of us. It's not the Sierra, but it's a good start. We're primarily concerned with scheelite, which is what houses the goods until they're refined. In the future we'll worry about setting up an interior machine shop, but for now any maintenance will be done outside here at the base."

Kearney once more scrutinized the map, which Sam struggled to get a view of. He'd be sure to photograph it if the opportunity presented itself. Kearney said, "The jumbo arrives tonight. Until then, there'll be no blasting. Once it's here, we'll set up an alarm system to make sure that any employees are back at the assembly point before any blasting has begun. Tan team, whoever knows how to use a rock mover should see Rudy about moving the debris through the ore passes. The first chute will handle the initial breakup for hauling, so make sure we've got ore hoppers on standby. We don't have a rotary dumper yet, so for now we're going to collect the rock before we start crushing." Kearney turned to the map, then fixed his attention on the landscape around the base of operations. "Rudy, see to it that we find a good location for the mill where the conveyor will connect. Make it a short trip." Rudy barely offered a nod. Sam was beginning to wonder if the man even had a brain inside his head or if Kearney had hired Frankenstein's monster to run the show. Kearney readdressed the men gathered around him. "The processing team will start to trickle in over the coming weeks to oversee the construction of the mill. Any questions?"

"Who do we see about pay?" one of the men asked. The question prompted yet another bout of laughter in the group.

Kearney smiled, then said, "That'd be me. Until we've got a proper accounting office setup, I'll be delivering checks next Friday, and every other Friday after that. I appreciate you all starting on a holiday weekend," Kearney said. "I know we've all got better places to be, but time is of the essence here. The faster we can start separating waste rock and producing concentrate, the better. Any questions?"

None came from the group. Sam wanted to ask, 'Yea, who are you *really*?' That would surely put him in his place and shut the operation down indefinitely. A good unmasking of this mystery man might cause a work stoppage, but that was just wishful thinking. And despite his and Brandt's propensity for being right about shifty characters, Sam still wasn't certain Kearney wasn't just a businessman looking to make a buck. The spy had to be *sure*.

"Alright, then," Kearney said. "Rudy, let's start looking around, shall we?" Rudy nodded. "Mr. Ives," Kearney said, addressing the landowner, "would you like to learn a thing or two about what exactly you're selling us?"

"I'd very much like that," Ives said.

"Follow me," Kearney said. The crew dispersed, each gathering around one of the men Kearney had introduced based on their individual skill sets; Kearney, Moreno, Ives, and Rudy headed toward the already carved-out mineshaft. Sam would be unwise to follow them in right away, but as soon as the rest of the men started to get to work, he'd be going inside, too. The spy aligned himself with the men in tan suits. Though Sam didn't foresee himself doing any rock breaking, he would be poking around as much as he could until he was satisfied he'd retrieved enough information.

Photographing the mine and some of the men involved in its construction was only half the battle.

Later, when the big boys gathered to discuss the operation at the main house—and he was sure they would—that'd be his chance to poke around further. Though Sam was always confident he wouldn't be caught—he had to maintain that attitude—he'd keep the suit on while wandering about the main property to blend in. No one there had any idea who he was as far as he knew, and he'd use that to his advantage. The man in charge of the group of tan suits waved his team on, and Sam followed. As the men dug through the mine, Sam would continue to dig for answers.

16

The old adage of the mice coming out to play when the cat was away didn't apply to Cat McAlister. If shady business dealings that could change the fate of the world at war were in play, then those who'd been sneaking around in the dark corners would be the mice, and Cat'd be the one having a field day in their absence. She'd unpacked both her own and Moreno's clothing into the armoire in the corner of the room, then changed into a light white dress. The exchange of clothing granted her a reprieve from the warmth she'd met upon arrival. Though she'd grown up accustomed to similar conditions, she'd been spoiled as of late while traveling in the circles assigned to her by Brandt. As the afternoon approached, the temperature outside only grew more intense, and a lack of cloud and tree cover wasn't granting the home any shade. A cool draft moved through the house every so often, but it was hardly refreshing.

At the bottom of Moreno's clothing bag, a

rectangular box was tucked between two pairs of pants: Sierra's Pride. Cat opened the box, anxious to get just one more look at the elegant piece. The diamonds, in the absence of the incandescent light in which she'd first seen them, took on a cool blue appearance. This unique property of the jewels made Cat even more eager to possess them.

The wheels in her head started to turn again, and she contemplated what she could get for each of the diamonds individually if she broke the string holding them together and traveled through the country from jeweler to jeweler. Selling the whole piece outright would be out of the question. Most jewelers would be unable to afford it, and those who could might be more apt to raise the red flag than make a shifty purchase from a traveling girl with *far* too many valuables on her person. Individually, though, well *that* was a different story. With enough money in her pocket, Cat could buy her own safety; she could *pay* to hide—but for how long?

Would Brandt turn the same resources that made his outfit efficient on her? Would he let her walk? Could she get out of the country? Surely finding solace in the arms of another country would provide her the cover she needed. Isn't that what the rumors about Sam had held, that he had fled to America? She could change her look, change her style—change her *name*. Were there any countries that wouldn't participate in the extradition of an American? She didn't know—but Moreno would.

Cat shut the small wooden case. Now wasn't the time. She needed to focus and stay on the straight and narrow. Brandt paid her well, and with the job came many creature comforts not only unavailable to the average citizen, but to even those who worked within the SSD operation. Even if she grabbed the jewels now and started running as fast as she could, she had no escape route, and no plan. *Focus, Cat. You've got work to do.*

Cat pressed her ear to the wooden door. She heard no footsteps outside, nor could she hear Adelaide, who would surely be coming and going from the house to accommodate Ives' guests. She opened the door, looked the second-floor balcony over, then surveyed the first-floor foyer. Only the light breeze of the afternoon wind could be heard rustling the fabric of the large curtains hanging along the windows. The gentlemen were all probably preoccupied with their work. *Now* was the time—she wasn't sure she'd get another opportunity.

Cat walked through the hall—barefooted, no less—and toward Kearney's room. Her soft, feather-like steps were necessary if she was going to avoid Adelaide, who would surely be informing Ives of Cat's activities if they were in any way questionable. Kearney's room was on the opposite end of the second-floor balcony, separated only by two guest bedrooms in between. Through the crack where the door had been left ajar, Cat spotted his luggage case resting at the foot of the bed. She took inventory of the main hall once more and, satisfied that there were no prying eyes, entered into the man's room.

How long did she have? Two hours? Three? It was irrelevant; either option was plentiful. Kearney's room did not contain a window in a spot conducive to see the comings and goings from the property, but she relied on her guess that she might hear an approaching car if the men arrived back at the guest house.

Cat grabbed hold of Kearney's luggage case, inhaled

deeply, then exhaled with a slow, soft breath to calm her nerves. In the quiet room, her heart raced, each thump pounding against her chest as if she'd swallowed a hammer. She'd snooped through the belongings of her targets before, but in each of the other scenarios Brandt had informed her of what she was looking for—or, as in Moreno's case, they'd been drugged into a sleep-like state. When it came to Kearney, she'd had no idea either what she might find. The infinite possibilities of what she might discover within his belongings made her more nervous than usual, and worse than that, there was no escape if she was caught red-handed. D.C. was a long way away, and so, too, any chance of rescue or salvation. The whereabouts of the only ally in her proximity were still currently unknown. For all Cat knew, Sam hadn't even arrived yet.

Cat unzipped the first of the zippers, opening the smaller section of Kearney's case. She employed a system of putting everything back where it had previously been like a puzzle—she'd learned it on the third floor of The Yard—in case Kearney became aware someone had looked through his things. She'd stack everything up on the bed in the reverse order of the way she'd found it. The miniature compartment contained clothing: slacks, collared shirts, two pairs of dress shoes, socks, under-wear, and ties—none of which were important. Under the pile of clothing was the first item of interest: a firearm. She had no idea what kind it was, though it didn't have the revolving magazine of most pistols she'd seen. Her suspicion was confirmed by the clip of ammu-nition beside it.

Beside the firearm was a blade with a rubber handle and ornately carved symbology along its hilt. Though the weapons cache inside the luggage case had already aroused Cat's most dangerous of suspicions, it wasn't enough to take home to Brandt. Moreno carried a gun too, and Cat knew that sometimes wealthy businessmen in transit sometimes armed themselves. She'd been party to a robbery at gunpoint herself at a younger age, and so she knew from personal experience that a man who displayed his wealth while traveling through Americana was a likely target for unsavory characters with no hard qualms about making a quick buck. Of course, it had not been she who had held the gun in that scenario, it had been her boyfriend, Buck, who'd brandished the weapon in the assailant's face, and she who had functioned as the bait to gain the sucker's attention.

Cat found nothing else of interest within the compartment. She carefully packed each of the pieces of clothing back inside the case, sure to match their initial arrangement as best she could, then closed it. Some slight deviation would be expected—the package had endured a lengthy trip, so she imagined Kearney wouldn't suspect anything out of the ordinary. Satisfied she'd discovered anything of value within the compartment, she moved on to the larger one.

Unzipping the compartment revealed an attaché case. *Isn't that what Moreno called it? No, a diplomatic case.* She recognized it as such because of the two combination lock codes located beside the handle. Locks often led to secrets. Cat instantly knew she'd found something worth looking at.

Cat interlocked her fingers and cracked the knuckles on her hands in one quick motion. This is what she was hired to do. Before even touching it, she scrutinized the dials to better approximate what technique to employ.

The first method of cracking—and one that required little tampering—was to look for evidence of use on the faces of the dials. Often one could see via simple wear and tear what a code might be. Each of the dials rested, from left to right, on the three-digit numbers "415" and "671." She attempted to open it, but it didn't budge. It was worth a shot. She spun the dials, focusing on the minute details surrounding each number, but was disappointed to find none contained any history of constant use. This was going to take more finesse.

Cat listened for any evidence of eavesdroppers. The home was still quiet. She dropped to her knees so her face was level with the dial. There were one million different combinations—Cat was going to reduce that number greatly, and it would require no hardware or tools. She rolled all of the dials until they each read "0."

Getting the lock set to the right combination was simple, really. All she needed to do was pull each lock while spinning the dials in linear order. The methodology would work for anyone with a little time, but most people invading the personal property of others were usually impatient. The lower the combination number, the less time the process would take. She pulled the pin as she went through the first nine digits of numerology on the left lock, then moved on to numbers in the teens, and the twenties, and the thirties, on and on like that until she reached the one hundreds.

A *crack* sounded from the hall. She froze. *It's just an old house*, she told herself. *Just the wood settling.* After a brief moment of pause, she refocused her attention on the lock. She continued to roll the dials, now working her way through the two hundreds, starting with the last dial, moving on to the second, until she rolled the third to make her way into the three hundreds.

The house settled again, *if* that's even what the noise had been. Cat ceased all activity. Now all could she hear was the sound of her own ragged breath. Sweat had gathered at her hairline, and she wiped it with the back of her hand and resumed the task.

Finally, when she reached the four hundreds, the lock popped. She wasn't even sure what number it had been that had released it, somewhere around four hundred and fifty, perhaps. She had to be sure. If she was going to tell Sam what she'd found, he'd need to get in, and she wouldn't dare force him to repeat the same process. She'd teach him, just in case Kearney changed the code again, but if he didn't, there was no reason to waste Sam's time. She rolled the dial back a few steps to "451," then continued slowly. The lock popped on "454." On to the next one.

She rolled the right dial to the starting point: "000," and repeated the same process, rolling each dial from right to left until she worked her way up the line. She'd hoped the old house had finally settled. Any more sudden noises might cause her to have a stroke.

After some concentration and patience, she heard a *pop*—the case opened. The lock currently rested on the number "239," so she set it back to "230." She rolled the third dial slowly, and the lock popped again on the number "237." *Four hundred and fifty-four and two hundred and thirty-seven, from left to right*, Cat said in her head. She let loose a sign of relief, if only because she'd gotten the hard part done. She'd still keep her wits about her.

Inside the case was a small leather diary, the clasps of

which were secured by a canvas strap wrapped from top to bottom, and she placed it down on the bed. The personal thoughts of Maxwell Kearney seemed valuable until she saw what else was in the briefcase: a folder which was packed with documents. Cat opened the folder and scrutinized the first of the papers.

A tremor of fear shot through her, causing her to drop the folder near her feet. She trembled as she stared down at the papers that spilled out over the floor. *Now I've done it.* Each of the papers slid from its original position.

Her focus turned to the door—had she made too much noise? Now her heart was pounding so hard she could hear each beat in her ears. Her temples throbbed, and her breath became uneven. Standing there swimming in her anxiety wasn't helping anything, so she started the process of collecting all of the papers and reassembling them in some meaningful order. There was only one problem, and it was the same one that had caused her initial burst of fear: they were all in German.

Brandt was right—Kearney *was* working for the Germans. Did that mean Moreno and Ives were, too? Cat wasted no time compiling the papers as fast as she could. There was no standard she could find for the order of the documents—the documents bore no page numbers. If the pages at least had been numbered, she might have been able to collect them in some organized fashion, but that was out of the question.

She wasted no time attempting to determine the contents of the documents. If Sam showed his face, she'd alert him to their whereabouts and put the job on his plate. She didn't have a camera, or a photographic memory, and her own reliability to reproduce the information she'd discovered was amateur at best. Just telling Brandt that the documents were written in German was enough to bring home as far as she was concerned. What dismayed her was that she had a whole weekend ahead of her to sit with that information before she made it back home. The thought of socializing with Kearney, knowing full well what she'd found in his case, only caused the fear to rise in her chest even higher. She felt as if she might pass out.

As she finished, her eyes fell to one document that gave her pause: a schematic. She analyzed the document, which was a blueprint of sorts for circuitry. Along the sides of the document, words had been printed that designated each of the sections of the mechanism, and likely, each of its parts. Because all of the information was in German, Cat still had no idea what the device was for or what it was about, but her best summation was that the machine must be in some way involved with a weapon.

Cat grabbed the last of the scattered papers, which she recognized as the first she had seen, and her eyes fell on the title of the paper which lay smack dab at the top and centered. In bold lettering, it read: *Bezüglich Wolfram.* Cat ruminated about the title for a moment. *Wolfram*, she whispered aloud. Where had she heard it before? *Newton*! Wolfram was the German word for tungsten. She remembered because Newton had said the letter assigned to tungsten on the periodic table of elements was "W," and she recalled that prefix: wolf.

"Everything alright?" a sweet, southern voice asked. Cat's heart nearly leapt through her throat and onto the floor. She dropped the folder once more, scattering the contents all around her feet. Adelaide lingered in the doorway, her hands clasped neatly at her waste and her face eager and attentive.

"What?" Cat asked.

"I'm sorry if I startled you," Adelaide said. "I asked if there was anything I could get for you? How are your accommodations?"

"Oh," Cat replied in a state of bewilderment. "No. No, I'm quite alright, Adelaide."

Adelaide approached, then knelt down and said, "That's my fault. Let me help you."

"No!" Cat snapped. Adelaide paused and released the paper in her hand. "I mean, it's no bother. It was my own clumsiness is all."

"Are you sure there's nothing I can do for you?" Adelaide asked, but now the tone of her voice was stern. Her face was only inches from Cat's, and her eyes had become intense and glaring. "Anything I can *help* with?" Cat lingered there for a moment, her own eyes darting between both of Adelaide's and their faces frozen.

Who is this woman? Why is she looking at me like that? Cat's mouth opened as if to speak, but no words came, and she was stuck in a daze as the attendant's gaze remained fixed on her own. "I'm sure," Cat said, then rose to her feet. Adelaide followed suit, smoothed her dress from the creases that had formed while she'd bent down, and took one glance at the scattered documents. "I was just ensuring that Mr. Kearney received correspondence from Mr. Moreno. I'd thought I'd forgotten it." *What a poor lie*, Cat thought. She was slacking.

"Well, you let me know," Adelaide said. "If there's *anything* you need."

"I…" Cat stuttered. "I will."

Adelaide left the room, and Cat double-timed the

cleanup of her mess. Once everything was secure again in the briefcase, she slammed it shut and spun the dials to no meaningful order. She'd completely blanked on their original settings. *Four hundred and fifty-four and two hundred and thirty-seven, from left to right*, Cat repeated in her head. *Four hundred and fifty-four and two hundred and thirty-seven, from left to right.*

How long had she been on Ives' farm? One hour? In one hour, she'd managed to potentially blow her cover. She had no good reason to be in Kearney's room, and now she'd be in a state of panic wondering if Adelaide would go and tell the man. It wasn't her business, but perhaps as the attendant to Ives' property, she might feel a responsibility to go inform her guest, or Ives himself.

Perhaps, if anything, the woman might think Cat had something going on with Kearney on the side. Cat could care less if that was what she thought, as long as it stayed hush hush. After she'd cleaned up the documents and ensured that they were in a condition close enough to the way she'd found them, Cat left the room, as well as the house. Though the conditions outside were undesirable, Cat needed to shed the anxious sensation welling up inside her and a walk of the grounds might be the ticket. A rendezvous with Sam might be required, and if he was there, she wanted to make her presence known.

17

S am had taken the opportunity to enter into the mine amongst the group of tan-coverall-clad men. Not only would it afford him the luxury of getting closer to the action, but the mine was dark and cool, and a welcome break from the sun. The stench of earth inside the rock cavity was ever-present, in addition to a musty, mildew-like smell that was pungent wherever moisture gathered. The team walked through the mine's entrance —a long, rocky tunnel braced on all sides with wooden beams along its entire length. Sam felt claustrophobic inside the enclosed space, and even more so as the voices of the men around him grew louder. He'd heard of mines collapsing and crushing those unlucky enough to be caught inside. He only hoped the men who'd done the initial work before Kearney had arrived had done a good enough job that he wouldn't suffer that type of terrible fate.

Without a train or car to cart them through the main tunnel, the walk was long. The group trekked deep enough into the hole that they saw very little light coming from the entrance, and near-darkness swallowed the path ahead whole. There was intermittent lighting—surely not enough to make working conditions safe in any way, but Ives' men had set up enough that the team could at least see where they were going. Several of the men had brought oil lamps to guide the way, but they did very little other than illuminate a very limited path ahead. Sam had no idea where the team was going, but he suspected it was probably to the first elevator shaft that had been installed so they could assess the situation and decide on a preliminary idea of what the next steps could be.

"Just a little further," the foreman at the head of the group called out, and Sam started to see a glimmer of light in the distance. They finally approached a hollowed-out, cavern-like stope where quite a bit of earth had been cleared to accommodate a large gathering. Sam suspected this would be the jumping-off point, or a sort of base of operations that lived inside the mine. In the center of the room, an elevator shaft rose vertically up into what seemed to be infinite darkness. This section of the cave was far better lit, and along the walls of the interior various tools had been strewn about, including shovels, pickaxes, and wheelbarrows.

"First group up the main pass," the foreman said, and a grouping of men shuffled one by one to the elevator. The lift didn't look as if it could accommodate many people, and Sam pushed his way toward it to be among that first group. Sam had seen no sign of Kearney, Moreno, or Ives, so he thought it likely they had already gone up to survey what lay above. Sam was the last one to make it onto the elevator, which was only able to fit eight to ten men.

The foreman pulled a lever, and a loud, grinding noise echoed through the cavernous room. The sound of metal scraping metal followed. Nothing about the operation felt safe, and he did not envy the men who would call this workplace home in the coming months.

As the elevator rose, the vertical shaft only grew darker. If Sam had felt claustrophobic before, he was *really* feeling it now. Hugging each of the four sides of the elevator were thick rock walls that left no escape should the elevator malfunction. Just the thought of being trapped at that depth in a rock box made Sam reconsider his eagerness to get inside of the structure. As the elevator rose, the pulley system groaned and rattled, and the loud clicking of the gears below dissipated until they could be heard no longer. The elevator was slow-moving and cumbersome. Sam wondered just how long it would take before they finally got up to the desired floor.

The elevator finally slowed just as Sam began to feel his blood pressure rise, and it came to a halt in a steel structure that functioned as a sort of carriage for its holding. When the motors ceased, one of the men opened the gate keeping them packed in, and the group fanned out inside yet another stope that had already been blasted out. Sam laid eyes on Kearney and friends, who were in deep thought about the next moves for the operation, their attention fixed on the upper sections of the room. The men paced around the chamber, Kearney and Ives in deep conversation, and Moreno simply along for the ride. Rudy stood by in silence, probably listening intently because he would be the one to facilitate any new construction within the operation. Finally, Sam could hear what they were saying perfectly. The shape of the room was excellent at bouncing sound waves in all directions.

"This would be north," Ives said, and he extended a finger out toward the wall of the room.

"Right," Kearney said. He turned to Rudy. "So our additional shaft will extend from here, and each of the first ore paths will extend in this northern direction. It would be wise to construct the first of our ramps in a southerly direction to anticipate proximity to the mill."

Another tunnel stretched south, and the group of men Sam had arrived in all followed the leader that way. Sam did so, too. Being stuck in the room alone with Kearney and company would be unwise. He didn't want to draw any unwanted attention to himself, so a better vantage point was in order. When the last of the men had disappeared down the south tunnel, Sam lingered back behind the edge of the rock mouth and watched as Kearney continued his survey.

Sam looked over his shoulder, ensured that he was as alone as one could be in the setting, and retrieved his camera once more. He snapped a photo, the shutter of which clicked loudly inside the room. Rudy immediately searched for the source of the click, and Sam ducked behind the edge and out of view. The sound had already caught his attention, and Sam checked his settings to see if he'd even gotten anything of value. The room was dark—far darker than the exposures he'd acquired in direct sunlight. He'd need to adjust his settings to compensate for the little light available. He'd only have one more attempt to get it right without raising too much suspicion; a camera's shutter was unique and easily heard, and he was taking an immense risk by attempting to shoot a second photo. Sam opened his iris as much as was possible, adjusted his shutter to meet the same low-light requirement, and aimed his camera when Rudy's attention wavered.

Sam pressed his body against the rock wall; a slow shutter would require a steady hand. He focused the camera, ensured he would get the best photo of the men possible, then pressed the shutter button. The *click* attracted the attention of Rudy once more, and his contorted face proved that he was becoming suspicious of the mechanical sound. Rudy approached Sam slowly. *Shit.*

Sam didn't think Rudy had seen him, but the spy didn't dare take another photo—even if it had come out poorly. Sam hoped his skills with the tool had improved enough that he'd gotten something worth bringing home, but he wouldn't know until he was able to have the film developed.

That was good enough for now—for both Sam and Kearney. "Alright," Kearney said to the men in his company. "I think we've got our work cut out for us."

"In that case," Ives said, "I'm going to go tend to my regular duties and let you gentleman sort out whatever else you need. I'll see you two for dinner, yea?"

"That sounds very good," Kearney replied. "Are there any other details that need to be worked out regarding lodging for the crew?"

"The lodge is at the southern end of the property," Ives replied. "There're enough beds in there for a small army, and it's not crop-picking season yet, so they should find plenty of room if they're staying here."

"Great," Kearney replied. "I'll see to it that any of the men who aren't from the area have somewhere to rest their heads."

"I'll follow you out," Moreno said. "It's far too cold for me in here, anyway."

"Follow me, Salazar," Ives said to the diplomat. "I'd like to pick your brain any-who—we're tilling some new beds, and I'm wondering what exotic crops we might be able to put in there next season." Ives turned back to Kearney and Rudy. "Eight sharp?"

"We'll see you there," Kearney replied.

Sam retreated once more behind the wall as the two men made their way to the elevator. His main interest wasn't in Ives—who Sam had still suspected was truly unwise to any foul play happening under his nose—and Moreno wasn't nearly as intriguing as Kearney. Sam already knew Moreno was dirty, and perhaps Cat would make headway in that department. Kearney was the man who truly piqued his interest, and Rudy stank of suspicion as well. Sam still hadn't heard the statue-like man say a word. The elevator whined, then descended, and left in its wake only the cold, stale air of the open stope.

Rudy checked his surroundings, ensured no one was eavesdropping, then said to Kearney, *"Es Gibt viel zu tun."*

It was the first time Sam had heard him speak clearly. His tenor was cold and matter-of-fact. *There it is,* Sam said to himself. *Germans.*

"Ja," Kearney said, massaging his chin in between

his thumb and forefinger. He frowned as he scanned the interior of the mountain.

Kearney was playing a character, *just* like Cat. Sam was flabbergasted at just how good the man's English was. The German had fooled Sam, that was for sure, and it seemed his act had likely pulled the wool over Ives' eyes, too. Moreno, Sam suspected, knew full-well who he was dealing with. The correspondence Sam had retrieved seemed proof enough of that.

It all made sense suddenly. Kearney was here to take tungsten right from America's stash pile, and he was doing it quite well. Ives, an unsuspecting businessman, was delivering his goods right into the enemy's hands. No red-blooded American who'd beat back the Germans in the first war would aid them this time around. The question Sam still had was, who was Kearney *really*? What was his *real* name?

"Wir versenden es jetzt, auch wenn es noch nicht fertig ist," Kearney said. *"Ich werde dem Führer eine Nachricht schicken lassen."*

Sam repeated the words in his head. *We'll send the ore as is, unrefined, and send a message to the Führer.*

God damn Nazis, Sam thought. *And they're right here on our own soil.*

Rudy, the man of few words, spoke once more: *"Vergeltung ist nahe."*

Sam lingered on the phrase. He'd heard it before: "Vengeance is near."

———

Cat's mind raced at a speed that would have rivaled a high-octane engine as she walked the grounds. She'd traveled north alongside several of the tobacco fields before her course took a westerly turn. The path edged closer to the ridge the further she continued. Soon she'd found herself near enough to its base that she'd managed to get out of the sun temporarily. She wagered that if she kept walking, soon enough she might find herself in Virginia.

It was already late afternoon, and she felt like she'd written a small novella of possibilities in her head. Could she get word back to The Yard? How? What was the closest Virginian town? Perhaps a call from the farm might be better, but what if someone was listening to the phones? Brandt's people did things like that, but would Ives? Would Adelaide talk? And damnit, where the hell was Sam?

Her discovery weighed heavily on her. She'd done what she'd been tasked to do, but normally she was discovering small morsels to bring back to the boss. She'd answered questions like "Who was with whom? When? Where?" Or followed commands like, "Let this one in the back door, see where this one goes, crack a safe." The discovery of plans for secret weapons—if that was even what they were—and for the Nazis, no less, made her suddenly feel as if she had become a larger player in this game than she had originally signed up to be. She was no soldier, and she certainly didn't know if she'd crack under the pressure of questioning from the likes of the men in her company. Dodging the guffawing jowls of the D.C. elite seemed like a cake walk compared to dealing with a guy like Kearney.

Get it together, Cat. There was still a job to do. She'd gotten the tidbit Brandt would have wanted, and now she had to press the issue as best she could. She had to alert Sam to the documents so he could do what he did best. She was thankful she wasn't the one who knew how to use a camera, because she wasn't sure if she could bring herself to go back into Kearney's room and rifle through his belongings again.

Cat discovered a small pond on the outskirts of the property. It was tranquil, and a row of large willows with long, thick foliage hanging from their branches reached over the water as if to welcome her to their shade with open arms. She'd been walking for miles, at least three, she thought. The size of Ives' property was overwhelming, and she took the opportunity to take a break.

Cat nearly collapsed on a large root jutting out toward the water. It was as if the tree had managed to plant its mouth directly into the pond for a steady drink. Cat considered that might be why the willows looked so magnificent. Under the arches, she felt as if she'd discovered the first true hiding spot on the property where she might be out of sight. She fanned herself to produce more cool air in addition to the relief the willow provided. A breeze howled, rustling each of the branches and making the leaves sing in unison. Around her, the sounds of insects and frogs in heated debate added to the tranquility of the hideout.

The crack of a twig sounded behind her. Cat looked over her shoulder—there was nothing there. In the quiet of the tree-covered bank, she could feel her heart begin to protest yet again. Ever since she'd discovered Kearney's true intentions, even the slightest prompt had seemed to send her adrenaline surging.

Another branch snapped, and Cat searched in the opposite direction. Her nerves were getting the best of her, and she sought to calm herself with reason. Surely the critters were lurking around the pond for the same reasons as Cat: shade, water, relaxation. These were just the sounds of nature—nothing to get all wired about.

The crackling came again, and this time the sound of wood splintering was so loud and forceful she was sure it had been from the weight of a foot. This was not the sound of a squirrel or fox stumbling across the forest floor—someone was *there*. She rose to her feet, searching through the low hanging branches. The foliage was so dense that looking through it yielded only more branches and leaves. She didn't feel hidden; she felt *trapped*. She'd lost sight of the farm in all directions. Was it Kearney? Had Adelaide spoken, and now the man had come to kill her? Who would know if she died? There were endless fields in which to dispose of a body. Her heart thumped with the fury of a jackhammer. *Boy, you've really done it this time, Cat.*

The leaves ahead rustled once more, but now the wind was not the cause. A figure formed, first in silhouette behind the abundant vines, and next taking the shape of a man. They'd *found* her.

She considered running—perhaps she could leap into the pond and hope the man couldn't swim. She could scream, but she was miles from the main house, so who would hear? Would they care?

She swallowed deeply, then took several paces backwards. If only she'd brought a weapon. Brandt had never provided her with one, and she wished she was permitted to carry a firearm like some of the other operators in the field. "That would be telling," Brandt had said. A lot of good her subtlety did now. Several branches parted, and the man came into view.

"Fancy seeing you here, Alley Cat," Sam said. Cat stormed up to him, balled up a fist, and punched him square in the chest. She raised another, but Sam caught the attempted strike in midair. She raised her free hand and slapped him across the face.

"Easy!" Sam said, and then he seized her free hand. Cat's teeth were clenched tightly, making her usually pleasing smile more closely resemble the snarl of a ferocious animal. "What gives?" Sam asked.

Cat pulled her hands free of his grasp, then wagged a finger in his face like a small dagger. She nearly screamed, "You scared me half to death! Why the hell couldn't you announce yourself?"

"Force of habit, I guess," Sam said. "I'm a spy."

"Where the hell have you been?"

"Spying," Sam replied.

Cat frowned. She looked Sam up and down, curious about the uniform he'd arrived in. "What's with the getup?"

"Camouflage," Sam replied.

"How did you find me?"

"I've been tracking you since I left the mine," Sam answered. "I saw you walking the grounds, but I kept to the ridge to see where you'd wind up. You were out in the open nearly the whole time—I can't just walk up to you in the middle of a field. When I saw you duck under these willows, I knew that was my chance."

"Well I'm glad you have the luxury of coming and going freely," Cat barked. "Some of us are in the middle of the snake pit with the cobras—and I almost got bit. You're up there galivanting around in the forest. Do you know just what the hell it's like keeping this act up all the time?"

"Are you done?" Sam asked.

"No!" Cat replied. "Kearney—"

"I know," Sam said.

"Know what?" Cat asked with confusion.

"He broke character," Sam said. "I overheard him in the mine speaking Deutsch to his goon."

"Oh," Cat replied. In a state of defeat, she attempted to one-up Sam. "Well you didn't find what *I* did."

"Do tell," Sam said, intrigued. Cat looked over both of her shoulders, unsure of whether or not this was a good place to be spilling the beans. "This is as isolated as its going to get, so get to it," he said at her reaction.

Cat sighed deeply, then wiped the sweat-soaked hair from her forehead. She slumped onto the bench-like tree root, and Sam sat, too. "Well, I opened his luggage, and he's got all these documents, you see?"

"What kind of documents?"

"I don't know," Cat replied. "Blueprints, or schematics."

"For what?" Sam asked.

"Circuits or electronics of some sort," Cat said.

"Describe them."

Cat rolled her eyes. "Isn't that your job?"

He dug into his pocket, retrieved two cigarettes, then handed one to Cat. He lit hers, then said, "Keep going," and lit his own.

Cat took a long drag. Sam could see Cat relaxing as the smoke did its work. Cat exhaled, then said, "I couldn't get much else other than that it was all in

German—and it was about that stuff, tungsten, only they called it wolfram."

"Well done," Sam said.

"That's it?" Cat asked as she rose from the root. She pulled at the cigarette once more, and the cherry flared, channeling the rage she'd been experiencing.

"That's it," Sam replied. "What'd you expect, a trophy?"

"Well, what did *you* find?" Cat asked.

"You," Sam replied.

A scowl crossed Cat's face. She said, "You know, I nearly got myself caught trying to get that information!"

"That's the job," Sam replied. "You seemed to be all for it when we left home."

"Well," Cat said, and she angrily flicked her cigarette, "that was before I realized I'd be sleeping in the same damn house as a bona fide Nazi."

"You get used to it," Sam replied. "That it?"

"Yes, that's *it*." Cat slumped onto the root again and nursed the cigarette, turning her attention away from Sam. Despite her pouting, Cat had more to tell.

"Alright," Sam said. "We're almost done. You've got the dinner tonight and then we just need to get through tomorrow."

"We should leave *now*," Cat replied.

"And blow your cover?" Sam asked. "What will you tell Moreno?" Cat didn't have a good rebuttal. "While you're at the dinner tonight, I'll get into Kearney's room —if Kearney's even his real name—and photograph the documents."

"You'll need the codes," Cat said. "Four hundred and fifty-four and two hundred and thirty-seven, from left to right."

"Thanks," Sam said.

"Don't thank me yet," Cat replied. "If he changes them, you're on your own. You'll need to cycle through the combinations. Do you know how to do that?"

"I don't."

"Jeez, if I knew how to use a camera, you'd be kind of useless, wouldn't you?"

"Get to it," Sam replied.

Cat explained the process. Once finished, she tossed her cigarette and said, "You'll find everything I saw in the briefcase."

"Good," Sam said. "Once we've got that, we're home free. You'll be on a train back to D.C., and before you know it you'll have a nice glass of scotch in your hand."

"Easy for you to say," Cat replied. "You get to hide and sneak around all over the damn place while I've got to share cocktails and conversation."

"We're all good at something," Sam replied.

"What's worse," Cat replied, "is that I think the attendant, Adelaide, saw me."

"Think she'll talk?" Sam asked.

"How should I know?"

"Hm," Sam replied.

"*Hm?*" Cat said with consternation. "That's all you have to say?"

"One night," Sam assured her. "That's all we need. Take the opportunity to press Kearney if you can. You didn't see anything that might hint at his real identity, did you?"

"I don't speak German," Cat said frustratedly. "And even if I did, it's *your* turn."

"You just get through the dinner," Sam said in the most comforting way possible. "Moreno doesn't suspect anything, and that's all that matters for now." Sam flicked the cigarette, then rose from the thick root. "I'd head back. You don't want to be away too long, and we certainly don't want them to see you with me."

"What if I need help?" Cat asked.

"I'm watching," Sam said. "You got your radio, right?"

"Yes," Cat said as she rose.

"Good. Turn it on at eight," Sam said. "Keep me alerted to any movement I might need to know about. That will buy me time." Cat nodded. "We're in this together, alright? You got my back, and now I got yours. One night." Sam offered Cat another cigarette, since the tobacco had helped put her at ease if only for a moment. "One for the road?" Cat nodded her head yes and took it, then Sam lit it for her before the spy disappeared through the thick sheets of leaves. He left Cat alone once more. Her suspicions were right: she was in the company of dangerous men—friend or foe.

———

Sam hiked back up to the ridge with a pep in his step. For all intents and purposes, everything so far had gone quite well. He'd managed to get a ton of photos of all the major players in short time, as well as of the interior of the mine, and he had the evidence he'd need to satisfy Brandt. But he'd still need more to make the spymaster jubilant, or maybe even secure some time off for himself. If he had some spare time, he might even take some leisurely photos of the countryside. He'd be sure to use a separate roll for that endeavor so that the men back at

The Yard didn't see that he'd been up to some fun during the mission.

All he'd need to do was get the evidence contained within Kearney's personal documents and he'd be on his way back home unscathed. He wouldn't even need to pull out his revolver. The only true opposition he'd faced since he'd arrived had been the harsh heat, and as the sun began to set below the ridge in the early summer evening, even that was starting to be less of a nuisance. He'd watch the action safely through that wonderful new zoom lens, and when the time came he'd trot down in the shadow of night and get what he needed from Kearney's room—bonus points if he could get his *real* name.

Sam got back up to the spot overlooking the mine's entrance. The crewmembers were packing up for the day, and the circus of diesel engines, carts, and rock movers below ceased their performance. Sam admired the violet hues of the sunset from his vantage point. A cloudy sky had crept in from the south in the late day and gave the atmosphere a bit of flare. He'd been stuck in the concrete jungle of the nation's capital for so long he hadn't seen much flora or fauna since he'd left Pforzheim, and setting up camp among the trees and critters didn't seem half-bad. If he didn't need to concern himself with getting caught, he might have even taken a stab at setting up a fire, but for now the small bag of nuts he'd packed would do.

After Sam finished his dinner—if one could call it that—he grabbed his bag and moved toward the edge of the cliff where he could secure his camera. His legs ached something fierce from all the walking he'd been doing, and he was thankful to have a short break where he could simply observe for the next couple hours until night fell and all of the major players were in the main house.

Sam secured the zoom lens to the camera, took a look through the viewfinder, and saw that all of the lights inside the main house had been turned on. Ives' wife and her staff were likely cooking up a storm, and Sam considered that he might be wise to grab some photos of the dinner meeting as well. He wouldn't know for sure whether that was worth the risk until he got down there. This job, unlike the last several he'd done that involved a *Nazi* element, was turning out to be quite easy.

Click. The mechanical noise was unique against the earthly sounds of the wilderness. The feeling of the cold metal of the barrel against the back of his skull came soon after. The source could only belong to one thing: the hammer of a revolver.

"Turn around slowly," a voice said, and the barrel of the gun was forced harder still against the back of Sam's head. He should have known better—should have known that it was *never* that easy. Sam turned slowly, expecting to find the stone-like face of Rudy staring back at him and ready to kill him where he stood. It wasn't Rudy, though—it was *Whelan.*

18

"Good to see you again, *Mr. Rilyeh*," Whelan said victoriously. He cranked the gun back without warning and lashed it across Sam's face. "That's for the other night." Sam collapsed to the ground, feeling the blood trickle from the corner of his mouth and the taste of iron on his tongue. Sam lifted his head and locked eyes with Whelan. The spy had given him a nice shiner during their last encounter and the left side of his face resembled a raccoon's. The federal agent drew the gun back and cracked Sam across the face with the butt once more. "And *that's* for meddling in my operation."

Sam massaged his jaw. "Isn't there such a thing as due process?" he asked.

"Not for foreigners," Whelan replied. Another agent stepped forward, removed his own pistol from its holster, and trained it on Sam. Whelan put his away, then started to pace in front of Sam in slow, contemplative steps. He brushed his suit jacket aside, displaying the FBI tin clipped to his belt. "That's right. I know all about you, *Sam*."

The announcement of his name did give Sam some pause. So few people actually knew his name that a stranger having this information felt supremely invasive. How long had these guys been watching him, and if so, what did they know?

"Here's how this is going to go," Whelan said. His face was silhouetted by the setting sun, which cast his features in a grim, shadowy light that made his eyes difficult to see. Sam, still on his knees and at the mercy of the gun aimed at his chest, had no choice but to listen. "You're going to pack up your little camera and your bag, and you're going to go back home before the last train leaves tonight." Whelan checked his watch. "There's one leaving just after nine that heads back north, and if you start walking within the next few minutes, you'll get on it with time to spare. You'd be *wise* to be on that train."

"Is nature photography against the law?" Sam asked.

Whelan's pacing ceased, then he turned to Sam. "Don't get smart with me. I'll give you one more so good you'll be begging for the pain to stop the whole way home." Whelan's knuckles were gripped so tightly Sam could see the white of his bones. "Now, I know your little lass is down there twirling around or doing whatever the hell it is she does, so you'd better hope she continues to stay in the good graces of one Salazar Moreno for the duration of the trip. If not, I'll have her in cuffs and on her way back to Pennsylvania where she belongs."

Sam didn't speak. Responding to the agent's threats would only confirm the man's suspicions, and Sam thought it better to neither confirm, nor deny, anything he was speaking about. "As it is," Whelan continued, "if I didn't have such limited resources down here and my partner and I didn't have our own investigation to see through, I'd have both your wrists locked up in bracelets and be taking you back to D.C. myself." Whelan sensed Sam's defeat. "Yea, that's right. Just by having you in his employ, I'm sure Brandt's breaking a whole slew of laws, some of which I'm sure it would be quite easy to peg you with. Skulking around in an enemy uniform, I believe, carries a hefty penalty." Sam grimaced. "Yes, I know about that too. But I can deal with you back in D.C. when the time is right."

"So you're onto Moreno, too, huh?" Sam asked.

"We're not in the business of sharing information, Sam," Whelan replied. "But yeah, we were on to Moreno long before you guys caught his scent."

"Hold on just a minute," Sam said. "We have someone on the *inside*. Let her do what she's got to do, and let's just let this all play out a bit more before we blow it."

"You're right," Whelan replied. "*We* have someone on the inside, and it's not *your* girl. We're several steps ahead of you and your boss, and I'm not going to let you go back down there and jeopardize the work we've done for the sake of taking some more pictures. You see, I've got pictures, too, Sam." Sam couldn't help but feel his face droop in defeat. "Oh yea, good ones—of you, your redheaded friend…" Whelan trailed off for a moment, then a snide smirk spread across his face. "Of your boss, and the girl at his desk…"

Of course, Sam thought. That explained Iris's behavior the morning before they'd left town, and subsequently, Brandt's. The feds had made a point to flex their muscles *before* the SSD continued to dig any deeper.

Whelan began to pace again. "Be a shame if his wife were to see those, or worse, the newspapers. Your whole operation might fold. Wouldn't that be a disappointment? Your boss would be back in the law offices taking cases where he belongs, the little lady with the fancy jewelry would be back behind bars, and you'd probably have to go back to wherever the hell it is you came from —*if* you don't face a military tribunal before you get there."

Bars? Sam sat on the comment for a moment as Whelan stood there. Had the crazy old spy chief pulled her *out* of prison? Whelan crouched down and looked Sam square in the face. He scrutinized the spy's eyes for a moment before he spoke again. Whelan pulled a cigarette from his pocket and lit it. He offered one to Sam, but for once in his life, the spy declined. He didn't want to take *anything* from this man.

"Yea, I think that might be better all around. Brandt's choice of personnel is a threat to the nation's security as it is. He's got a bunch of commies slithering about those hallways—seen 'em myself. That whole building's nothing but a bunch of degenerates, criminals, and the like, clacking away on keyboards and smokin' cigarettes while they fish through our scraps. One bad thing about rapid expansion is that there's no accountability. You ever find a good restaurant? One where the chef puts thought and care into every meal and they all come out as good as the last? Then someone comes along and says 'Hey, let's open up more of these.' Then, with every restaurant that opens, the chef has got less and less oversight of that food, and each new place's food gets worse than the last, each falling a little further from the standard that was set in the first place—that's *you guys*. You're the new restaurant."

"Moreno's not the one you want," Sam replied. Whelan knew what he knew, and there was no way to convince him otherwise, so Sam decided to go all-in.

"That's for us to decide," Whelan replied. "This is *American* soil. You can't just run around the country unchecked, pointing your guns and cameras wherever you please."

"But *you* can," Sam replied defiantly.

Whelan rose to his feet once more, took another drag of his cigarette, then flicked the ash into the breeze. "I think we're done here," he said. Whelan waved to his partner, a stringy man in a suit and tie with jet-black hair and sunglasses, and the man finally aimed away from Sam and deposited his firearm into its holster.

"What about Kearney?" Sam asked. If Brandt's people were going to have to absolve themselves of sin, they were going to need to have the goods to show their worth.

"Who?" Whelan asked.

"Ah," Sam replied with a smirk as if he'd put it all together. "You guys didn't have anything. You followed *us* here."

Whelan frowned dismissively. "Don't kid yourself," he said. "We've been watching Moreno since before he started corresponding with the man down here." His face become hard like stone. "Moreno's ours, Sam—it can't go any other way. Have a good night." Whelan set off away from the farm, then paused and took in the setting sun for a moment. Over the course of their conversation it had morphed into an intense rust color.

"Beautiful sunset, isn't it?" Whelan said. "Now *that's* a nice photo if I've ever seen one."

"And if I say no?" Sam asked.

Whelan and his partner continued walking away from Sam, and without turning, Whelan called out, "Pack your bags, Sam. You're in over your head."

Sam finally breathed easy when the two federal agents disappeared out of view. He was angry with himself. He'd allowed himself to be cornered, and had it been anyone else, he might already be dead. A bullet to the back of the head would have made quick work of the spy, and it would have been lights out before he'd even known what happened to him.

He was also angry with Brandt. All the work he and Cat—in addition to the people working around the clock at The Yard and the agents overseas—had done could be for naught because the old man couldn't keep it in his pants. Sam had nearly been killed on numerous occasions in the burned man's employ, and for what? The Nazis were pointing unimaginable weapons of war at the entire globe and the SSD was at risk of being exposed because the boss had had a fling with his secretary.

Sam wondered what Brandt would have him do. *Push forward*, Sam thought. Brandt already knew what the agents had on him, and he'd sent his team into the field anyway. If Brandt wanted otherwise, Sam and Cat never would have left the capital. He had made it clear that unmasking Kearney was the top priority. What Sam was really concerned with was whether or not Brandt could protect them. Sam could run—he'd done it before, and he could do it again—but could Cat?

Brandt, no matter how much money and how many

resources he could provide, was not above the law in the states. If his pseudo-enemy over at the FBI had the president's ear and wanted him shut down, Sam could see himself in an American penitentiary, or worse, a prison camp. It'd be no different than if he were captured in Germany. In the last several days, Nazis and shady diplomats seemed to be no match for American bureaucrats.

The sun finally drifted just below the ridge to Sam's west, and now the farm below was cast in the cool shadow that only came with the arrival of night. The main house was lit up like a field of stars, ready to accommodate and entertain the guests who'd arrived. The guest house, too, was busy with movement. Sam turned the camera toward the dormitories where the non-locals were staying.

Outside, propped up in wooden chairs and grilling around a fire pit, the mine workers had set up their own little party of sorts as they relaxed the day away. The dormitories were a wide, horseshoe-shaped arrangement of small, ramshackle structures that less resembled homes and mores semi-finished barns. There were quite a few beer mugs in attendance, and among those enjoying the festivities, Rudy was present. Apparently he wasn't awarded special accommodations as the man in charge in Kearney's absence.

The infiltrator trekked over to the opposite side of the peak. Whelan and his lackey had disappeared, but Sam knew from experience, they were *watching*. If Sam made a move, they'd know. He could leave with what he had so far—it would be something, but it wouldn't be enough. *Well that's just too bad*, Sam thought. *This one's ours.*

Sam packed up his camera gear, made sure it was all

secure in the pack, then slung it over his shoulder. He'd wanted to take as little with him as possible, and had debated bringing the whole bag, but the clouds traveling north might bring rain, and unlike Cat, Sam didn't get endless resources to use for his troubles. He liked that camera, anyway, and he didn't want to see any of its finer electronics suffer damage. Below, the farmland grew darker still.

Sam removed only two items from his pack: the radio earpiece, and his revolver. It would be ill-advised to fire any shots, but he had to protect himself if necessary. If Cat was in danger, he'd need to do the same. Unlike his mission in Germany, he actually had an escape route, which was in any direction where the enemy was not. On American soil, the rules that were putting roadblocks in his path were also the same ones that would protect him from Kearney and Moreno.

Sam loaded six bullets into the cylinder of the gun, then armed the earpiece. The device emitted only static. Cat had not turned her own on yet, and Sam turned his off to conserve the battery. Below, Sam saw several people exit the guest house and trek toward the main house. Though he couldn't see their features without the aid of the telephoto lens, the cream-colored dress flowing in the breeze made him sure Cat was among them. The time was near. He set off down the ridge under the cover of approaching night and headed straight for the guest house.

———

Large glowing lanterns lit the stone road leading to the main house, and Moreno tightly interlocked his arm with Cat's as they approached the main entrance. The archway of trees looked magnificent lit by the lanterns. Even in the South, Cat was in the company of wealth unlike any she'd seen before. Moreno looked handsome in his suit, which was an olive-colored tweed style fabric that was appropriate for the evening, but not too showy. Kearney accompanied them to the main house, wearing a pastel blue dinner jacket which was appropriately formal. The abusive heat had finally subsided, and Cat was looking forward to a drink to calm her nerves. Though she could smell the food being prepared all the way from the guest house, she had no appetite whatsoever.

"Did you enjoy your leisure time?" Kearney asked Cat as they continued down the stone path.

"Very much so," Cat replied. The brief eye contact she made with him was uncomfortable. He fixed her with that sinister stare whenever he spoke to her, and in the dim orange light, his features, especially with the scar, looked ghoulish.

"Any interesting activities to speak of?" Kearney asked.

"I'm sure you boys don't want to be burdened with the silly activities of a lady's day," Cat replied.

"On the contrary," Kearney said. "One could get into quite a bit of trouble having free rein of a property like this. Surely you've got some valuable anecdote to speak of."

Cat choked on her response. She hadn't even been seated at a table yet and the German was already pressing her for information—that was supposed to be *her* job. What remained unknown was whether or not the man suspected her of being untrue like himself, or if he was genuinely just a curious individual. "I'd much rather hear about your own endeavors, Mr. Kearney," she said. "You're the one who's traveled all this way to prospect the resources of this wonderful farm. Your day was productive, I hope?"

"Indeed," Kearney replied. "I learned much."

"Mr. Kearney has his work cut out for him," Moreno added. "A great new relationship was forged here today, one which should prove fruitful for all of us."

"That's just wonderful to hear," Cat replied.

"You're not off the hook yet, Ms. McAlister," Kearney said to Cat with a devious grin. "I'm very much looking forward to hearing *everything* about your own business. I'm fascinated to learn the character of a woman—so young, I might add—who has acquired such an entrepreneurial spirit, and who's managed to capture the attention of my good friend Salazar. You'll have to humor me with the details over dinner. I'll be sure to sit right next to you. Would that be alright, Salazar?" Kearney asked the diplomat.

"As long as you don't get any ideas," Salazar said jovially.

"I wouldn't think of it," Kearney replied. "I'm just an intrigued man looking for interesting company."

Cat giggled nervously. "Then it's a date."

"As funny as you are charming," Kearney said to her. Cat's gaze drifted from Kearney's and to the stone road ahead. But she could *feel* him still looking at her. She might have attributed the sensation to anxiety about the documents she'd spilled across his bedroom floor, except he'd been behaving in that manner since she'd first met him. Kearney, if he was skilled at all, was probably good at spotting the enemy a mile away. Was he military?

Abwehr? Even if she made it out alive, part of her didn't even want to know what Sam would discover. The stress of this mission might just be enough to force her to call it quits and go on the run once more. The spy games she'd signed up for were suddenly proving too costly.

The door to the main house opened as if magically when they arrived, and Adelaide was there to usher them through. Standing by the door, Rudy, to whom Cat hadn't even been properly introduced, lingered in shadow as he puffed a cigarette. Unlike Kearney and Moreno, he had not changed into his dinner best and was still wearing the dirt-covered overalls he'd been working in. Moreno held Cat's hand delicately as she climbed the steps, but Kearney remained behind and made a beeline for Rudy. Cat turned to watch the rendezvous, and noticed that Rudy had an uncanny bulge beneath his shirt: there was a firearm tucked into his waistband. She'd been taught to look for things like that.

Kearney whispered something to Rudy, then the man nodded without a response. Rudy tossed the cigarette and made his way down the tree-covered path. When Kearney's gaze met Cat's once more, she realized she'd been staring and diverted her attention clumsily as Kearney climbed the front stairs.

The interior of the home was more stunning than the last. The floors were carved from marble, and a large double staircase spiraled along either side of the foyer and up to the second-floor balcony. It was a larger, more ornate, version of the architecture found in the guest house. The wood along the banisters featured the most intricate of details featuring leafy plant life. Candelabras decorated the hall as well, casting the room in a romantic, elegant glow. A player piano in the corner of the room accompanied their entrance with a classical tune.

"An absolutely stunning dress," a woman called out. The sound of stomping heels approached, and Cat turned to see a white-haired woman in a rose-colored gown coming toward her with a large, welcoming smile spread across her face. She reached her hand out. "Abigail Ives."

Cat took her hand, then said, "Cat McAlister."

"Wonderful to meet you, my dear," Abigail said. "It's nice to see another woman around here." Abigail turned to Moreno. "Salazar, it's been so long."

Moreno took her hand in his own and kissed the back of her palm. "Abigail," he said. "I'm always charmed."

"And Mr. Kearney, I presume?" Abigail asked the man.

"Indeed," Kearney said. "Thank you very kindly for both opening your home and lending your husband's time."

"My pleasure," Abigail replied. "God knows he's got so little of it, if he's willing to provide some to you, I'm sure you must be as worth it as he claims. I hope you've all brought your appetites." Cat's stomach churned at the mention of food. She'd only been in Kearney's company for several minutes and she was already feeling a nagging sensation in the pit of her stomach.

"Adelaide," Abigail said. The woman had been standing by, ready and waiting for her next instruction with a permanent smile fixed to her face. "See to it that each of our guests has a glass of Chardonnay in short time."

"Yes ma'am," Adelaide replied with a slight bow,

then scurried off and through the swinging kitchen door.

"She's new," Abigail said, tilting her head toward Adelaide. "A recent hire that just sort of fell into our lap, but she's quite good—exceptionally educated and worldly. She needed far less breaking in than the last handful we hired."

A hand clap originating from the top of the grand spiral staircase in the large foyer nearly gave Cat a heart attack. The sudden noises attacking her nerves were becoming too much to bear. Ives walked excitedly down the set of stairs, eager to see his guests once more. For the first time, he had ditched the large hat. "Are we ready for dinner?" he asked as he approached the bottom step.

"Thank you, dear," Abigail said softly. Ives patted his hair—which had been combed to the side—with a hint of embarrassment on his face. She addressed the guests, "I always tell him that if he's going to bring company into this home and be seated at my dinner table, he's going to have to mind his manners. The dinner table is no place for that ridiculous hat."

"Old habits die hard," Ives replied. "I'm still working on which side the forks and knives go on."

"You'll learn, dear," Abigail said, and she patted his chest with her hand lovingly. "Please, this way." Abigail began the trek through the deep hallway that led to the dining room, and the rest of the guests followed suit.

The table looked as if it cost more than a luxury apartment. Like the rest of the woodwork in the home, it was carved in incredible detail. Cat became acutely aware that Abigail had instilled an air of class in Ives that might not have been present otherwise. All of the glamorous presentations were likely her doing, while he was probably responsible for cutting the checks. The table was decorated with a long gold runner from end to end on top of which two large vases of fresh cut flowers had been arranged, and at each place setting an abundance of gold silverware surrounded a series of plates. Cat wondered whether it was *actual* gold. If she managed to swipe a spoon or knife, would anyone notice?

"Mr. Ives will sit right here at the head," Abigail said she as gestured to the far end of the table, "and I'll sit side-saddle here." Abigail pointed to the other end of the table. "And Mr. Kearney, you'll take the other end."

"Wonderful," Kearney replied, but instead of pulling his own seat out, he beat Moreno to the punch and reached for Cat's. He pulled the chair out from under the table, then said, "Ms. McAlister," and waved his hand over the seat cushion. Moreno looked disgruntled by his gesture, since he'd normally been tasked with doing the gentlemanly things, but he made no stink about it. Cat was just happy that she'd sat to Kearney's right.

Before she left her bedroom, she'd put the radio earpiece in her right ear, and she'd been concerned that sitting to Kearney's left would tip him off to it. Moreno, she believed, wasn't observant enough to notice a detail like that, and though it was small enough to escape notice, Cat still had the overwhelming feeling that Kearney was on to her. As Cat took her seat, she whipped her hair around her shoulder nonchalantly, then activated the earpiece as if fixing her mane. She couldn't make contact with Sam just yet, but she'd be sure to alert him to Rudy's whereabouts when ready.

Adelaide materialized through the double doors that

led into the dining room, a tray of glasses bearing white wine balanced on her hand. She made her way around the table as the guests took their seats and deposited a glass in front of each of them. Cat, breaking character if only for a moment, wasted no time sucking down half of the glass. Abigail noticed and Cat saw the downward curls her lips. Cat quickly returned the drink back to the table in front of her. Abigail looked to Kearney. "Mr. Kearney, didn't you say your foreman—Rudy, was that his name?—would he be joining us?"

"I'm afraid not," Kearney replied. "Far too busy. He'll be up until the late hours preparing for the next steps."

"A shame," Abigail replied.

"Well, then," Ives said, and he rose from the table with his glass in hand. "To distinguished guests and new friends." His eyes wandered to each of those seated as he toasted, then onto the empty seat. "And more wine for us!"

Everyone raised their glasses in unison, and Cat finished hers in one quick gulp. Kearney swirled his around before sipping, sniffed eagerly to absorb the aroma, then took a sip and smacked his lips obnoxiously. "Where I come from, this would be considered a rarity."

"Is that right?" Abigail asked curiously. "I thought it was quite common in California."

Kearney paused, and Cat watched his reaction eagerly. She didn't know about grapes or regions or whatever the hell these people considered good or rare, but she knew a lying man when she saw one, and Kearney's eyes widened in the same way every man's did when he'd been cornered. "Northern California, yes,"

Kearney quickly course-corrected. "Not as abundant where our factory is, though."

"And where is that factory, specifically, Mr. Kearney?" Cat asked as if to piggyback on Abigail's inquiry.

Adelaide appeared through the double doors, now bearing a tray of small salads delicately draped with shredded vegetables. Kearney refocused his attention toward the food, then said, "Oh, look. I spy a first course." Kearney then turned to Cat, his eyes flaring with intensity, and a cruel grin stretching across his lips.

19

Sam had made it onto the homestead property. A thin chill crept through the air, and the wind rattled the tobacco plants as he approached the guest home. Under the cover of night, he was just another shadow among many. He'd used the tall plants as cover, specifically traveling among the rows that had been carved out to separate different sections of crops. The light from the house—the only source present above the dark plot of land—acted as his guide. *Home free.* He'd be catching the morning train out of town.

He was due for a short vacation that Brandt had promised him upon return. It was nothing to brag about —only three days—but if he was honest, after all of the walking—and enduring the southern heat—a snooze on the action was warranted. The spy thought he might even fire up that camera on one of his days off and see if he couldn't get some exposures of D.C. life. The capital was rife with photographic opportunities for a man looking to develop his craft.

Upon finding a break in the plants, Sam laid eyes on the main house. It was lit up like a miniature city, and though Sam could see no one inside, he imagined that dinner had commenced. He shifted his gaze toward the guest house. Unlike the main house, its interior was shrouded in darkness. *Perfect.*

He checked his watch: it was eight. Sam clicked his earpiece and listened for the hiss of the answering sister piece. There was a pause, then a moment of silence, and the radio crackled and tuned briefly. Then, he heard the sound of people engaged in conversation. A woman laughed, but the sound did not come from Cat.

"How's the food?" Sam asked.

"Very *rich*," Cat mumbled.

"What's that, dear?" the woman asked.

"The wine," Cat replied to her. "It's very rich."

"This is from the south of France," the woman said, then veered off on a tangent about the novelties of the region.

His attention moved to the guest house once more. No movement was visible through the dark glass. The absence of light in the house would make for some difficulty if he was going to acquire good photos, *if* he even found Kearney's belongings.

The woman was still going on *ad nauseam* about vines and wood and the sun. Every time she gave an anecdotal piece of information about the country she'd follow it with a nasally little laugh that sounded like the call of an exotic bird. "Who the hell is that cackling?" Sam asked his partner.

"Abigail," Cat said loudly. "You must tell us about the history of this home."

"Right," Sam said. "Ives' wife?"

"Are you familiar with plantation homes?" Abigail asked.

"Yes," Cat said awkwardly. Now Abigail launched into a description of the construction of the home, and Sam decided that making Cat juggle two conversations at once was unwise. She'd done her part and now he had to do his.

"I'm all clear, right?" Sam asked, eager to get some sort of confirmation that he wasn't walking into trouble.

"Are you from the South, dear?" Abigail asked. "I think I can hear the twang in your speech."

"No," Cat replied. Her response was confusing and unconvincing, and Sam was unsure if it was intended as a reply to his own question, which made him second guess whether or not he should be proceeding forward into the house.

"No?" Sam asked, but Abigail and Ives had launched into a back and forth about the home's history and construction, and Sam knew Cat had no good opportunity to continue to give him information. "Cat?"

She didn't reply. Sam dismissed the conversation as he snuck through the front of the property. He kept low to the ground, hunched over and shuffling his feet with soft but rapid steps. When he arrived at the front door, he paused and took stock of the foyer through the front-facing window. He was met with only darkness.

He grabbed the main door's handle and lifted it slightly as he opened; this was an old spy's trick. The action was virtually noiseless. When one wanted to open a door, the weight of the door was often the stressor on the hinges, in turn causing screeches and whines. If one wanted to keep a noisy door quiet, they need only lift slightly so that it met less resistance as it moved along its hinges. Sam closed the door behind him and found only the still air of the empty hall.

He waited like that—quiet and tranquil and perceptive—for several moments before he moved again. Then, when he did, he continued stealthily through the room as if he was a specter. His attention remained fixed on the second-floor balcony.

He entered the first bedroom to the left of the top of the staircase. It was an easy find because he'd glimpsed the attire Kearney had been wearing earlier in the day hanging in the open armoire. Sam entered the room, closed the door quietly behind him, then placed his bag down on the floor. His movements, though sharp and purposeful, remained feather-like while he surveyed the Kearney's belongings. The window at the side of the room was visible from the main house, and Sam quickly pulled the floor-length curtains over the glass. Sam scanned the room as if installing a memory of each of Kearney's items and their placement into his brain. Then, he got to work.

He opened the small desk drawer to the disappointing discovery of stationery for guests. He then explored the armoire, which contained several changes of clothes. The man was well-dressed. Each of his suits was finely tailored, and he'd brought options which suggested he might be something of a fashionista. Sam, aware he was unlikely to find an S.S. uniform or any damning clothing, moved on to the rest of his goods.

The luggage, Sam thought. Cat had mentioned she'd found the documents in his luggage. Sam found a case under the bed and pulled it across the wood floor. He opened the large flap: the case was empty. He moved on to the two smaller flaps where one might keep paperwork, but was distraught to find each of those contained nothing of interest.

Damn, Sam thought. His eyes wandered around the room. *If I were a war criminal, where would I keep my secret paperwork?* That Kearney had even brought documents with him across seas was a surprise—Sam knew there was strict protocol regarding the removal of paperwork from military bases—but Cat had *seen* it.

The spy lifted the mattress and ran his hand along the surface of the box spring, but found nothing there, either. He turned the lights on in the bathroom, searched beneath the sink, the shower, and even the toilet, then ran his hands along nearly every square inch of the walls carefully, wondering if just maybe there were some secret hatch or safe where Ives' guests could secure their belongings. After checking the entire room once, then twice over, Sam bit his lip in defeat and cupped his hand to his ear before saying, "Cat, you there?"

Now that his attention was focused on the dinner conversation, he heard Kearney holding court, saying, "We can take the material in the raw for now. There's such high demand at the assembly line that refining on the premises will be costly—specifically in regards to transportation—but *necessary*. Within the next month, will set up a crude refining process, and that will mean that much less of the material will need to be carted away. We'll be able to transport more per truck, and that will mean fewer trips."

Oh, it'll be costly alright, Sam thought. Shipping anything to Germany would be costly.

Kearney started again, "Within a couple months, hopefully we'll have been able to build a station right within the mine itself that will separate the tungsten from the ore.”

“So exciting,” Abigail replied eagerly.

“She’s already been telling anyone that’ll listen what we’ve found,” Ives added. He said playfully, “I’ve advised her against that.”

Kearney cleared his throat, then said, “Let’s not alert too many people to what we’re doing here. There’s a lot of red tape around these…“ He paused, then said, “*Things*.” His tone became illusive and stern, but then he said warmly, “That’s why we’ve got our friend Salazar here.”

Abigail interrupted, “You know, Wade, you’ve never told us how you met Salazar, have you?”

“Cat!” Sam called into his microphone. She didn’t answer.

“The year was ’15, I believe?” Moreno replied.

“February,” Ives added. “Jesus, it was cold.”

“Wade,” Abigail said as if warning him.

“Yes, ma’am,” Ives corrected himself. It took Sam a moment to realize that she’d reacted to him for taking the lord’s name in vain.

“Cat!” Sam yelled again. He tapped the radio, which only delivered a staticky, garbled mess.

“If you’ll excuse me,” Cat said to the group. ”The ladies room?”

“Down the hall, second door to the left,” Abigail directed her.

Sam paced around the room, anxiously waiting to hear if Cat had secured a safe location in which to speak. As he heard the sounds of her heels clicking rapidly against the home’s wooden floors, he continued his fruitless search just in case he’d missed something. He worried that perhaps Cat's compromised search had jeopardized the mission at hand. Maybe Kearney had been keeping his documents close to him.

"Any time now," Sam said.

"Quiet!" Cat hissed. Sam turned toward the bedroom door and checked the hall once more. All clear. He rested his hands on his hips, then saw an unusual gap tucked neatly between the mattress and the foot of the bed frame from his new vantage point. *Got you*, Sam thought.

He dug between the mattress and the bed frame, found the briefcase, and placed it on the bed. Sam repeated the numbers in his head as he rolled the first dial. *Four hundred and fifty-four*—the first lock popped open—*and two hundred and thirty-seven*. The second lock popped, too, and Sam opened the lid—the briefcase was empty. *No.*

"Cat," Sam said. There was no response. "Cat!"

He heard Cat close a door behind her, then she spoke again, "Sam—"

"I've got nothing here," Sam said as he paced. "I thought you said the folder was in his travel case."

"Sam—"

"It's empty. Where else could it be?"

"Sam!" Cat barked.

"What?"

"Listen!" Cat said in exasperation. "You've got to get out of there."

"Why?" Sam asked. "I haven't got anything yet. Where else could it be—"

"Rudy," Cat warned. "I think he's got it. I think he knows…" The sound of a creaking door behind the spy made him lose track of what Cat was saying. Whoever was entering did not know the door trick he used to keep quiet. Sam turned his head slightly: out of the corner of his eye, he saw the black mass approach swiftly.

Sam spun around, braced himself for an attack, and lurched backward to dodge a shadowy fist that came straight for his eyes. His attacker's other fist hooked across his chest, and Sam barely dodged that one, too. The figure swung again, and Sam tumbled backward and into the wall. The attacks came with fury, each faster than the next, until Sam tilted his head and a rock-like package of knuckles pounded through the sheetrock wall.

"Sam!" the spy heard his partner say over the radio. There was no time to respond.

Sam threw his own fist toward his attacker's face, but the man quickly blocked it with his forearm. The absence of light in the room only made the clash more disorienting. Shadows and fists cutting with rage through the darkness. Before Sam could even prepare to strike again, the man hit him square in the face. The impact felt like a rogue fastball. Even in the dark room Sam saw stars circulating in his vision.

Another strike came, sharp and quick, and it rattled his skull like a jab to the face from a heavyweight champion. Unlike a padded glove, though, he felt as if every square inch of bone had connected with his face. The attacker pinned Sam to the wall by his shoulders, and Sam used the only thing left he had available, his knee, as his next weapon of choice.

The spy's leg connected with the man's gut, sending him staggering back toward the center of the room. Sam's enemy, as if he'd felt no pain at all, lunged back toward Sam before he could even prepare his next defense. Sam raised a fist, but the figure hooked Sam one good across his cheek so hard he felt the pain return in the same area where Whelan had already punished him. Sam had already been hit in that cheek—the left—enough times that it was just perpetually sore.

Broken bones supposedly healed stronger, but Sam was beginning to wonder if his had suffered far too much over the years. A broken plate could only be fixed so many times before the cracks were irreparable. Sam turned his face to reorient himself, but another jab connected with the bridge of his nose before he even regained awareness of the attacker. The assault came *fast*: one punch to the gut, another uppercut that made his head dance, then yet another jab to the sternum that knocked the wind out of him and sent him gasping for air.

The attacker grabbed Sam by the torso like a rag doll and hurled him across the room. His body plummeted into a small desk, shattering the legs and forcing it to collapse. The spy attempted to rise to his feet, even if he didn't know which way was up or down, but a heavy boot smacked across his jaw and put him back down for good. The kick caused his radio earpiece to fly out of his ear, and he heard the plastic clatter across the wood floor as his head smacked down against it in unison. He reached for the small piece, but the same boot that had ended his chances of fighting back came down hard on his wrist, and Sam turned to find the tall man towering above him.

Sam gasped, looking to snag just one good breath of air. He'd been stuck somewhere in between coughing and choking. The oxygen came back slowly, as if he'd needed to jumpstart his lungs into working again, and the figure walked swiftly across the room. Sam was momentarily incapacitated. The man flicked the switch on the desk lamp, turned toward Sam, and he saw the face of the man he'd already known was responsible for the brutal assault: Rudy.

"You will stay down," Rudy said in broken English rich with his Germanic enunciation. He removed a pistol from behind his waistband and pointed it toward Sam to ensure he'd understood the command. Sam hadn't even considered fighting again, especially not with a gun drawn on him. That was the second time he'd had the barrel of a gun pointed at him in only a few hours—and by two different *sides* no less. He'd finally achieved some decent respiration and the starry-eyed effect from the beating subsided in the now well-lit room.

"Help," Sam tried to say with ragged breath toward the radio. "H-Help." Rudy's attention turned to the tiny radio earpiece near Sam's head. He walked over to it, and though Sam tried to grab for it once more—if only to sabotage it—Rudy swiped it before he could reach it and examined it between his fingers.

The spy had been blindsided by the man. His instincts that the foreman resembled a soldier more than a miner were correct—his fighting style was quick and efficient. Sam, as confident in his own methodology of fighting as he was, stood no chance against the warrior. Rudy hadn't even drawn the gun in the first place, because he hadn't *needed* to. Or perhaps, Sam thought, because he also couldn't afford to blow his cover. Now the gun he pointed at Sam was only there to keep him in line. Sam had been bested.

Rudy crouched above Sam, pressed the barrel of the gun against his chest, then searched the spy with his free hand. He discovered Sam's revolver, emptied the cylinder of its bullets, then tossed the firearm on to the bed. He found Sam's bag and dumped its contents carelessly all over the floor. The camera and lens hit the wood floor, both with loud *cracks*. Sam shuddered when he heard the sound of shattered glass—his poor lens.

Rudy grabbed the exposed rolls of film, then tore at them vigorously. He opened the camera's rear door, ripped the half-exposed roll of film from its body, then tossed that aside, too. He carelessly dropped the camera onto the floor, which made Sam wince at the crunching sound once more. The ache of his precious gear suffering damage was beginning to hurt more than the pain in his body.

Rudy pushed all of the contents from the bag around with the toe of his boot. The documents Sam had received from The Yard spilled from the folder. He wished he'd disposed of them as directed, but he hadn't. That was an amateur move. Sam found it all quite invasive—he should know, he was a master of the art.

"You are taking pictures," Rudy said. "No more." Rudy dug into the pocket of his coverall, retrieved a pair of handcuffs and tossed them to Sam. "You will put these on."

"And if I don't?" Sam asked. Rudy drew the gun at his head. Sam had no choice. As humiliating as the whole ordeal had been, there were no further options. Sam put the handcuffs on.

The sound of the opening foyer door below echoed through the main hall. *Cat.* Sam opened his mouth to speak, but Rudy drew the gun to his face and said, "Quiet."

He wanted to scream, to tell her to run the other way. Maybe she'd play it cool and act as if she knew nothing. After all, Cat's cover hadn't been blown yet.

Sam heard Cat's heels traveling up the stairs, then Rudy pointed the gun toward the door. Cat barreled through it, a look of shock and confusion spread across her face as her eyes darted between Rudy and Sam. "Quiet," Rudy said. He waved her over toward Sam with the gun, then retrieved yet another pair of handcuffs from his pocket. He threw them to Cat, who caught them clumsily in her hands.

Cat looked to Sam for the next step. He only nodded to encourage her to do what she was told. As Cat placed the handcuffs over her wrists, the look of defeat and humiliation that formed on her face was unlike any he'd ever seen.

Rudy told her, "Sit."

It occurred to Sam that Cat was no stranger to handcuffs, and the familiar feeling of cold metal clasped around each of her tiny wrists must be an unwelcome memory. When she slumped to her knees, her head fell forward in a melancholic bow. Rudy reached toward her face, then ripped the earpiece from her ear. Cat turned to Sam with the sad, drooping eyes of a confused dog.

"Up," Rudy said, and he waved the gun toward the door. Both spies descended the spiral staircase, and he marched them outside with the firearm aimed at their backs.

The end of Rudy's gun barrel did all the talking the German did not as he led Sam and Cat from the guest house. Their captor paused for a moment on the front lawn, then scratched at his chin as he considered his options. He hadn't thought his plan through so well, it seemed, and was probably contemplating how to get the attention of his boss. If he took Kearney away for a moment, perhaps leaving Ives and his wife behind with only the company of Moreno, it might seem suspicious. After some time they'd certainly start to wonder where Cat was, and shortly after that, Kearney—that was *if* Ives wasn't in on the mess. But Sam still didn't suspect him.

Sam considered that Rudy might just take them both off into the woods and do the job himself. It was unlikely Kearney would give a damn if Rudy did them both in. Once Kearney's operation was in motion, he'd probably have liaisons taking care of the rest and intermediaries to see to it that any supply ready to ship made its way to the fatherland.

"What's going to happen to us?" Cat asked Sam, her voice shaky.

"We'll be alright," Sam replied sympathetically. He was lying. There was *never* any guarantee that spies were going to be 'alright,' but he didn't need to let her know that. "I've escaped worse situations."

"No more talking," Rudy said, and he reminded both parties that he was armed by directing the barrel of the gun between both of their faces. Rudy's attention turned to a small wooden outhouse at the corner of the guest house property. Though the magnificent homes had been retrofitted with proper bathrooms, the old habits of the farm died hard, and Sam was sure that the workers still used them frequently.

"There," Rudy said, and he pointed the gun toward the slim wooden shack. It occurred to Sam that Rudy would attempt to lock them both inside. Sam took the opportunity to consider how he might finagle his way out of the hostage situation as he and Cat walked toward the shack. Even with his hands cuffed behind his back, there were still ways to draw attention to their predicament. If Ives was still on the good team—and Sam strongly considered he was by the way Kearney had weaseled his way through the transaction—then Sam could alert the homeowners to the foul motives of the men who'd infiltrated their lives.

When they arrived at the outhouse, Rudy said, "In." Sam shook his head to signal Cat to go first, then he made like he was going to follow her in. He'd have to make a scene. Though the worst thing spies could do was draw attention to themselves, he didn't have much choice left. Undoing the work that had been done in D.C. was not in Sam's best interest, but Rudy was likely running out of options himself—and where the hell was Whelan now that Sam actually *needed* him?

Rudy made to close the outhouse door, and the moment he was down a free hand, Sam delivered a swift crack to his enemy's skull with the front of his own. The attack worked—Rudy fell clumsily to the grassy lawn and blind-fired his pistol into the open field. The shot would be heard for miles. Sam, though his hands were useless, charged his captor once more to prevent him from rising to his feet. Rudy scrambled for the gun frantically, digging through the shadowy grass and feeling around, but before he could find it Sam fell onto him with both knees.

"Run!" Sam commanded Cat, and she barreled out of the outhouse, then set across the field toward the guest house. He was merely buying time, enough for Cat to get out of harm's way. Rudy delivered an iron fist to Sam's jaw that sent him falling to the ground. The spy wound up flat on his face and unable to climb to his feet. Rudy retrieved the gun, aimed it at Sam to remind him who was in charge, then kicked him once more to the ground with a punishing thrust of his foot. He took aim toward Sam's fleeing partner.

Sam searched for her, and found her sprinting across the lawn, a silhouetted figure obscured by darkness caught somewhere in between the main house and the guest house. Sam swung a foot toward the back of Rudy's leg, and his captor fell backward. Sam's lack of a free hand was making for a difficult fight, but he'd use his teeth if that's what it took to see that Cat fled safely.

Rudy rose to his feet again, Sam to his knees. The

spy was struggling, desperately attempting to subdue his enemy despite a lack of any appendage of value. Rudy, fond of his boots, delivered a heel to Sam's mouth that put him down once more. The creak of a door opening in the distance gave Sam hope—had the noise he'd made sent in reinforcements?

Sam watched the German take aim. A shot rang out, another crack that rippled across the farm. *No*, Sam thought. *Not again*. Fear boiled inside of him—a worry that yet again an asset had been killed on his watch. But when Sam caught sight of Rudy's gun, it was not aimed toward Cat any longer, but held pointed to the sky in submission, along with his free hand.

"What the hell's going on here?" Ives demanded to know. Sam looked to the homeowner, and saw Cat frozen in the middle of no man's land between the two parties. Now, Ives was the one with Cat in the sights of his rifle, and Abigail, Kearney, and Moreno trailed behind him. Ives took inventory of the players, his cheek snug against the rifle's stock as he redirected the gun toward Sam. No one spoke. "Somebody better start talking or I'll let the rifle start."

Kearney stepped forward, and with a slithering, snake-like quality in his voice, he said, "It seems that everyone is not who they *say* they are." He sauntered toward Cat. "Rudy is quite good at determining who is and is *not* what they seem." Kearney stopped in front of Cat with a smirk on his face that seemed to say, 'I've got you.'

"Who the hell is he?" Ives asked, nodding toward Sam.

To tell Ives the truth wouldn't necessarily free him. He was the one in cuffs, and at the moment Kearney was still in good standing. He'd had a long-lasting relationship with Moreno and it was likely to be the Spanish *infante de gracia's* word over Sam's own. He'd also risk Kearney denying the information and fleeing. To lie further might see to it he and Cat would wind up six feet under—the burden of proof lay with the spy.

"He's an infiltrator," Kearney said. "Which organization do you work for, my friend? Who has paid you to come steal the secrets of these innocent people? Tell us who you are."

"You first," Sam replied.

"What's he talking about, Kearney?" Ives asked.

Rudy reached into his pocket, then presented the two radio earpieces to Kearney. The menace scrutinized them in the palm of his hand, then displayed them for Ives to see. "Impressive technology," Kearney said. "No doubt proprietary."

"What in the hell is it?" Ives asked, never relaxing his grip on the gun he held aimed at Sam.

"A radio, it seems," Kearney replied. "And judging by the fact that Mr. Moreno's guest is currently the other party in handcuffs, I'd say it's safe to assume the two were communicating."

"What gives, Salazar?" Ives asked.

"I know nothing of this," Moreno said. He marched toward Cat, towering above her as she attempted to hide her guilt. "Is this true?" he asked.

"No, Salazar," Cat cried. "I don't know who that man is."

"Of course she does," Kearney replied. "That's why she arrived to the party with him last night." Moreno turned once more to Cat, who couldn't hide her surprise that Kearney had been aware of their presence. "Paul Rilyeh, am

I correct?" Kearney smiled deviously at Sam. "A quick check of the guest list told me everything I needed to know." Now, Kearney focused on Cat, then said, "Catherine McAlister, convicted offender in the custody—or *formerly* in the custody—of the Pennsylvania State Penitentiary. She's got a list of offenses, documents of which could stretch across the Atlantic—armed robbery, theft, extortion, breaking and entering, accomplice to murder. I wonder how she got into *this* game." Moreno couldn't have hidden the shock on his face if he'd tried. The man was utterly perplexed, and the rapid movement of his eyes signaled that not only was he dumbfounded, but embarrassed. He'd been the one to bring her on the trip, and he'd fallen for the ruse.

Sam was blindsided by the information as well. How *much* had Brandt known before placing her in his employ? Had the crazy bastard broken her free? But despite his confusion, she was on his team, and right now they were *both* in trouble.

"Since we're talking fake names," Sam said, "perhaps Mr. Kearney will tell us his own." Rudy brought the gun down against Sam's brow with a painful crack. Sam's face hit the ground, his cuffed hands unable to break his fall, but he quickly rose once more to his knees. Sam shook the blow off, then turned to Kearney and asked, *"Ist Vergeltung nahe?"*

"What'd he just say?" Ives asked. He questioned Sam, "You some kind of Kraut?"

Kearney's eyes glowed with rage, the dark spheres of his pupils widening as Sam waited for a response. Sam addressed Ives, whose barrel was still pointed directly at his face. "No use prancing around it any longer," Sam said. "If you're in the business of dealing with Nazis, then by all means, make it quick and don't let that gun linger in my face. If not, then I'd point it just a few feet to my left."

"It's true," Cat blurted out. "Kearney's a liar. They want your tungsten for war machines. Go dig through their belongings. They've got a briefcase with the plans and they're going to ship it all to Germany."

"That's a lie!" Kearney growled.

"But it's not," Sam retorted. "Mr. Ives, if you go up to Kearney's room, you'll find my bag. Inside of it, you'll see your friend Salazar's correspondence with the Germans. We've been on to him for months. If that's not proof enough, then I don't know what is." It seemed the paperwork Sam had kicked himself for not disposing of *had* proved handy.

Ives turned the gun toward Salazar with an expression of utter betrayal forming on his face. "Salazar?" he asked. "Is that true?"

"Point that gun away from my face," Moreno warned Ives.

"If I go up there, what am I going to find?" Ives asked.

Moreno's eyes shifted nervously toward Kearney, then without warning, Moreno grabbed the barrel of the gun from Ives' grip and pushed it away from his torso. Ives fired, and the shot ricocheted with a chaotic *ping* off of the roof of the guest house. Moreno shoved Ives with the butt of the rifle, then pulled it from his grasp and turned it back on the Carolinian. Abigail gasped in horror.

"Now just what the hell is this, Salazar?" Ives asked through panting breaths. The attack had knocked the wind out of him, but Ives had instinctively stepped backward to shield Abigail from harm.

Kearney shook his head from side to side, then said, "*All diese Arbeit. Wozu?*" Ives looked dumbfounded as Kearney spoke. When Kearney spoke again, it was with the thick dialect he'd been hiding all along. "So much time invested in making this a feasible transaction. Mr. Ives, you could have made a fortune. Now, things have become *difficult*."

"So it *is* true," Ives snarled. "I'd have put a bullet through your head myself had I known what type of shit you were pulling." Ives spat, turned to Moreno, then said, through gritted teeth, "And you as well."

"Of course you would," Kearney replied. "I'd have done the same myself. Now we must see to it that no one is able to talk about this mishap. This has turned into quite a mess."

"*Töte sie?*" Rudy asked.

"No," Kearney replied. "We've made enough ruckus already." Kearney sighed deeply, his eyes wandering to Sam, then to Cat, then to Ives, who was still shielding Abigail with a nasty scowl plastered on his face. "We'll need to make a *different* kind of noise." He said to Moreno, "Salazar, see to it that Mr. Ives and his wife keep quiet. If anyone comes asking questions, take care of it. Rudy and I will handle this. If Mr. Ives or his wife give you any trouble, kill them."

"You're a son of a bitch, Salazar," Ives said.

"That may be," the Spaniard replied.

"After all that time," Ives said. "How much is he paying you? How much is selling your country—your *friends*—worth?"

Moreno said nothing. Instead, he waved the gun

toward the house. Without options, Ives grabbed Abigail's hand and walked toward it.

Kearney placed both of his hands on his hips and gave Sam a disappointed look. "Do we have the materials to begin blasting currently on site?" he asked Rudy, who nodded. "Good, then I don't see why we should have to wait any longer."

21

___

The captive party set out across the field under the watchful gaze of their enemies and made the trek toward the mine on foot. The dark property made it difficult to see even their own footing, but they followed the road carved out by the trucks as it snaked up the side of the ridge. Rudy trailed behind them with his pistol in hand, and Sam and Cat walked side by side with Kearney nearby.

"Don't suppose you're willing to let us walk?" Sam asked.

"I'm afraid not," Kearney said with a soft laugh. "You're nuisances, like flies." He'd given up the American performance completely, and even though his voice now had the tinge of his mother tongue, he still spoke English exceptionally well. "I'm not going to let two little flies buzzing about ruin all the work it took to get this far."

"Seems like quite a mess if you ask me," Sam said.

"On the contrary," Kearney replied. "It is a simple

tragedy. Two bandits arrived late one evening to the Ives' ranch, killed Mr. Ives and his wife, then ventured into the mine where they were crushed in an unfortunate collapse. It seems the two bandits thought the mine was rife with gold. They were inexperienced, and after they'd brutally murdered the farmer and his wife, they ventured late into the night into unstable tunnels where blasting had been scheduled. Their bodies were discovered quite some time afterwards."

"So that's how you're going to play it?" Sam asked.

"Something like that," Kearney replied. "I'll have plenty of time to work out the narrative while we take what we can."

"By the time you've gotten what you came for, people will start asking questions about the whereabouts of Mr. Ives," Sam said.

"It seems that Mr. Ives bequeathed his estate to his old friend, Salazar Moreno," Kearney replied. He had it all figured out.

"Moreno's already in deep," Sam replied. "His usefulness will be short-lived."

"No matter," Kearney said. "The gun pointed at his head—metaphorical, of course—will keep him in line. Moreno is an unfortunate puppet being pulled by strings he can't even see. His strings *will* snap, but by that time I'll be back home."

"And where's that?"

"Peenemünde," Kearney replied matter-of-factly.

"Peene-what-a?" Sam asked.

"*Peenemünde.*"

"Never heard of it."

"Few have."

"You put on a good show, Kearney," Sam said.

Kearney smiled, then tilted his head to Cat. "Haven't we all?" Cat's gaze averted his. "It's Ramm," Kearney said. "Udo Ramm, *Ressourcenbeauftragter der Forschungseinrichtung Peenemünde.*"

"Sounds like a made-up title if I've ever heard of one," Sam said. "Sometimes I think you guys just get kicks out of formulating new titles. The more complex the better."

"You are funny, Mr....." Ramm realized he didn't know his enemy's name. "What is it? I know that Rilyeh is too silly a name for a real man to take."

"Sam Abel," the spy replied.

Ramm's face glowed with liveliness and curiosity. "Abel, you say? *Kommst du aus Deutschland?*"

"Among other places," Sam replied. "Your english is good. What gives?"

"I was here before the war broke out," Ramm said. "The fatherland called, and I answered. When opportunity knocks, you open the door. Now it seems I've found myself here again. What's your excuse?"

Sam didn't answer. Instead, he pivoted. "So, *Heer*? *Luftwaffe*?"

"A little bit of both," Ramm said. "The exact translation of my occupation is a bit difficult, but..." Ramm ruminated on the title for a moment, then said, "Something like, Resource Officer for the Peenemünde Research Facility."

"Fancy title," Sam replied. "And what do you research there?"

"No, no, Mr. Abel," Ramm said, and he wagged a finger back and forth as he smirked. "Some secrets are better left untold. I might afford you the luxury of knowing *who* delivers your death, but nothing more."

"Thanks for the courtesy," Sam replied. "Let me parlay with you."

"I'm listening," Ramm said. Sam looked back toward the captor in the rear—Rudy's gun was still fixed on both him and Cat. Without a way out of the cuffs, he was left with no alternative but to try to get Cat out alive with whatever information she could funnel to Brandt. "Let the girl go. I'm the one who put her up to it. She knows nothing other than what's been said here tonight."

"And that is far too much," Ramm replied. "It's unfortunate that she has been caught up in this scenario we've found ourselves in, but no one will be leaving knowing anything about what's taken place. Besides, she's become far too valuable to the narrative, what with her history and all." Cat's ears perked up, and Ramm slowed his step to address her. Ramm smiled. "Yes, my dear. You've ruined this plan, and now you'll be the one to fix it. I can read the headline now," Ramm said, and he waved his hand in a grand arc as if imagining the newspaper title: **"Escaped Convict Allies with Nazi Expat to Steal Gold."**

Cat had no poker face. She looked to Sam briefly, as if to see if he'd noticed the guilt in her expression. Ramm frowned, "Oh, did he not know? My, my," he said, then he smirked once more at Sam. "All the actors in the little play with their big secrets."

"They could have cast someone better for you," Sam replied defiantly. "There's no way you'd be a leading man with that face."

Ramm drew his hand down the side of his cheek, "Oh this. A dueling *schmiss*, as I'm sure you're aware— and I should note, the only exhibition I've *ever* lost. I was quite handy with the blade. My first duel was the only in which I was scarred. I was undefeated thereafter. I've set that particular hobby aside, though. It's all a bit barbaric when you get down to it. Still, where I come from, the *schmiss* is a sign you should be shown respect."

"Name a price," Sam said. "My boss can pay. What do you want? Immunity? Asylum?"

"You're missing the point completely, Mr. Abel," Ramm said. "I'm not for hire. I'm here to ensure these resources get to where they need to go. No amount of coaxing could turn me against the project."

"Why such loyalty to *them*?" Sam asked.

"As I said," Ramm replied, "loyalty to the *project*."

"Why here?" Sam asked. "Why go through all the trouble to get them from us?"

"Supply and demand," Ramm replied. "Tungsten is an invaluable resource—and one which we have become quite dependent on. It is clear that we will not have an ally in Spain for long, and the only other large reserves exist on Chinese soil. That puts us in a bind. One cannot ensure the weapons are produced in mass without it. The tools required to *machine* the weapons are reliant upon the material. Tungsten is incredibly resilient. Other lesser metals bend to its will." Ramm stopped himself, then a thin smile formed on his lips. "I've said too much already."

"The last time I was in the proximity of one of your weapons, I blew it to high hell, along with a company of your men."

Ramm stopped walking immediately, then approached Sam slowly and read his face. Suddenly, he showed great interest in the spy. "You?"

Sam nodded coyly. "How about this?" he said. "Tell

me where Eichler is and I'll spare you when this is all over."

"*You*," Ramm said with great intensity. He surveyed Sam's figure as if it was the first time he was meeting him. Ramm was analyzing him all over again with renewed interest. "What a trophy I would earn if I was to deliver you up. You made great waves, Mr. Abel— great waves *indeed*." Ramm continued walking, and the rest followed. "But no matter. It's not worth the risk of whisking you back to the fatherland. To kill you here would be just as meaningful. I'll be sure to tell everyone at home about the great prize I captured in America." Ramm set his sights on the dirt path ahead. The road was becoming steeper with every step they took. "We're almost there."

They paused at the mouth of the deep hole, and Rudy gathered dynamite. The grunt also grabbed a long cord Sam knew would be used to blast the mine from a safe distance. There was irony in the idea that he might meet his death in the same way in which he'd destroyed the super tank only months earlier. They were going to be buried alive. If they were lucky, the blast might make their deaths quick and painless. There was the option of the pill, a quick, painless exit to be utilized if necessary, but Sam was not sure Cat had been given one.

Sam whispered to Cat, "It's going to be alright." Her eyes looked as if they'd shed tears at any moment. He could see that she did not believe him, but it was in Sam's nature to maintain a good attitude. "Nothing to say?" Cat shook her head from side to side. As Rudy continued to collect the resources needed to dispose of the spies, Sam was attempting to convince even himself that there was still a way out of this.

They traveled through the dark shaft where the tunnel had been bored out, Rudy in the rear leaving no route of escape, and Cat and Sam wedged between him and Ramm. They rode the elevator to the floor where Sam had first learned more about Ramm's true identity. Sporadic, barely adequate lighting made the trip gloomy. If doom awaited Sam and Cat, the ambiance would prove aesthetically appropriate.

When the lift stopped in the cavernous stope, Rudy waved his gun toward both parties, instructing them to walk down yet another tunnel Sam had not explored. Inside the tunnel, Sam noted that small holes had been drilled in very precise patterns. Sam took stock of one of the patterns as he continued through, which had been shaped in the form a plus sign of five holes, with one reaching in each cardinal direction and one in the center.

"Here," Rudy said, and he pointed to one of the rock walls that had been drilled out.

"Good," Ramm said, then turned to Sam and Cat. "Well, I believe this is as far as we go." Rudy secured a fuse to each of the cylindrical sticks, then shoved them into the corresponding holes. "If we're going to do the job," Ramm said, "then we might as well do it right. There's no use wasting good explosives."

Ramm smiled at Cat. "Ms. McAlister, though I don't appreciate your meddling, it all seems to have worked out." Cat grimaced. "Mr. Abel," he said, and a victorious grin crept from ear to ear as he stared at the spy, "we all lose at some point or another."

Ramm set off back toward the elevator, and Rudy kept the gun pointed at the spies, slowly unwinding the spool of fuse line as he retreated down the dark corridor.

He grabbed a large sheet of wood that had been resting against a nearby rock wall, then placed it over the mouth of the hole and tapped several nails through the support beams with a hammer. Soon the Germans were out of view, and the two spies were shrouded in near-darkness. Sam, though he could see nothing, wasted no time searching for an option. A small sliver of light crept through a crack where the pieces of wood didn't meet, which provided just enough light to see their surroundings.

"I need your help," Cat mumbled.

"We need to find a way out of here," Sam said, "And fast."

"Then help me," Cat said again as if chewing on tacks. Her lips parted slightly, and the reflection of gold appeared between her front teeth. Upon closer inspection, Sam discovered it to be an earring.

She undid the clasp with two teeth, then turned the piece over in her mouth and bit down to slightly bend the metal. Sam hustled over, then Cat said, "Turn around." Sam turned his back to her. "Hold out your hands and cup them." Sam was intrigued, and he followed the direction without protest. "I'm going to spit this into your hands—*don't* drop it. I can barely see a damn thing in here. Ready?"

"Ready," Sam replied. She spat the earring out, and Sam felt the moist jewelry fall into the palm of his hand.

"So that's why you were so quiet," Sam said. "I was beginning to think you were actually worried."

"I was," Cat said. "I thought *you* had a plan." Then she turned her back to him and said, "Alright, now hand it back to me. Sam fidgeted with the earring between several of his fingers, then carefully made the hand-off.

"Got it?" he asked.

"Yes, now stand still." Cat pressed the earring against Sam's cuffs, and he could hear the small tin pin rattling around inside.

"You've done this before," Sam said with a chuckle.

"Quiet!" Cat snapped. "I'm concentrating." Cat bit down on her lip, fiddled with the small earring once more, then the clasp fell and Sam's hand was freed.

"And here I was thinking that was the end for us," Sam said.

"It *will* be if you don't get mine off," Cat barked. "Do you know what you're doing?"

"No," Sam replied.

Cat huffed, then handed him the earring. "Alright," she said. "Insert the pin until you feel the small clasp. Press as hard as you can and depress the pin. There's a small ratchet in place that you need to disengage."

"You should be teaching this to our operatives," Sam said.

"A girl's got to keep *some* secrets," Cat replied. Sam fiddled with the mechanism clumsily. The tunnel was silent save for the clatter of the pin inside the cuff. He went on like that for some time until Cat huffed impatiently. "What's going on?"

"I'm trying," Sam said.

"Turn it a bit when you do it," Cat said hastily. Sam did so, and the cuff finally fell off. "Gimme," she demanded, and she took the earring from him. She undid his other cuff, then finished the one on her other wrist and tossed both cuffs aside. "Now you're up."

He was impressed. Perhaps Brandt's gratuitous spending did provide some value after all. With all the fancy tools at The Yard's disposal, it had been a simple piece of jewelry that had freed them—jewelry that Brandt had surely paid for.

Sam searched the interior of the cave. Without any tools, he'd be forced to rely on brute force. He sprinted toward the makeshift door, and attempted to pry it with his fingers. It didn't budge. "Stand back," he instructed Cat, then thrust a heavy foot into the wood panel. It budged, but didn't come free. He lifted his foot again, then slammed it into the wall with more might—still nothing.

Despite the danger in doing so, he resolved to use his shoulder to add more weight into the impact, and thrust all of his weight into the door. The nails screeched. He tried again, but the force wasn't enough.

"On three?" Cat asked. Sam nodded.

He counted the numbers out loud, and on three, both partners plowed into the wood panel. Their inertia was so great that when the wood finally came free they tumbled on top of it. Sam helped Cat up. "Let's go," he said. "Carefully."

They traveled with caution down the long tunnel until finally they saw the elevator shaft. Of course, the machine had been used, so all that was present was a seemingly bottomless pit that provided no point of safe exit. Sam pressed the "call" button, but no noise came from the shaft. "They turned it off," Sam said.

"Ives said they'd already cleared some of the mine, right?"

"That's right," Sam said.

"Well then there's got to be some other way out of here."

The long tunnel that the miners had disappeared into earlier in the day drew Sam's interest. It was the only other exit he could find. A hissing sound emanated from the long shaft below—the fuse cable rattled.

"What is that?" Cat asked.

Sam looked down into the black abyss. The noise grew louder, and next he saw a faint flicker of light climbing up the dark hole. He squinted to get a better look. He didn't need to see it to know: Rudy was prepping the demolition.

Sam grabbed Cat forcefully by the hand, and the two ran away from the shaft and into yet another long, dark hole.

"I can't see a thing!" Cat yelled.

"You'll never see anything again if you don't keep moving!" Sam argued.

After several moments of traveling down the corridor—the interior of which was a cool and unwelcoming rock prison of its own—Sam perceived a change in the light toward the end. Whatever lay ahead, it was the only option left for escape.

"There!" Sam yelled, and both he and Cat double-timed their speed when Sam yanked her hand. Just as they approached the mouth of the hole, a blast rocked the ridge with a rolling roar like thunder. They both leapt from the opening of the mine, and Sam pushed Cat to the floor and covered her with his own body. Dirt and debris spewed from the hole, and tiny rocks pummeled his back and torso. The explosion grew silent as the dust settled, and when the cloud of shattered rock finally dissipated, Sam helped Cat to her feet.

"Happy Fourth of July," Sam said. Cat scoffed at the comment. He'd finally gotten a rise out of her. Both spies wiped the dirt from their bodies, then Sam stepped forward to get a better view of the farm below. They were on another ridge, higher even than where Sam had set up his camp to watch the action below. Sam looked at Cat, his eyes flaring with ferocity and determination—a callousness that appeared every so often—then he said, "Let's try this again, shall we?"

The path back down the ridge was a series of thin switchbacks. Foot traffic had carved it out neatly as it sloped back down, and without much available light, it was the only route Sam and Cat had available. Taking a direct route back to the farm would be treacherous—the ridge was thick with foliage and so steep that one bad fall could send them tumbling down the cliffs. Sam couldn't see where the path led, but the overall route seemed to be taking him back near the mine's main entrance. Once they were there, the path back to the farm would be easy to navigate.

"Wait just a minute," Cat pleaded. "Do you have a plan?"

"Rarely," Sam replied.

"I can tell."

"Stopping Ramm would be a good start," Sam said.

"What about Moreno?" Cat asked.

"He's a bonus." Sam growled, "I want *Ramm*."

"I didn't sign up for this," Cat replied with trepidation.

His eyes narrowed in that callous way again. "Then sign off."

Sam continued on the path, and Cat followed reluctantly. The final descent led to the clearing where the trucks had been parked, and Sam placed a hand in front of Cat's chest to stop her from proceeding. "Wait," he cautioned. Cat did so. She'd appeared to have had enough action for the night, and perhaps, her career.

Sam walked softly into the clearing using one of the nearby trucks as cover. The enemy was still lurking, and Sam had the element of surprise no longer. Though they'd left them for dead, Sam knew his enemies would remain on high alert. He flanked one of the trucks—a flatbed with a massive auger strapped to it—skirting along its side.

Only the sound of his own footsteps displacing dirt met his ears. The property was quiet. That might mean the path ahead was free and clear. Sam knew that quiet could also mean danger. His senses sharp, particularly his hearing, he paused and listened momentarily for the sounds of movement.

The *crack* of a gunshot ripped through the dirt field, and the ricochet of sparks that followed sprayed Sam's face. Sam recognized the sound of the gun instantly: it was the .38 revolver he'd brought with him. Now they were trying to kill him with his *own* weapon. He darted behind the nose of the truck, which caught the next two bullets that followed, and instinctively dropped low to the dirt floor. A pair of feet shuffled along the path, then disappeared behind a set of massive rubber tires.

Sam rolled under the truck, leapt to his feet, then ran to take cover. He climbed up the step to the truck's driver-side door, peeked into the side view mirror on the passenger side, and saw the faint black figure of a man's shadow briefly before it disappeared into the darkness: Rudy. This time, Sam *knew* his enemy was lurking.

Inside the cabin of the truck, the sharp edge of a pickaxe twinkled. Sam opened the door quietly, retrieved the tool, then hopped back down from the truck's step. The axe was heavy in his hand. Either side had a point sharp enough to penetrate a man's skull. It wasn't a .38, but it was better than nothing. Feet hitting dirt pattered beside him, and Sam choked up on his grip of the axe, then brought it close to his chest.

At the rear of the truck, a shape appeared, and Sam took cover behind the open driver's side door. Rudy fired another two shots, both of which clanged against the steel door chaotically. Sam ran around the front end, then searched below for Rudy's location once more. He saw nothing.

This game couldn't last for long, of that Sam was sure. Rudy had fired five shots, and the firearm only carried six rounds of ammunition, so Rudy only had one more attempt to shoot him—*if* he was only armed with one gun. He prayed Cat would stay silent under the cover of night.

Sam approached the rear of the truck's semitrailer with the most graceful of steps. The spy had mastered the art of producing virtually no sound when walking, but so too had Rudy it seemed. Despite the man's large stature, he had been incredibly adept at getting the jump on Sam *twice* now. His enemy had military training— very *good* training—and Sam understood why Ramm had chosen him as company on his trip to America. He wasn't just a miner—he was Ramm's *muscle*.

Inhaling softly, Sam gripped the axe, then turned the corner of the semitrailer. The next bullet came fast and without warning, and almost tore through Sam's bicep. He barely had time to react to the shot before he realized that Rudy was standing right in front of him pointing the gun in his face.

Rudy pulled the trigger, but the gun only produced a thin *click*. Sam barely flinched. The German's face twisted into a contorted expression of surprise.

Sam swung the axe, the sharp point of which connected with the gun in Rudy's hand with a metallic clang. The gun went tumbling into the dirt, and Rudy gripped his hand. Surely the impact had caused him agony, but when Sam swung the axe once more in the opposite direction of his torso, Rudy leapt back instinctively.

Sam swung once more with the opposite end of the blade, shuffling toward Rudy with large strides every time he attempted a strike. The smile on Rudy's face grew larger with every attack he made—he was *enjoying* it. Sam's arms became tired, and the last swing connected with the wall of the semitrailer, showering sparks across both of their faces. Rudy saw his window and grabbed the axe himself. Now both his and Sam's hands were gripping it, and the men met face to face as each attempted to direct one of the two points into each other's face. One man would break, and Sam was unconvinced he could force the opposing end toward his attacker.

"I assumed you were clever," Rudy said through gritted teeth. "That is why I stayed behind." Sam attempted to force the axe forward with all the force he had, but the pointed edge of the blade only grew closer to his own face. The spaghetti-like vein in Rudy's forehead throbbed, and even in the darkness Sam could see Rudy's face grow more red. Sweat gathered on the man's skin, and the smile on his mouth became only more maniacal as he pushed harder.

Sam roared to try to gather more power, a guttural, primal growl that beckoned the strength deep inside him. Rudy only laughed as Sam attempted to push the axe forward. It was a *game* to Rudy, who was probably using only half of the muscle groups Sam currently was. Sam felt the sweat in between his fingers making his grip on the wooden handle less than adequate, and Rudy growled himself as if to match's Sam's own animalistic cry.

The axe would slip from Sam's hands at any moment. The edge of the tool was right between Sam's eyes, so close that the sharp point lost focus in Sam's vision. Rudy pushed harder, and now the blade was almost touching Sam's skin. The muscles in Rudy's forearms flexed grotesquely, and both men's arms began to tremble from the demands of the battle.

Rudy said, "First, I will drive this spike into your eyes, then I will go find the woman." His eyes flared, and Sam felt weakness in his arms that could cost him the fight at any second.

"Which woman?" a voice said from beside Sam, and Rudy turned to see who had spoken. Sam looked, too, expecting to see Cat standing by and ready to save his skin—but it wasn't Cat. It was *Adelaide*, and she was holding Ives' rifle in her arms and aiming at Rudy. She fired, but only delivered a warning shot into the air. Rudy lost focus on the battle at hand, and Sam twisted the butt of the axe up into his face. Rudy fell to his knees, then raised both of his hands in submission. Adelaide ejected the shell from the rifle, then cocked the bolt and loaded another. She looked at Sam, then announced herself: "Adelaide."

"Sam," the spy replied through struggling breaths.

Adelaide turned to the edge of the lot, then called out, "It's safe now." Cat materialized from the dark foliage, her face full of surprise. "We should get down there," Adelaide said to Sam. She grabbed the empty revolver and tossed it to him. "He's got Moreno under watch, and Ives and his wife are safe. I think Kearney fled."

"*Who's* got Moreno?" Sam asked.

"Whelan," Adelaide replied.

"You're FBI?" Sam asked. Adelaide gave him a thin smile, then handcuffed Rudy.

———

At the main house, the dining table still remained full of food and booze, but new guests had arrived, including Whelan and his unnamed partner. Ives and Abigail paced nervously around the table, and Moreno sat cuffed to the arm of the chair slouched in defeat. Whelan casually puffed on a cigarette when Sam, Cat, Rudy and Adelaide entered. He tilted his head toward Rudy, then nodded proudly toward Adelaide.

"Look who I found," Adelaide announced.

"Two out of three," Whelan replied.

"Where's Kearney?" Sam asked.

"Gone," Whelan replied. "Once he saw us coming," Whelan patted Moreno's shoulder gleefully, "and he knew his friend here was in for it, he skipped off and made for the hills."

"We've got to go after him," Sam said forcefully.

"Where to?" Whelan replied. "Don't even know the man's real name, do ya?"

"It's Ramm. Udo Ramm. Isn't that right, Salazar?" Sam asked Moreno mockingly. Moreno grunted, then an indiscernible mumble followed.

"What was that?" Whelan asked.

"I said you've misunderstood!" Moreno replied. "I know nothing of this man. I am innocent."

"Bull shit, you are," Ives said, and the Carolinian hauled off and hooked Moreno in the jaw. Moreno, unable to defend himself, took the full force of the punch. When he'd recovered, Ives moved to hit him again.

Whelan and his lackey restrained Ives—who looked like he was ready to go to town on the Spaniard. "Easy, now. We don't hit men that can't defend themselves," Whelan said.

Ives shrugged it off, fixed his tie, then paced away from the table to cool down. He called out toward Moreno, "I'd kill him dead right here if y'all weren't keeping guard."

"Be that as it may," Whelan said, "this man's got a whole lot of questioning coming his way, and he's no good to us if he can't talk."

"He'll talk alright," Sam said. He eyed Rudy. "We already tried him." Rudy scowled. The spy marched toward Moreno, bent down so his face met the man's, then asked, "Where did he go, Moreno?"

"I told you," Moreno replied through bloodied teeth. "I know nothing."

"Think you can convince a jury?" The spy nodded toward Whelan. "Your word against his?"

"Can *she?*" Moreno asked, and he smiled at Cat with his red-stained teeth. Cat hid her face shamefully. "Yes, I know things, too, now."

"Talk," Sam said with a snarl, but Moreno only flashed his crimson teeth.

"Your man's long gone," Whelan said to Sam. "Be happy you drove him away and let sleeping dogs lie. He ain't coming back."

Whelan's words didn't matter to Sam. The German had let slip that he was privy to high-value information. Ramm had known exactly what Sam was talking about when he'd spoken of his little "trip" to Germany, which meant that he was in with the upper echelons of Nazi society—Brandt would want him. Sam had been sent to gather information, but—as usual—he'd found himself in a much larger pickle. It was beginning to become a habit, but if Brandt could nab Ramm, who knew what types of information the man could cough up?

Sam grabbed a cigarette from his case. He hadn't had one in hours, and it was the only thing that would give him the clarity to decide whether to do what he was *itching* to do. Whelan was watching closely, and whatever action Sam took next would be scrutinized heavily. Regardless, there was no way Sam was leaving North Carolina with his hat in his hands—an FBI victory, compromised spies, and an escaped Nazi just wouldn't do. Sam casually sauntered over to Whelan's partner, then asked, "Got a light?"

The man nodded, then pulled a lighter from his pocket and cupped his hands around the tip of Sam's cigarette. As soon as the cigarette flared, Sam grabbed the pistol from the man's holster and pointed it against Moreno's thigh. The federal agent gasped, then Sam redirected the gun toward him briefly before saying, "Get back." Sam returned the gun to Moreno's thigh.

"*Ay Dios mío.* What are you doing?" Moreno yelped as he shifted nervously in his chair.

"I don't know if you want to do what you're about to do, son," Whelan warned Sam.

Sam ignored Whelan, who'd shifted his own hand to the pistol holstered on his belt. Sam said to Moreno, "This is the femoral artery. Do you know what that is?"

"N-no," Moreno replied.

"It's the major artery in your leg," Sam said as he pressed the barrel of the gun tighter against the man's thigh. "I pull this trigger, and you'll bleed out in short time." Moreno's body shuddered uncontrollably. "Mr. Ives," Sam said without breaking eye contact with Moreno, "how far are we from the nearest hospital?"

"*Too* far," Ives replied.

"Wade!" Abigail cried.

"Quiet," Ives snapped abruptly. "This man don't deserve no fair chance. He was gonna sell us down the river. As far as I'm concerned, I don't care if he becomes feed."

"Please, Wade!" Moreno cried out. "It's not my fault. I was forced—I *swear* it."

"Convince him," Ives said with a flick of his chin toward Sam. Moreno's old friend showed no remorse.

"You'd be making a big mistake, Abel," Whelan called out. He undid the strap that secured his gun in the holster. "That man's federal property now, and if he don't get home back to D.C. with us, there's gonna be hell to pay."

Sam pretended there was no one else present. It was he and Moreno now, and no one was going to come between them. He pressed the gun harder against Moreno's thigh, then inhaled from the cigarette that was tucked between his teeth before mumbling, "Where is Ramm going?"

Moreno, through wet, blood-spattered lips, cried, "You wouldn't shoot me. You wouldn't kill a consul. It would be treason!"

"Treason doesn't apply to me," Sam said. His eyes narrowed, and Moreno trembled. "Last time—where is Ramm going?"

"I have information," Moreno cried. "I can tell you so much."

"I don't care what you have to say about your cohorts," Sam said. "Not right now, at least."

"If you're going to kill me, then kill me," Moreno said defiantly. "You would be doing a disservice—"

Bang. The shot made everyone in the room flinch. Moreno screamed, but Sam remained focused. The gun was still pressed to the man's leg as he writhed in pain, flopping around in the seat like a fish out of water. Whelan removed his gun from his pistol and pointed it at Sam. Adelaide drew the rifle on the spy, too, and Sam heard Cat gasp from the corner of the room. Even with every gun in the room pointed at his face, Sam only saw Moreno and himself.

"Please, Wade!" Moreno cried out again. Ives couldn't help him. He, too, had been caught in the maelstrom that was Sam Abel. "I will give you names—names of those who give the orders!"

"That's just short of the artery," Sam said to Moreno. *Names are good,* Sam thought, *but Ramm is still in reach.*

He pressed the gun harder against Moreno's thigh, causing him further agony. Blood began to pool, seeping through Moreno's pants and forming a red stain that grew larger by the second. "You'll be alright if we patch that up in good time—the next one..." Sam took another drag from the cigarette. "I can't be so sure."

"Abel, you don't put the gun down and I'll kill you myself," Whelan said. Sam still showed no interest. He'd had enough of Whelan and his games. He'd let Brandt sort that out later. Right now, there was *only* Moreno.

"N-New York," Moreno choked out through whimpers.

"*Where* in New York?" Sam asked.

"A hotel," Moreno said, and tears started streaming down his cheeks.

"Be more specific," Sam demanded.

"I-I don't know!" Moreno cried.

Whelan yelled, "Damnit, Abel!"

Sam blocked the federal agent's request out. He said to Moreno, "Last chance."

Whelan pressed his gun against Sam's temple, and now it seemed as if *everyone* was pointing a gun at someone.

"The Park!" Moreno said as if pleading for Sam to stop. "The Park Hotel on Park and Madison!"

"That wasn't so hard, was it?" Sam asked, and he removed the gun from Moreno's thigh and handed it back to Whelan's partner. The man instinctively pointed it right back at Sam, but the spy showed no fear or remorse for his actions. He only took another satisfying drag from the cigarette. Whelan holstered his firearm.

Sam looked toward Cat and said, "Come on."

"Where are we going?" Cat asked.

"New York," Sam replied.

"The hell you are," Whelan yelled. "Only place you're going is back to D.C. in cuffs."

Sam ignored Whelan once more, grabbed Cat's hand, and exited the dining room without even acknowledging the agent's comments. Whelan, flummoxed, chased after the two spies.

"Hey!" Whelan yelled. "Abel!"

Sam stopped dead in his tracks in the main house's foyer, then turned to face Whelan, who nearly bumped into his face when he, too, stopped. "You want to shoot me, shoot me," Sam said. "But there's a man out there who's likely about to board a plane, and if we don't stop him, he's going to flee back to Germany with Nazi secrets—*good* ones." Sam exhaled the smoke from his cigarette, then stepped forward and locked eyes with Whelan. "Now I know your boss has got it out for mine, and their opinions of the rules differ greatly, but the truth is we're on the same team whether they like that or not. That man knows a lot about a lot, and there's no way in hell I'm going to let you hold me here while he prances off. I'm running out of time. You want to help, help, but if you're not going to see to it that he's stopped, then get out of my way and we can sort the rest of this out in D.C."

Whelan didn't respond. Instead, he only stared back at Sam with a skeptical intensity in his eyes. The federal agent gnawed on his lip for a moment, then slowly nodded. "Alright," Whelan said finally. "Then let's get to it. I'll get you there."

"You got a car?" Sam asked.

"Don't need one," Whelan replied.

23

The C-47 parked in the dirt field only a few short miles from the farm made Sam feel like he'd hit the lottery. It was a large plane, primarily designed for cargo and troop transport and ready and able to fly them back north. Despite all of the wonderful goodies Brandt had been able to afford for the SSD, he had yet to produce a vehicle like that.

The plane was painted an olive green, which meant that somehow Whelan had been afforded the luxury of some of the military's vehicles for his use. Just because Brandt didn't have many friends in D.C. didn't mean Sam couldn't make any. Whelan's partner had stayed behind with Moreno, and Abigail, who had a cursory knowledge of nursing, assured the men heading to hunt down Ramm that the injured party would be fine if she patched him up quickly. The bullet would need to be removed at a hospital, but she promised to stop any blood loss the man had suffered in its tracks.

Ives volunteered to take the trip back to D.C. with

Rudy, the agents, and Moreno. He'd told Sam and Whelan that it was to ensure that Rudy and Moreno didn't try anything stupid, but Sam suspected the farmer turned entrepreneur wanted to take the opportunity to clear his name. Sam didn't blame him. He'd been mingling with war criminals, and there was no way to do good business with a stain like that.

"Change of plans," Whelan said to the pilot. "We're going to Newark." The pilot gave him a thumbs up, then climbed into the plane. The propellers started up as soon as Sam, Cat, and Whelan took their seats. The pilot had been standing by, surely to allow for the speedy transportation of the apprehended Moreno, but the plane had been freed up when Ives offered up his own car to escort their captive to D.C.—the trip wouldn't be long if they drove straight through the night. Once the engines had gotten some good momentum, Sam could barely hear any noise other than the speedy rotations of the propellers.

"Let's get one thing straight," Whelan yelled as he buckled his seatbelt. "Moreno's ours. You can have this Ramm or Kearney or whatever his name is, but don't get any other ideas. Moreno's a federal case, and I'm going to have enough questions to answer about this as it is."

"Deal," Sam said.

"And keep your mouths shut," Whelan said.

"We're very good at that."

Whelan lit a cigarette, then waved it at Sam and said, "I knew there was *something* about you. You're a crazy son of a bitch."

"I've been told," Sam said.

"I just happen to like crazy," Whelan said with a smirk.

Despite the clear airways ahead of the C-47 and the luxury of priority travel, the trip to Newark wasn't quick. Sam thought the aircraft was a bit of a lumbering dog. He was nervous that Ramm had gotten a head start, and unless the plane could land in the middle of Central Park they'd be cutting it close. Heavy thunderstorms from a wave of heat forced the plane to circle the runway for nearly two hours. Every minute that ticked by forced Sam's heart rate to increase. The watch Sigrid had given him ticking away on his wrist was only another reminder of how badly he wanted to catch Ramm, and it only worked to make his rising anxiety worse.

Sam would still have to get to New York, and that would take another hour. Once he'd arrived, he'd have to actually discover where Ramm was hiding. If the man, who was going by an alias that would not raise any flags, was able to flee from the hotel before Sam arrived, he'd likely be on a flight to an occupied territory, or somewhere near one, before slipping back into his native land. Where would he go? Spain? France? Any option was *too* far.

Whelan stormed up to the cockpit and, Sam assumed, pulled rank. Eventually the pilot gave the signal that they were cleared to land, and Sam felt a fleeting moment of victory. Whelan had given the spy a change of clothes: olive aircraft fatigues for maintenance personnel that happened to fit Sam acceptably. He was happy to get out of the moist clothing. He hadn't had a shower in two days, and the coveralls were starting to stick to his skin. When he walked down the plane stairs and onto the runway, the temperature in New York started the sweaty cycle all over again. Luckily Whelan had called in another favor, and there was a government-issued sedan, black of course, waiting to pick them up right off the tarmac.

Before Sam climbed in the car, Cat hustled down to the bottom of the staircase, then stopped. Her eyes could not hide the worry she felt. The dress she'd been in since the early hours of the night rippled in the breeze of the idling propellers and made her appear angelic. Sam approached and placed his hand on her cheek affectionately.

"You did good," Sam said.

"You be careful, Sam Abel," Cat said. "You still owe me that dance." Sam smirked, then backed away slowly, unable to take his eyes off of her. He'd been impressed with Cat's abilities. She'd been thrown into an op that was out of her league, and though she'd shown the cracks of stress on more than once instance, she'd been the one who got them out of the jam. If he made it back alive, and he damn well was going to try, he'd give her that dance.

Sam climbed into the car, and Whelan grabbed a briefcase from the driver before he joined the spy. "Park Hotel—double time," Whelan told the driver. The car tore off, leaving only the vaporized particles of smoldering rubber on the glistening tarmac. Inside the car, Whelan opened the briefcase, which wasn't filled with documents, but ammunition.

"Anything for me?" Sam asked. Whelan held up the case, and Sam spotted ammunition for his revolver, which he then filled up. Whelan armed up, too. A combat knife caught Sam's attention, and he took it for good measure.

The trip was treacherous, but Sam uttered no complaints. The driver had taken Whelan's command seriously, bobbing and weaving in and out of traffic where necessary, tearing through intersections so fast that Sam gripped the seat with a white-knuckled fear, and skidding around any turn that presented itself. Whelan showed no hint of unease—he was obviously used to the sensation of whipping around and countered the harsh movements with a gyro-like balance.

The driver made good time. When they arrived alongside the emerald lawns of Central Park, Sam told the driver, "Stop here." They'd make the rest of the trip on foot in case Ramm was watching.

"Wait for us," Whelan told the driver. "If we don't come out in the next hour, call it in."

"Roger," the driver replied, and Sam and Whelan leapt from the vehicle, guns in hand, and ran across 5th Avenue with disregard for oncoming cars. Soon they arrived at Madison Avenue, and they hugged the north side of the street to remain out of view of any of the building's windows. The Park Hotel was wedged right on the corner of Park and 68th Street. A large plaque with gold lettering and a maroon awning greeted their arrival. The building was a magnificent titan of finely molded concrete. So many floors rose into the sky that Sam wouldn't dare count them.

At the front entrance, a doorman in a burgundy jacket tailored to match the awning tipped his hat toward two passersby. He hadn't noticed either Sam or Whelan, and Sam ducked behind a large stone column resembling a gargoyle. Whelan followed suit. Sam thought it foolish to try to enter through the front door. Ramm might have Americans on his payroll, and the spy wasn't foolish enough to think the criminal might not have considered paying off hotel employees. Anyone could be bought for the right amount of money, and the man who opened the front door for arriving guests was probably a cheap sell.

Sam peered around the column; there was a drive which led into an underground garage that sloped down under the building, and that would be the path of least resistance. "Alright," Sam said to Whelan. "You cover the door. If he sees me coming, I need someone on the outside."

"My trigger finger's quicker than any Nazi's footwork," Whelan replied with a chuckle.

"Whelan," Sam said, and he locked eyes with the man he'd been exchanging blows with for the last couple days, "thanks."

"Quit yappin' and get in there," Whelan said, and smacked Sam on the back with a heavy hand.

Sam descended into the garage. The cavernous structure echoed the clacking of each of his footsteps, and he hugged the corner of the ramp that bent around and descended further below the building. He kept his gun at the ready. Though he hadn't planned on finding Ramm in the hotel's garage, no one could know how many more Rudys there could be lurking in the hotel.

Once Sam had a clear view of the garage, one car amongst the rows stuck out in particular: a truck. Not only was it much larger than most of the other vehicles beneath the building, but it also bore the Thornton & Sons text and emblem. Sam recognized the two criss-crossing thorny branches instantly. *Got you*, Sam said softly. A stairwell at the opposite end of the garage caught his attention. Next to it, a plaque read "Lobby," and an arrow pointed upward.

Sam heard the growl of a car engine approach from behind, so he ducked for cover behind a parked car's rear. The car stopped at a small kiosk, then two hotel patrons—a man in a tuxedo and a woman at his side wearing a fur coat that looked like it had been composed of a small forest of animals—exited the vehicle. The attendant hustled out to the roadway, and Sam hoofed it behind a row of automobiles and out of sight. As the parking attendant catered to the two guests, Sam slipped into the stairwell and climbed the concrete steps. The single door at the top of the stairs was unguarded, and Sam holstered his gun under his shirt and bolted through the door.

The hotel lobby buzzed so vibrantly with guests that Sam was confident no one had seen him enter. Wealthy couples traveled along the marble floor and chattered jubilantly, each of them dressed in the most extravagant of classic fashions. Most of the men were clad in tuxedos, and Sam suspected he might have stumbled into a wedding. Waiters zig-zagged around the room bearing plates of small bites and liquor. Most of the commotion stemmed from the hotel bar, which flanked Sam's left side and was the focal point of the room. The wedding was likely just beginning. Though he was underdressed, Sam slipped in amongst the crowd and searched for the front desk.

When he found it, two clerks were busy tending to more guests. Sam approached the desk, shoved his way forward and to the front of the line—much to the dismay of several people—and made eye contact with one of the clerks. Sam said, "Pardon," to the clerk—who immediately looked Sam up and down and wrinkled his nose at Sam's attire—then asked, "I'm looking for a Mr. Maxwell Kearney."

"The line starts back there," the clerk said and pointed toward the tail end of the waiting group of people.

"I have very urgent information to give him and I'm afraid I forgot his room number."

"I'm sorry," the clerk said, then snidely added, "*Sir*," after a brief pause. "We're unable to give out information concerning our guests."

"It's *very* important," Sam replied.

"I can call up to him if you'd like," the clerk replied.

Sam frowned, then said, "No. That's alright." The clerk grew suspicious of the spy, and rightfully so. The information couldn't be *that* important if Sam didn't want a call to be made. The clerk dismissed Sam, then returned to cater to the guest with whom he'd originally been in conversation.

Sam searched the lobby for another way to figure out where Kearney was. The open floor plan was overwhelming. There were elevators in every wall, and there was no way Sam was going to go door to door. He had no inkling of which room Ramm was in. There could be a thousand rooms for all Sam knew. He could wait for Ramm to exit the hotel, but trying to catch him in the street would cause a scene, and an escape attempt could lead to a dangerous chase, or worse, the injury or death of an innocent bystander. Sam had to corner him now, and *alone*.

Just as Sam felt the feeling of defeat creep in, he saw a bellhop grab two luggage cases from two guests and place them on a luggage cart. The bellhop grabbed the cart, then pushed it down a hallway perpendicular to the concierge. Sam followed the bellhop as he turned around the corner, then set off to see where his trip would end. When he got to the mouth of the hall, Sam grabbed a gold-piped luggage cart and pushed it in front of him. He followed the sound of the rattling cart ahead and did his best to obscure his face with his own cart. He peered around the next corner. The sound of the party in swing in the lobby dissipated slowly, leaving only the quiet hall as he progressed.

On the wall next to him, a series of garments belonging to the bellhops hung from hooks. Sam grabbed one of the jackets, tossed it over his shoulders, then threw the cap on his head and continued forward. He could add "hotel attendant" to his list of disguises. The bellhop stopped at a room and unloaded the luggage, then retrieved his cart and turned around. As he exited, he nodded to Sam, but the spy only tipped his hat down and gave him a slight nod in return. The bellhop passed him, and Sam quickly ditched the cart and hustled into the room.

The deep, closet-like space contained a wealth of luggage. Just going through every single tag that had been tied to the pieces would take several minutes. Sam looked above the luggage, and there were two plaques that narrowed his search: one read "Arriving" and the other "Departing." Sam dug through the luggage cases in the "Departing" section hastily. Kearney likely wouldn't be staying long. Luckily there were fewer pieces of luggage in that pile than in the "Arriving" pile. Most of the guests present were probably staying for the wedding.

He flipped through tag after tag, sloppily tossing the

cases about with disregard for their contents. His wishes were granted when he found a brown leather case with a tag on the handle that read "Kearney, M." Sam felt his heart race. He turned the tag over, and on the backside the characters "30G" had been written in black ink. Sam ripped the tag from the case with a quick snap and threw it in his pocket. If anything, the confusion with Kearney's luggage might buy him some time.

When he exited the storage room, he turned to his right to find an elevator with a sign that read "Employees Only." *Perfect*, Sam thought. He kept the bellhop's uniform on, then tapped the button to call the elevator. The employee elevator was a good find—no elevator operator was present to obstruct him from the upper floors. The doors opened, and Sam stepped in. He scanned the series of buttons and hit the one that would take him to the thirtieth floor. The elevator rose.

24

The lift climbed for what felt like eternity. Sam felt the sensation of his stomach stretching toward his feet with every floor he passed. When the machine finally slowed, the doors opened on two quiet, intersecting halls that stretched outward in three directions. A sign beside the elevator directed Sam: rooms A through H lay straight ahead. But that still wouldn't get him *into* the room. A knock on Ramm's door would not give the spy the element of surprise he was looking for, so he headed left toward a service cart beside one of the guest rooms. The carpeted hall had a dampening effect on Sam's steps—for once he wasn't working so hard to keep quiet as he snuck around; now he had to remain unseen.

Inside a nearby room, two hotel staff members were busy at work tidying up from a guest's recent stay. Among the soap and toiletries on the cart, Sam found a hanging ring with keys on it. It didn't take long to deduce which was the staff's skeleton key: it was the only one with a series of tapered teeth whose edges made a "V"-like shape. He imagined it would open any door in the building, so Sam swiped it from the hook and set back the way he'd come. He traveled down the hall, passing by the rooms of no interest until finally he arrived at the last rooms in the hall.

Room "H" lay to his left, and he soon discovered room "30G" on the opposite wall. A tall, floor-to-ceiling window stood in between the doors. Sam, against his better judgement, took a peek through the glass and toward the busy street below. Park Avenue was bustling with action, but most of it was indiscernible due the incredibly long distance to the street level. If Sam had had any breakfast in his stomach, the view might have forced it up. Any fall from that height would kill a man instantly and leave a mess in the street.

Sam pressed his ear to the door: quiet. He placed the key ever-so-gently into the lock, then twisted softly to open the door. The key worked, and soon Sam found himself in a small vestibule. A pair of dressy black shoes had been set neatly beside the coat closet, and they still bore the dirt of farm-life around the edges. Sam pulled his firearm out and closed the door softly behind him.

Not a sound could be heard inside the wide room. The suite was fit for a king, and spacious enough to accommodate a sizable gathering. A large picture window at the far end of the living room displayed a series of equally massive buildings that obscured the East River skyline. The only view one would get from this end of the hotel was of glass and concrete.

On the kitchen area counter, a passport lay among a series of scattered papers and a folder. Sam opened the flap and cautiously flipped through the papers, one eye trained on the room and the other paying half-attention to the documents. On full display were the files Cat had spoken of—Sam recognized the circuitry schematics immediately, and though he'd have liked to snag some photographs, Rudy had damaged his camera. He hadn't even been given the opportunity to collect his belongings before fleeing the South.

Sam grabbed the passport. The document bore Kearney's name, along with folded travel visas and stamps from frequent trips around the world. Sam pocketed the passport and the visas—Kearney, or Ramm, wouldn't be going *anywhere* without them. The spy directed his gun around the room as if it were his primary set of eyes. He walked slowly, taking careful, deliberate steps.

The bedroom contained another briefcase that lay open on the comforter. Sam directed the gun forward, then heard the soft trickle of water emanating from the bathroom. He proceeded forward, the gun always one step ahead of him, then recognized steam curling through the bottom of the doorway leading to the bathroom. Sam couldn't have planned it any better. If Ramm was in the shower, or on the toilet, Sam wouldn't have so much as a scuffle. How lucky could he be?

Sam crept forward, his index finger gripped against the trigger, then he grabbed the doorknob. He twisted delicately, made sure the bolt was free of the door jam, then kicked the door open and pointed the gun toward the shower. The empty bathroom was a deflating discovery. The steam had fogged up the room heavily, but not enough so that Sam didn't see the blurry mass speeding up behind him in the cloudy mirror.

He turned on his heel, but the attack came hard and swift. Ramm knocked the gun out of his hand, then rushed the spy. Sam felt the impact of all of the man's body weight against his chest, then the sharp, crunching sensation of his spine bending in a way it did not want to go. Sam had been pinned against the bathroom counter, and he'd lost sight of his gun. Ramm threw a fist, and Sam just barely dodged the strike. Ramm's hand went crashing into the mirror, forcing a web-like series of cracks through the glass.

The German let out a grunt as he clutched his bloodied hand. Sam backed out of the bathroom. He spotted the gun in the shower, but saw no chance of retrieving it. He turned his attention back on Ramm, who abruptly ripped several shards of glass from in between his knuckles with a quick swipe. There was no way Sam was going to squeeze through the door and grab the gun without grappling with the man once more. Sam back-stepped swiftly, pulled his combat knife from its holster, then readied it under a tight fist.

Ramm pulled his own knife from his suit jacket. It was an elegant dagger, not so dissimilar from the kind Sam had wielded in Pforzheim. It was thin and razor-like, and even from afar Sam could see the finely detailed hilt.

Sam had at least gotten the first strike—blood speckled Ramm's stark white shirt. The German gritted his teeth, held the tip of his knife forward as if to challenge Sam, then stepped forward on his right foot. He placed his left forearm behind his back as if prepping himself for a proper bout of *mensur*, then extended his arm out over his head and bent slightly at the knees. Sam continued his retreat back out into the large suite and extended one hand out to grapple, retracting his armed hand for maximum leverage. The two dueler's stances couldn't have been more different.

Ramm smiled nefariously, then said, "Good then, Mr. Abel. We'll settle this the old way."

Operation: Shiny Toys, indeed, Sam thought.

Sam was always prepared for a knife fight. If that was the way it had to be, then he'd be obliged to accommodate Ramm. There was only one weapon the spy liked better than a pistol: a good knife. Sam could wield a knife unlike other men; it was just another extension of his body. He didn't even realize he'd been smiling himself until Ramm said, "I see you agree."

How the spy's fighting style would fare against Ramm's, he did not know. What he did know was that the enemy had a scar to prove he could be defeated, and that was enough. Ramm took two quick steps forward, and Sam retreated with two of his own in reply. Sam watched Ramm's eyes carefully. He'd let the German take the first strike, if only to see how the man fought.

"That blade's kind of short," Sam said mockingly. "You're going to need to get in close if you want any action."

Ramm instantly challenged Sam's bravado. He leapt forward in a whip-like charge and swiped the dagger furiously toward Sam's face. Sam felt the whisking sensation of displaced air against his skin, and quickly regretted his comment. Before he even had time to strike back, Ramm swiped with wide, sweeping slashes with the knife that forced Sam to pivot on his foot and parry the attack. The two men's locations had been switched completely. Sam considered retreating toward the gun and making quick work of the fight. He would feel no shame in shooting the man rather than dueling him. Rules were for suckers, and when the matter was of life and death, the only man crying about rules was the one who'd been defeated.

Sam hesitated to strike. He'd told Ramm that the key to victory was to get in close, but the same was true for himself. He'd need to look for his opportunity within Ramm's own attempts to attack him. Ramm twisted the knife above his head, rotating it in teasing circles that Sam knew were only for show. Sam was unaffected by his distractions. Like the German, he remained calm and steadfast.

Ramm thrust the knife forward once more, and Sam leapt backward in response. Before Sam could find his window to attack, Ramm swiped hastily in rapid motions, forcing Sam against the dining table. Sam swiped himself, but his attempt was only met with an ear-ringing *ping* when his knife clashed with Ramm's. Ramm quickly slid his knife downward, breaking Sam's weapon's hold on his own and jerked it furiously, slicing right through Sam's sleeve and down his forearm.

Before Sam's injury could even register, Ramm put all his force into a strike, and Sam dipped away from the attack with little room to spare. The German's knife sank into the table. Though Sam thought he might have found his moment to strike when the point of the knife penetrated the wood surface, Ramm tore the knife from the table and quickly attacked once more with a broad, scythe-like sweep. Sam had spoken too soon—the man was better with a blade than he'd thought.

"Come, Sam," Ramm said with a provoking purr. "I'm not going to have to do all of the work, am I?"

Sam took the bait and attempted to slash the man,

but Ramm countered the attack with a parry and took another swipe with his weapon. That attempt grazed the back of Sam's arm, slicing only through the fabric of his clothing, and Ramm delivered a kick to the back of the spy's leg that sent Sam tumbling to the floor. Ramm followed with another jab toward the spy's face; the tip of the blade narrowly missed Sam's nose when he rolled across the floor. Sam hopped up on both feet and thrust his knife forward. His blade met Ramm's with a *clang*. Thankfully Sam's blade had a tiny crossguard built into the hilt—Ramm's knife might have slid down and cut straight through four fingers had it not.

Sam felt the trickle of blood down the corner of his right eyebrow and dabbed at it to see that he *was* bleeding. Ramm grinned. "I see you're getting an education, Mr. Abel." Sam wiped the blood from his eye, nervous it might leak into the duct and obscure his view. "I can now call you a member of the club," Ramm said, gesturing to his own *schmiss*. "Traditionally we might count that as a defeat, but we can both agree that this bout is not finished."

Sam circled the man, his knife held tightly and his free hand extended forward in anticipation of Ramm's next attack. The spy was beginning to sense that to get in close was going to mean risking injury. If he wanted to get the man where it counted, he might need to offer up his body and hope for the best. As they moved around the wide space, Ramm's eyes never breaking with Sam's, he searched the German's movements for any tell he might make.

Sam jabbed forward, and Ramm redirected the spy's weapon with his own with a wand-like flick. Sam rushed forward once more with a wide swipe, but as expected, Ramm saw the attack coming from a mile away. It was as if he could read Sam's mind, always one step ahead of him, and if Sam made an attempt to strike, Ramm was quick to fend off the attack. Now neither man spoke; only the two clattering knives made conversation.

Sam realized that his enemy could do this all day. He'd still never even removed his hand from behind his back, maintaining his traditional stance as if to brag to Sam that he was the better fighter. Sam's extra hand was doing him no good.

The only other hint he had of how to defeat Ramm was that the man, like any braggart, liked to talk. Ramm waved the knife as if to entice Sam to approach. If Sam was going to get his shot, he was going to have to make it count. Now Sam's back was to the massive picture window, and Ramm was forcing him toward it.

Ramm said, "I told you, Mr. Abel," then smirked deviously, "I've only lost—"

Sam shot forward, slashed the knife with a back-handed motion toward Ramm's face, and managed to slice the man across the unmarred right side of his cheek. The victory was short-lived—Ramm thrust his own knife into Sam's shoulder. The piercing wound forced Sam to drop his weapon, but now both of his hands were free. Sam felt the sharp, searing sensation of the knife cutting through several ligaments, tendons, and muscles that were supposed to hold things tightly in place.

The pain was instant and unbearable, yet it was the exact advantage the spy needed. He grabbed Ramm with both hands, then shoved him toward the picture window with every ounce of strength he could manage.

The knife left Sam's shoulder with a wet *thunk*, and Ramm flew backwards toward the window and smashed into it with a heavy crash.

The glass shattered under the man's weight, and he fell backward. Sam reveled in the surprise in his enemy's eyes as he registered what had happened. Shards fell in unison from the large window, and Sam hoped that none would hit any people thirty floors below. Ramm's feet rose into the air, and his tie flapped upward as his torso attempted to carry the rest of his weight out of the window and down to the street below.

Sam snatched the small end of Ramm's tie, instantly arresting his fall. Ramm's hands were thrashing wildly in panic, half of his body inside the hotel room, and the other dangling from the New York City skyscraper's window. "Stop moving," Sam said. Ramm ceased his flailing as the tie tightened around his neck. Sam let the man dangle there for a moment so that he could savor his defeat. The veins in his neck raged in the vice-like grip of the continually tightening tie. Blood trickled from the wound Sam had inflicted on the side of his face. The long slash, unlike the vertical one on his left side, was wicked and diagonal. It was anything but a clean cut, and even with medical attention, would heal poorly.

"Let me go," Ramm said. "You've won—those are the rules." A crowd began to gather in the street below. Onlookers' gazes remained fixed upward toward the man dangling from the windowsill. Then, Sam's attention turned to the face of the building on the opposite side of the street when he heard a bevy of windows opening. Now there were many witnesses to what he might or might not do.

Sam had never intended to kill the man, though. He'd like him gift-wrapped and handed to Brandt. " Only dead men care about rules," Sam said, then yanked the tie forcefully and sent Ramm tumbling to the hotel room floor. Sam retrieved his knife while Ramm loosened the tie around his neck in search of air. Then, Sam stepped forward and pressed the knife to Ramm's throat.

"How did you know?" Ramm asked between gasps for air.

"Stealing secrets is easy," Sam replied. "Keeping them is hard."

"I don't suppose there's any way of convincing you to let me go," Ramm said. "Many courtesies could be extended to unlikely allies." Sam shook his head, then loosened the tie completely from Ramm's neck, keeping the knife pressed against his trachea, and forced the man to his knees. He maneuvered behind Ramm's back, secured the tie around both of his wrists, then kicked him back down to the floor face-first.

The hotel room door burst open, and Whelan entered with his gun drawn. Once the agent recognized that Ramm had been subdued, he holstered the gun and hustled over to the living room area. Sam slumped into the seat, winced when he was reminded of the pain in his shoulder, then set about constructing a makeshift tourniquet from a pillow sham. A flustered bellhop sprinted through the door, and Whelan commanded him to go find a doctor.

"Thanks," Sam said to Whelan.

"For the doctor, or for him?" Whelan asked while nodding toward Ramm.

Sam smiled, then asked Whelan, "You got a cigarette?"

25

———

S am Abel and Cat McAlister swayed softly in each other's arms as a needle danced along a wax cylinder. The old phonograph in Cat's apartment was playing a standard that Sam had heard a hundred times, but couldn't for the life of him remember the name of. A light breeze flowed through the apartment, a welcome reprieve from the never-ending heat the two had endured. Neither spoke, but they enjoyed the comfort of stillness and quiet. Cat's head rested against the bandaged area where Sam's shoulder had been injured. That one would take a while to heal, and it still throbbed something fierce, but something about Cat's touch made it better.

Whelan had offered the C-47 up for the trip back to D.C., and they'd delivered Ramm to a jubilant Brandt. The spymaster had been pining for information, and Sam had brought him Christmas in July. Brandt had instructed both Sam and Cat not to come back to The

Yard until they'd gotten good and plastered and slept off a hangover. There were no trophies for people working in the SSD, only pats on the back and time off earned.

When Sam delivered up Ramm, Whelan had sat the exchange out, but Sam had made the agent's involvement known to Brandt. Rudy had been detained by nameless agents for Sam to present to his boss, and Adelaide had handled his delivery. It wouldn't smooth over the spymaster's opinion of the federal organization, but it helped to know that his best operative had made a potential friend. Having contacts inside opposing organizations was part of the business, even if the road ahead was still bumpy. Whelan could make no promises about his orders to take down the spy chief, but he'd done Sam and Brandt a solid by promising he'd destroy the copies and negatives of the damning photos he'd taken.

Sam didn't know the fate of Moreno just yet, and truthfully, he didn't care. He'd cast his line into the pond and rather than pull out a minnow, he'd caught a hefty bass. It was a possibility he might read about it in the paper, but something told him the feds were going to milk Moreno rather than make his criminal activities public. Much more could be gained from men that talked than from those who were made an example of. Sam imagined Ramm would endure the same fate.

The record continued its serenade, and Sam reveled in the brief spell of calm. Soon he'd be back to work, but right now he was here in the moment with Cat. No one had spoken for quite some time, then Sam felt Cat's head shift against his chest and press tighter.

"I'm sorry I didn't tell you," Cat said. "He told me not to tell *anyone*."

"The less I know, the better," the spy replied. "In *this* case at least."

"Sam," Cat said softly, and her eyes met his with grave concern. "What happened to the girl? The one from Germany?"

Sam inhaled to buy time as he prepared his answer, then released the air softly through his nose and said, "She never left." He gave no further details. To relive her gory death would be hard enough, and there was no use explaining to Cat exactly *what* happened to those who played "the game," as it had been termed. Her eyes squinted slightly, scrutinizing those of the spy's. She gazed intensely into them as if to search for the truth in the answer. She pressed it no further, but returned her head to his shoulder and remained in the moment.

———

Sam woke the next day to find an empty bed. The linens still smelled of her perfume, and though sleeping with partners was ill-advised, he suspected that the information his mission had yielded would soon send him far away from her, wherever that may be. They were two different operatives with different skill sets, and though they'd been thrust together for one particular mission, there was no likelihood they'd work together frequently now that it had ended. It had been some time since he'd been with a woman—in fact, Sigrid had been his last.

"Cat," Sam called out. No one answered. She'd left behind all of her belongings as far as he could tell. He considered that perhaps she'd gone out for breakfast, and he made his way to the kitchen to look for more signs of her. The rest of the apartment was quiet, too. What was most peculiar was that Cat had left the keys to her apartment on the hook by the door. *How would she get back in?* The phone rang, but Sam didn't dare answer it. The bells chimed once, twice, then a third time before it finally stopped.

Sam started his day with coffee and a cigarette. He sat shirtless in the dining room and removed the bandage from his wound to check its status. The white gauze was still tinged with a spot of blood, and he hoped it was healing. It was just another to add to the road map of scars his torso had been covered in.

He waited in the apartment for another hour. Two cups of coffee and four cigarettes later, he put his clothes back on and decided to go see what Brandt—who was likely having a field day with his catch—was up to. Sam had no hobbies to speak of, so he did what he always did when no other tasks remained and walked the streets that led to The Yard.

———

Udo Ramm sat alone in a dingy cell, slumped over in a chair surrounded by three concrete walls and a two-way mirror. Brandt chewed on the pipe stem clutched between his teeth, unable to hide the smile curling around his cheeks as he admired his holiday catch. Sam enjoyed yet another cigarette. The German stared directly through the glass, and though he could not see Brandt or Sam, it was as if the man knew they were there and was looking directly at both of them with a sinister scowl of defeat. Brandt slapped Sam on the shoulder admiringly as if he were a proud father.

"Ouch," Sam cried.

"Oh," Brandt said. "Sorry."

Sam massaged the shoulder, then returned his gaze to Ramm. "Is he talking yet?"

"Some," Brandt replied. "We'll press him harder—and his friend. Now we need to do some recon and see just what we're dealing with at this Peenemünde. The Brits have heard murmurs about the weapons, but no one's taken a look-see."

"What weapons?" Sam asked.

"Rockets," Brandt replied. "It's not the first we—or they—have heard of the place. They think it's all hearsay—just a diversion they've been fed by whackadoos."

"What do you think? Sam asked.

"I think *anything's* worth a look-see," Brandt said.

Sam ashed his cigarette on the concrete floor, then asked, "Why is he talking?"

Brandt shrugged. "Said if we sent him back he'd be dead anyway—something about Himmler eating his own. It was either go home empty-handed or stay here. The more he gives us the better shot he's got at the creature comforts one might hope for in captivity."

"What might those be?" Sam asked.

"Cigarettes, booze," Brandt replied. "Maybe a nice steak every so often."

"Is he under arrest?" Sam asked. "*Officially*, I mean."

"As far as I'm concerned, a man who isn't officially here doesn't get official treatment."

"He says he's American," Sam said.

Brandt shrugged. "He's in our custody, and we'll treat him alright—far better than they'd treat one of ours, I suppose."

"I'm sorry about Moreno," Sam said with a hint of shame. "The way it all shook out…"

"No matter," Brandt replied. "We got a morsel and ran with it, and we pulled a prize by the skin of our teeth. It's rare that things like that happen. You throw as many lines into the water as you can, and you hope you catch a good fish." Brandt paused as if deep in thought, then said, "We got *lucky*." Brandt gave the spy a nod of approval, then inhaled from the pipe before he continued. "You did what you could. This one's a better prize anyway. Moreno would've been a good catch," Brandt turned to face Ramm, "but this one's going to give us far more to bring to the table—already *has*."

"And Brigham and Thornton?" Sam asked.

"They'll be filed away," Brandt replied. "I'm told Mr. Ives had a change of heart regarding who he'll do business with."

"How'd you hear that?" Sam asked.

"I've got more than two ears," Brandt said coyly. "I'm sure the other two will be more than happy to oblige when faced with the consequences of their ignorance."

The slash on Ramm's face had been tended to, and like Sam's injury, the clean white bandages had been blotted with red stains where the wound had spotted. Ramm still hadn't gotten the opportunity to change his clothing, and his skin glistened with the traces of days-old sweat. Sam thought the least Brandt could do was give the man a shower, but then he remembered what Ramm would have done had he had his way, and he quickly dismissed any sympathy he might have felt for his enemy.

"Have you heard from your partner?" Brandt asked.

"No," Sam replied.

Brandt inhaled from the pipe, then scrutinized Sam's face with a trace of skepticism. He snorted, and with the exhalation came a plume of smoke. "We called in this morning…" He paused. "No answer."

"Probably slept in," Sam replied.

There was another long pause before Brandt told the truth. "She's *gone*, Sam." The spymaster's face drooped shamefully for a fraction of a second. He'd lost her, Sam thought, but he wasn't going to pout about it—he quickly stiffened his jaw and stood straight, almost at attention. Yet it was as if the spymaster knew something Sam *didn't* know.

"Are you sure?" Sam asked.

"I've got more than two eyes, too."

Sam knew better than to begin to spout about virtues or ethics—he'd be preaching to the wrong congregation. There was an inherent risk using the type of personnel in Brandt's employ. Sometimes the ugly side showed itself.

There was another awkward pause as the two men stared at Ramm. Sam couldn't help but speak up to break the tension. "Respectfully…"Sam hesitated.

Brandt motioned his hand to proceed, then said, "Get on with it."

"I still don't understand why you put her in there with him."

Brandt's judging eyes corrected Sam swiftly before he even spoke. "I put her in there with *you*." Both Brandt and Sam refocused their attention on Ramm, then the spy boss said, "Besides, do *you* know someone who can crack a safe, beat a lock, or finesse a dial?"

"I don't," Sam answered, and the tension was

momentarily defused. Sam felt an incredible urge to blurt out his frustration with Brandt's lack of due diligence. "You *knew*," Sam said. "You knew and you sent her in anyway. Couldn't you at least have changed her name?"

"Remember what I told you when you first started?" Brandt asked.

Sam didn't reply. In his head he turned over some of their earliest conversations. He landed on two simple words Brandt had mentioned several times: plausible deniability. Who better to pin a crime on than an *actual* criminal with a history. At this point, Sam wasn't sure who in his atmosphere was telling *any* truths.

They both gazed at Ramm for a moment longer in silence. He was a defeated man, scarred and weak. His skin had turned a dark plum color where it had swelled. "I'm sure she'll turn up," Brandt said after the silence had become unbearable.

Sam didn't reply, but he could feel Brandt watching him, perhaps judging him. Who was Brandt to talk? Sam had endured Whelan's pursuit, and why? Because Sam was villainous? Perhaps. But also because Brandt had himself been unfaithful and revealed a weakness in the outfit.

Anyway, there was no need to give the spymaster *all* the details—especially if they had nothing to do with an operation. If Brandt's team was as good as they claimed to be, they knew everything there was to know about Sam. Perhaps that was the nature of the business when it came to the war, but some secrets were better left untold if they could be. Sam wasn't aware of the protocol when it came to interoffice relationships, and maybe the chief's own extra-marital affairs reflected his concern for Sam's involvement with Cat.

Sam turned to Brandt, then said to his superior, "Sir." He used the title respectfully as if he might gain favor with the man. Brandt turned to face his favorite spy. "Anything?" Sam asked. Brandt knew what he meant.

"Nothing," Brandt replied.

———

Sam took the rest of the afternoon off. It wasn't his job to interrogate Ramm—there was a special, rarely seen group of people for that job they called hornets, rumor had it because they knew how to *sting*—and he didn't want to stare at the man's mangled face any longer. He'd run out of cigarettes, and he went to a corner market in the center of the city to get some more.

After paying the clerk, he stepped out to the sidewalk and lit up. He savored the cigarette while observing the comings and goings of the locals as they went about their days. Preparations were underway for a holiday parade, and an abundance of red, white, and blue decorated nearly every storefront in the form of flags, streamers, and flowers.

A woman with her hair done up to the nines pushed one child in a stroller, and dragged another by the hand. Two men patched a hole in the sidewalk, unloading cement from a mixer and patting it flat with shovels. A newsie waved a paper at several passersby, exhorting them to stay up to date on current affairs abroad. Along with the smell of smoke, Sam caught the whiff of baked apple pie wafting from one of the storefronts. The aroma was comforting, familiar and warm and a signifier that all was right—at least for *today*.

He considered how nice the ignorance must be for the people at home. Most had enjoyed their holiday weekend without so much as a hint of the enemy. Such was the privilege—or curse—of the spy's knowledge. Sam was well aware of all the nefarious things going on around the world while these people tended to their own personal crises that were far more pressing in the day-to-day than any war ramping up overseas. Midway had only been a month earlier, but soon European soil would meet American boots.

Sam caught the front page of the paper as a black woman on a bench read through the events. The headline read **Germans Push East**. The reader flipped another page, then the paper fell slowly. She stared back at the spy. Sam cocked his head as he looked at her face, and he couldn't help but feel the sensation of familiarity. He stared back himself, and both watched each other from opposite sides of the street. For a moment he thought perhaps he might have seemed rude, but as he scrutinized her hair style—a bob cut with a small cap resting on the head—he suspected she was wearing a wig. He recognized the face immediately: it was *Adelaide*.

"Nice day," a voice behind Sam said. Sam *knew* the voice. He turned to find a smoking Whelan standing beside him.

"You're almost as good at sneaking around as me," Sam said.

"Not good enough, I suppose," Whelan said with a chuckle as he nodded toward Adelaide.

"I'm assuming everything went alright on your end?" Sam asked.

"As well as we could hope."

"Good, then I suppose both of our bosses will stop bickering for a moment."

"Oh, come on now, Abel," Whelan replied as he exhaled a cloud of smoke. "You and I both know those old dogs *love* the old tricks."

"Glad to see this morning's paper only concerns *important* events," Sam said.

"Today," Whelan said. Sam understood.

"What of Moreno?" Sam asked.

"I'm sure we'll do the same thing you're doing over there," Whelan replied. "Squeeze him until there's no juice left, then squeeze him some more. We'll let him stay in the job. He's more use to us as an informant—he goes on with business as usual, his friends are none-the-wiser, and we get a man on both sides of the fence. Seems he was telling the truth: his friends at home had dirt on him too—his hands were tied. Of course, you didn't hear that from me." Whelan gave Sam a sidelong look, as if to say, 'We're all in the same club *really*.' But then, he said, "We wouldn't want the wrong people finding out we know what we know. Pulling him will raise too many red flags, and we want him right where he is, *don't we?*"

"That's a really long-winded way of saying 'stay the hell away,' Whelan," Sam said. The federal agent shrugged. "I hope you struck up a nice deal with Ives."

"Deal?" Whelan asked in surprise. "Better than that, my friend. Mr. Ives was so distraught about his little predicament that it seems he thought it fit to deliver his entire tungsten supply into the hands of the federal government—*free of charge*."

"Is that right?" Sam asked.

"Indeed. Let's hope Mr. Brigham and Mr. Thornton are suddenly feeling charitable, too."

"Glad I could help," Sam said.

Whelan laughed, then said, "You're alright, Abel." Across the street, Adelaide folded her paper into a neat square. Whelan tossed his cigarette to the street and tamped it out with his toe. "Of course, there's one little loose end that gave me pause."

"What would that be?" Sam asked.

Whelan dug into his pocket, retrieved a photo, then handed it to Sam. Sam looked down to the photo: the image was of an open—and empty—safe. Sam recognized the safe—it was Moreno's. He and Cat had broken into it only a few days earlier, and it was hard to forget.

"Lose something?" Sam asked with a thin smile he found it difficult to hide.

"Moreno's all out of sorts that a necklace he recently procured seems to have just up and vanished. I wouldn't care so much myself, but anything he had in his possession is evidence and, *of course*, property of the federal government. You wouldn't know anything about that, would you?"

"Can't say I would," Sam replied. The two men stared into each other's eyes. Whelan knew Sam was fibbing, and Sam knew the agent knew. Men who'd mastered the art of lying had few *real* secrets.

"Haven't seen your friend around since we got back," Whelan said. "Have you? It's like she just *disappeared*."

"I haven't," Sam replied. Whelan only nodded with a thin smirk.

"You hang on to that," Whelan said as he stepped away. "I've got copies." Whelan turned to fix the spy with accusatory eyes for a moment more. "I'll see you around, Abel. Happy Fourth." Whelan set off. Across the street, Adelaide collected her purse and walked parallel to Whelan before each went separate ways.

Sam looked down at the photo once more, then said to himself, *Good girl.*

AFTERWORD

Thank you for reading *Everywhere and Nowhere*. If you've made it this far, you've probably already been on an adventure or two with Sam Abel, and if you haven't, I'd recommend checking out the two prior stories that feature him, *A Whisper in the Oaks* and *The Shadows of Might*. You can find both in ebook, paperback, or hardcover formats wherever books are sold. This is the fourth of many books I have planned for release. I'll be offering both stand-alone novels for those like me who like contained reads, as well as series for those who like to stick with a longer story. If you're enjoying my books, feel free to leave a review wherever you review them.

As I write this in the year of 2022, most days the world seems fractured. I notice the constant pull of split and fragmented sides, people caught in a constant tug of war that seems never-ending. Sometimes I wonder if it's just the nature of things, an ebb and flow and back and fourth of a world in a perpetual state of disagreement in which all parties assume virtue. It can seem fruitless at times, but when I wrote *Everywhere and Nowhere*, I set out to write a story in which maybe, for one moment, if the characters put down their megaphones, or in this case, their guns and knives, and rallied together for one brief moment to solve a common problem, there could be a small semblance of victory. That is not always the case in the real world, and perhaps, wishful thinking.

In the case of the story, both parties at odds might have valid points for disagreement, but a single thread unites them. Maybe I was fantasizing about what that could look like, visualizing feuding sides shaking hands for a hot second and finding common ground where they might not otherwise. It's possible that I was just trying to imagine a fictional world in which momentarily all was okay if there was a boogie man two sides could point a finger at. The truth is often far more messy, and as one can see through the actions and intentions of my fictitious characters, difficult to navigate. I consider *The Shadows of Might* to have anything but a happy ending. Were problems resolved? Sure, but that didn't mean all was well. At the end of *Everywhere and Nowhere*, all is well, but as with any small victory, the question that follows immediately is, "For how long?"

At this point, I ask myself, "What can I count on?" The only thing I can say for sure is, "Sam Abel will return…"

You can look for updates (and join my mailing list) at www.clarkemayer.com

ABOUT THE AUTHOR

Clarke Mayer is a filmmaker, photographer, and writer from New Jersey. Most of his day is dominated by a Black Mouth Cur named Pam who doesn't ever run out of energy. He likes to write, hike, and run, but most of all he likes to read and watch crime, spy, horror, and thriller stories.